The Mune

Gold SF
Series editors: Una McCormack and Paul March-Russell

ALSO IN THE GOLD SF SERIES

Mathematics for Ladies: Poems on Women in Science
by Jessy Randall
Empathy by Hoa Pham
The Disinformation War by S.J. Groenewegen
The Ghostwriters by M.J. Maloney
The Other Shore by Hoa Pham
Merchant by Alexandra Grunberg
Little Sisters and Other Stories by Vonda N. McIntyre
The Headland by Abi Curtis
Schrödinger's Wife (and other possibilities)
by Pippa Goldschmidt
*The Path of Most Resistance: More Poems on
Women in Science* by Jessy Randall

The Mune

Sue Dawes

Goldsmiths
Press

Copyright © 2025 Goldsmiths Press
First published in 2025 by Goldsmiths Press
Goldsmiths, University of London, New Cross
London SE14 6NW

Printed and bound by Short Run Press, UK.
Distribution by the MIT Press
Cambridge, Massachusetts, USA and London, England

Text copyright © 2025 Sue Dawes

The right of Sue Dawes to be identified as the author of this work has been asserted by her in accordance with sections 77 and 78 in the Copyright, Designs and Patents Act 1988.

Every effort has been made to trace copyright holders and to obtain their permission for the use of copyright material. The publisher apologises for any errors or omissions and would be grateful if notified of any corrections that should be incorporated in future reprints or editions of this book.

All Rights Reserved. No part of this publication may be reproduced, distributed or transmitted in any form or by any means whatsoever without prior written permission of the publisher, except in the case of brief quotations in critical articles and review and certain non-commercial uses permitted by copyright law.

A CIP record for this book is available from the British Library

ISBN 978-1-915983-24-4 (pbk)
ISBN 978-1-915983-25-1 (ebk)

www.gold.ac.uk/goldsmiths-press

'It comes to this, that unless Heaven should send a new planet alongside for us to export our superfluous women to, we must make up our minds to keep them at home.'

> Jessie Boucherett,
> 1868

Part 1

1863

The Ship

MOLLY

Betty's baby, when it finally comes, is the same blue-grey as the London sky the night they set sail. Betty fights like a wounded animal, tearing at Molly as she cuts the cord with the knife the men use to gut tuna. It's better if Molly takes the baby away now, than leave it for the daily checks, when it will be ripped from Betty's arms like a dead fish from a net.

Betty sobs, the sound so deep her body shakes.

'Do you have a keepsake?' Molly asks, clutching the limp little body to her.

She takes a small red gem from Betty's stiff fingers and, wiping away tears, shuffles around the ropes and to the stairs that lead to the ship's deck. Taking one of the petticoats piled near the hold doors, she cloaks the fragile body in it, tucking the small red token inside the shroud: as if the child is to be delivered to the foundling hospital and might someday wish to seek out its mother. Despite Flora saying a few words of scripture, as Betty would want, how God heals the broken hearted and binds up their wounds, when Molly lays the dead baby gently down on the steps, ready for collection, it doesn't feel like they've done enough.

The storm returns that evening, and the wind blows its rage, screaming down through the gaps in the wooden deck above. The cold air wakes Molly and she raises herself up on the thin straw mattress but can see nothing; the few oil lamps that line the hold are snuffed out.

Anchoring herself as the ship starts to rock, feet pressed tight against the bunk, she curves her body to protect her baby, who whimpers in sleep. In the darkness, she can hear snatches of prayer, sobbing, and the unrelenting cries of other newborns. She clings on. It will no doubt settle down soon.

An explosion of thunder, and the ship starts to keel. Molly is launched from her bunk. Splintered wood strikes her as she falls. Arms protecting her baby, she hits the deck sideways, in a tangle of rope, canvas and broken bunk, feeling the punch in her ribs.

The hold doors crash open, water tearing through the bolts as if they are nothing more than strips of paper, and outside the moon hangs full and red.

A bubble of panic as the water rises in the hold. Women screaming with terror, lift their babies above the salty line, holding their breath to save them.

Molly closes her eyes as the water takes her down.

Then there is light, warm and bright, rushing over her.

The Island

MOLLY

Molly stirs at the sound of a cry. Her baby. She recognises the urgency of its hunger. Blinking, her eyes sensitive, used to the dim light in the ship's hold for so many weeks, she searches for her child but there is nothing but black sand. Molly winces as warm salt-water washes up to her knees, stinging as bad as if she's been walking barelegged through nettles. There's weed in it too, silken and coiled around her ankles in restraints. She shudders, kicks it off and pushes herself back from the shallows, over the sharp sand and past a line of smooth white shells. She looks again for her baby, squinting against the light, which is brighter than the sun that glinted on crystal in her husband's house.

The baby cries again, making Molly flinch. Two milky circles appear on the bodice of her soaked, brown woollen dress. She must find her baby. Rubbing her eyes to get some relief from the dazzling light, the coarse black grains of sand stick to her damp skin and graze her. There's nothing in front of her, no blanket-wrapped bundle floating in the water, just an unmarked, deep green sheet of sea. Rolling up her torn skirts, she knots them at the side and following the path of white shells tracing the curve of the shore, staggers towards where she thinks the cry came from. Desperate, ignoring the splinters, shards from the shattered bunks on the ship, that dig into her skin with each footstep, she searches for a dent in the black sand ahead of her: evidence of her child.

Another cry, closer now, and there's movement in the haze, a small arm punching upwards into the cloudless sky. There must be something wrong with Molly's eyes, because every time she looks, the ground beyond the shell path seems to be shifting. Maybe she's confused by the water lapping on the sand and the heat, which in her thick dress, is stifling. Anxious to hold her child again, Molly dismisses her doubts and crosses the beach, her feet sinking. Her baby is half-buried beyond the tideline marked with purple weed, mouth opening and closing like a fish.

She tries to dig her baby out of the sand, but the grains slip through her fingers, sharp as tapestry pins. The baby cries again, and this time Molly sees the sand shift with the sound, rippling, tugging the baby under. Panicking, because the sand is also moving beneath her, Molly grabs at her baby, no longer caring about protecting its delicate skin, now just trying to save it and herself from being buried alive. She will not let another child be taken.

The baby released, Molly clutches it to her chest but there's no reprieve because the hole fills up, as if the baby was never there. The baby is silent for the moment, snuffling and sucking at the milky stains, spreading across her chest. Molly wants to run but she remembers watching a pig sink in mud on her parents' land, how its squealing and kicking had buried it deeper. The tenant farmer said the trick was not to panic or fight but to make yourself as big as you could be, to spread your weight. He'd blown his cheeks out, called himself a jollocks, and made Molly laugh. What if this sand is the same?

She glances around. Where are the other women who were on the ship? The beach ahead is flat and bare. There's nothing to grab on to, no rock pools or driftwood, just twists of weed and a few dead silvery fish. She must decide and fast, because the sand has her in its clutches, filling in the spaces around her ankles. Remembering a childhood game, when you had to trust there was someone behind to catch you, Molly holds her baby tight, bends her knees and falls backwards. The sand is harder than she expects when she smacks down on to it, and she feels it dig through the thick weave of her dress, but the position gives her enough purchase to pull her feet free. Spreading her arms and legs in a star, her baby balanced on her chest, she presses herself slowly backwards, tiny crab-like movements as the sand nips her.

Finally, Molly reaches the line of smooth white shells. Exhausted and frightened, she sits up, safe for the moment. Unbuttoning the bodice and easing the heavy dress from her shoulder, Molly lets the baby latch on to her nipple. Her burning discomfort recedes.

It's silent here, deathly, with not even the shriek of a gull. Molly shivers, despite the white-hot sun blistering down on her. Is she alone? Where is the ship? Shielding her eyes, she looks back along the path. The white line of shells ends abruptly at rocks, jutting out of the sea, sharp black lumps thrown there by giants. Behind her are trees, a kind she doesn't recognise, heavy with red fruit, and with huge glossy, green leaves. The foliage is so dense, Molly can't see what's behind it, but she can smell burnt eggs: an aroma, which bubbles up around her. Apart from the smell, there is only the black sand and the sea ahead, the green of which reminds Molly of the lawns at the Institute that looked so lush through her small, barred window. Locked in the tiny room, she used to dream of burying her feet in those blades.

She picks debris from her baby's hair as she smooths it down, and tries to focus her thoughts, but nothing makes sense. She felt the sea draw her under when the ship sank.

How has she survived? Where are the other mothers? Where the devil is she?

A woman screams, and the sand beyond the strip of shells ripples in reply. Molly shudders, looking towards the sound, but she cannot see past the bend in the shore. It is proof at least that someone else has been washed up further along the beach. She's not alone.

Molly stands up and, clutching her nursing baby close, stumbles further along the path towards the scream, careful not to lose her footing. The white path bends, separating the forest and the shoreline. As Molly rounds the corner, feet lacerated and bleeding, she freezes.

The ship lies marooned, sideways in the sand. Its hull is cracked in two like a walnut, and the mast with all its ripped rigging juts out: huge wooden fingers on the sand. Even through the haze, Molly recognises the curved outline of the vessel she boarded in London. They were promised a fresh start in the New World, but that, like everything else she has been fed since her husband sent her to the Asylum, has been a lie.

There is noise behind the broken wooden panels of the ship: other survivors, and they're moving. Tattio is arguing with Betty and Ada.

'Us must help one annudah to de shore.'

'Better we wait for rescue. Men will come.'

'Was men what got us 'ere in the first place. Talking don't do nowt. I ain't risking me babby stuck in 'ere.'

Molly waves to catch the three women's attention and to warn them to be quiet. She cannot shout, because if what she has witnessed is real, a raised voice will put them in danger. She's too late. There's a crash as one of them staggers through the broken hold doors. Ada, stumbling forward, holding a baby-sized bundle in her arms. The sand buckles beneath her. Molly can't help her, even if she were able to get close enough, because the sand will also draw Molly down, like before.

'Ada!' Betty shrieks. 'Someone do summat!'

The sand swells in answer, sucking Ada deeper.

Molly's never been the lady her parents or her husband hoped for and refuses to be now as she removes her dress, lays her baby in the damp woollen nest on the shell path, and runs away from the shore in her soiled petticoats. The forest floor is thick with claggy mud, clutching at Molly's feet, but she fights against it. Using all her strength, she drags a fallen limb back across the path, pushing it out over the sand towards the woman. But Ada is too far away and now there is only the pale curve of her shoulders above the black unstable mass. The sand is a monster and it's swallowing Ada whole.

Molly wants to call out to Ada, she shouldn't feel alone, but every syllable spoken aloud seems to make the sand angry. Ada's cries are enough to cause ripples without the added cracks and creaks as the ship breaks further apart. Panicking, unsure what to do next, Molly doesn't see the silent girl at first, balancing on the mast, which stretches out over the path, several feet away, until she starts to remove her shoes.

The girl is wiry, slight and determined, even with her baby strapped to her back and one of the ship's tin buckets in her hand. She reaches Ada quickly but all that is left of Ada now, is her head and arms above the sand, with her baby held aloft. She's spitting sand out, but however hard she tries, shaking her head from side to side, it continues to run into her mouth like beetles.

The girl uses the rigging, which has formed a tight net across the sand, and laying down, pulls herself towards Ada.

Molly watches, open mouthed, her hands clenched tight, as the ropes shift.

The girl reaches the end of the rigging and, legs clamped around the boom, stretches further out, scooping the baby from Ada's arms. She drags the bucket back over the sand, which pulls back like the sea. The baby kicks with determination, red-faced and screaming. Molly sees gratitude in Ada's gaze before, with one final breath, she's sucked under. Molly looks away, can't bear to look at the pale arms, sticking out of the black sand, two white poles of surrender.

The silent girl uses the mast to reach the path, carrying her heavy burden. Ada's baby is safe.

When Molly looks back, there is nothing to suggest Ada was ever there, no dip, and no memorial to her passing.

The girl, still clutching the bucket, is frowning at the line of women who have started to follow her path to the shore. Molly winces, watching them slip and slide in wet, ill-fitting shoes, as one by one they carefully step onto the mast. Some seem reluctant to journey but are pressed onwards with gestures and shouts of impatience from those behind.

'We must tell them to be silent,' Molly whispers to the girl.

The girl puts the bucket down and starts to clap. Each meeting of her hands makes the sand jump as if startled. Molly joins in, making as much noise as possible. The sand puckers and surges through the rigging.

The women on the beam pause, seeming to finally take notice.

As Molly and the girl cease clapping, the sand quietens to a swell.

The scowls that follow, Molly thinks, are from fear not anger, because every so often, one of the babies screams and the ship shifts, the women jolted, forced to grip on, whilst trying to hold tight to their offspring.

Molly cannot suffer to watch, so takes Ada's squalling baby from the bucket and places it next to hers on the woollen cloth. Wounds on their skin from the sand are like claw marks from a giant bird. She needs to bathe both babies in salt water, so they don't sicken, but there is no time now and the waterline here is too far away to attempt to reach it.

The more women that step onto the white shells, the more noise there is. Babies cry, desperate and hungry, the women too exhausted and terrified to tend to them.

Molly tries to get them to quieten again, her finger pressed to her lips, but they are too focused on their own trauma and in one last crescendo, the last of the ship's cargo, a lone pregnant woman, her foot tangled in the rigging, falls from the beam and is sucked under.

Molly's shoulders have already started to blister in the heat: small white bubbles of water-filled skin. Of the thirty-odd women she's counted on the shell path, only Sugar, Tattio and the silent girl seem unaffected by the sun, but even their dark skin is sand-whipped and dry. They need to find shade and water, if only to maintain the flow of their milk, and to keep the babies from crying.

The path is barely a serving tray's width and Molly struggles to move down the line of women collapsed on its smooth white surface, without stepping on the sand or the boggy earth behind. She reaches Betty, whose hands are free of burden, limp and resting in her lap. Molly cannot carry Ada's baby as well as her own.

'Betty,' Molly whispers.

Betty, like the others, is staring ahead at the ship, as if she can somehow will it back on the ocean with her gaze.

'Betty.' This time Molly hisses her name. Her voice carries across the sand in a wave and it's enough to snap Betty out of her reverie.

Betty looks at Molly, her eyes wide and red-rimmed. She looks in shock, barely blinks. Her brown hair is matted at her scalp in a thick coil, speckled with salt. It must be heavy, but she does nothing to correct it.

'Are we dead?' Betty whispers, raising her hands from the folds of her dress and staring at her bruised palms. 'Is Ada alive under the sand? Will I find my babby here?'

Molly's never believed in much, except the tarot cards, but she knows the body does not survive death. It rots. Betty's child is buried at sea, wrapped in petticoats. They will not be reunited, despite the red token she folded into the shroud.

In this place they are breathing, moving, and thinking. Molly intends to keep it that way. She's had too many years under someone else's lock and key to give up so easily.

'Are we under the sea?' Betty asks, her face as white as scrubbed linen.

Even when Betty was helping Molly with the women who were labouring, trapped in the hold of the ship, her mind seemed to drift to places Molly could not understand.

'We have to find shelter,' Molly says. 'I need you to help me.'

Betty was so tender to the women during birthing: holding Vera's hand until she passed, even though blood was emptying out of her like a pump; sharing her rations of sauerkraut, salt meat and dried biscuit; reciting passages from the Bible. People don't forget kindness. If Molly can just raise Betty to stand alongside her, the others might follow.

Betty stands, refusing Molly's proffered arm as she smooths down her heavy skirts. She clears her throat, spitting debris into her hand and then grimacing as she looks around for somewhere to wipe it.

'God has saved us,' she says, 'and we must follow his path.' She gestures to the line of white shells that stretches away from the shore and bends into the forest behind them.

'Praise be the Lord,' Rosie, a small, red-headed girl, replies.

Molly bites back a response. They need to put trust in themselves, not some man in the sky who is careless and cruel. She says nothing as, one by one, the women start to move, standing up, shaking away sand and lethargy. Molly catches Sarah, two women down from Betty, muttering into the crook of her elbow as she settles her baby: 'We ain't saved, we're damned to hell. Bit o jam ain't twigged it yet.'

Molly stays as silent as the girl that saved Ada's baby. It's better to let someone else do the talking.

BETTY

They've been walking for an age. Betty winces in pain with each footstep but it's nowt physical, it's Ada's babby. She's got to do summat to stop the wailing, which clangs in her head like church bells. Betty knows she should feel sorry for the child, losing its ma like it did to that deadly sand, and give praise to the miracle of its survival, but there's nowt but a tingle of irritation and an aching throb between her legs.

She holds the child in the crook of her arm and grapples with her memory, desperate to find words from Cook's Sunday readings to fill her head, aught to dull the sound of the babby trying to suck her dress, and the high-pitched buzz of the insects that land on her like April drizzle. Her babby is somewhere, alone, drifting in the sea. Betty blinks away the tears that start to spill, imagining them tracing a white line down her dirty face.

'God is our refuge and strength, an ever-present help in trouble.'

But the words, which so comforted her in the chapel at the Manor, make her think of Master's thick lips, puckered with text. It were her fault. She tempted him. She should never have been in the stables on her own, but she liked the horses, feeding them carrots from the kitchen, with their hot breath and silken coats. Cook said Master were a godly man and it were a moment of weakness, as men are prone to. Perhaps, like those moments, pushed up against the hay bale, this loss will pass into numbness.

Betty tries to see what's ahead, but the silent, primitive girl's wild frizzy curls block her view. It feels like they've been walking forever along this narrow white path. The trees either side of her are so close and thick with leaves she can barely breathe. She needs to stop and adjust herself; her arm is starting to ache from clutching the babby and she's sweating with the effort and the burning heat, but she will not remove her dress and expose her undergarments like so many of the others. There could be savages here, hiding in the forest, or men with webbed hands, and it will not do to offer encouragement.

'Need me some bloody gas pipes,' a woman behind her says.

Betty shudders at her language. Breeches are for men. Sarah's got a foul mouth and no decorum. Probably dragged up in the gutter. Cook used to talk about women like her: unfortunate women: vessels for disease. Betty's not sure exactly what were meant, but with Sarah's sagging breasts, lank hair and pock-marked face, Betty decides it's better to keep her distance.

Betty walks faster, urging the quiet girl forward with a prod in the back. She can feel the knobs of her spine under her fingers. When the girl turns, frowning, Betty tries for a smile, because at least she still wears her dress. She's not forced to witness the girl's full, brown, milky breasts. Her stomach clenches with distaste. As soon as they are able, they must baptise the children. Perhaps she has been saved for this purpose—like the adventurers in the stories Master liked to read to her—to stop the others behaving like animals.

The trees grow less dense further along the path, fanning out to smaller, flatter bushes with frayed green leaves and deep orange berries. The air smells sweeter, fresher than before. Small yellow creatures dart over the white shells, which end abruptly at a clearing. One creature runs over Betty's foot. She screams, setting the babby off again.

'Take it!' she says, thrusting the babby at the silent girl, heat rising in her cheeks. She can't look at its scrunched-up face no more.

When the silent girl takes the child, it quietens. Ada's babby hates her. She's useless. Maybe it's a good thing her own babby is dead.

Betty turns away from it all, thinks about running back down the path to the sea, to lose herself in the sand like Ada, but Sarah blocks her passage.

'You queer in the attic girl?' Sarah asks, a sneer on her red, pitted face.

Betty struggles to breathe. The air feels as thick as treacle in her throat.

Tattio puts a hand on Sarah's shoulder. She's Sarah's opposite, with darkly silken, smooth skin, deep brown eyes and eyelashes that curl as if they have been set in rags.

'E's lost a babe,' Tattio says gently, using words Betty don't altogether recognise.

Sarah shrugs Tattio's hand off. 'Ada's dead. Her brat ain't good enough for her?' She spits onto the dirt, and it lands with a slap on the toe of Betty's shoe.

Betty swallows down her disgust. None of this is fair. She should be at home, chopping herbs, cleaning Master's silver. She were good at that and he were teaching her to read. Betty realises now that Cook had tried to help her. If she had taken Cook's phial of medicine to remove the blockage, there would have been no reason for her to leave the big house and Master. No reason to be here with these women.

There's pressure on Betty's waist as someone draws her away from Sarah and into the clearing. Molly, with a sour milk smell.

'Time will heal,' Molly whispers, her breath hot on Betty's ear. 'I should know.'

Betty do not believe Molly because she has the same tone Cook used when agreeing with Master, sniping about his ways the moment his back were turned.

'Trust in God,' Betty finishes, her voice flat as crinoline without a cage.

MOLLY

The clearing is nothing more than a patch of damp earth framed by black rock and flat dry bushes, but it is cooler, and firmer underfoot than the shore. The women that are injured or have little milk can at least rest, whilst others take charge of feeding their own and others' babies. Molly cannot sit. Her attention is caught by the rhythmic drip of water coming from somewhere close. She knows that sound. In the Asylum, in her small room, looking up at the stained rose cornice, at the brown damp which fingered the intricate leaf design where water leaked through, she'd listened to it splash into the metal bucket below.

Molly adjusts her baby, asleep on the fleshy pillows of her bosom, and steps away from the group and further from the clearing. The ground is different again here, covered with a fine grey dust which holds tight to her footprints. She sneezes, the sound echoing back at her.

'To thy health,' Betty mumbles, half asleep, slumped somewhere behind her.

Betty's barely said anything since the silent girl took Ada's baby from her. She refuses to wet nurse others. When she does speak, it's as if she's reciting psalms on Sunday. Maybe the short rest will have lifted her?

The silent girl moves next to Molly, her finger on her lips, pointing in the direction of a tall tree, covered in shells.

'What should I call you?' Molly asks.

It isn't right that she doesn't have a name.

The girl shrugs.

'Call her Newt,' Sarah shouts across the clearing, her voice a hard thud against Molly's ears. 'Like one of 'em mutes that go to 'em funerals ain't she? They pays good money for that.'

It doesn't seem right. Molly can't call her that, but the girl shrugs again, like she doesn't care.

The silent girl steps cautiously forward ten yards, until she's an arms-length away from the tree. It has a thin beige trunk with papery bark and branches at the top that brush upwards like the girl's hair, but in faded green spikes. She plucks one of the violet shells from the trunk and there's a sucking sound, like a baby finding the nipple. From this distance the shells look the same as the clusters of snails that climbed the Asylum walls; their fragile shells dotted on damp and crumbling brick.

The silent girl returns with the creature, turning it over and showing it to Molly. It's the size of her dirty palm and has a fleshy insert, tucked inside. The violet shell is coated with a dark red, sticky sap. The girl pinches her fingers to her mouth.

'Wallfish,' Betty says, now awake and leaning past Molly to get a better look at the shell. 'Good for the breath.' She breathes out, touching her chest where the eyelets of her bodice begin. 'Master Henry had special forks to eat them.' She blinks and a tear traces the mound of her plump, youthful cheek.

'We can eat them then?' Molly checks.

But Betty's withdrawn again, back to the place where she has been taking refuge since they arrived in the clearing. Molly's worried about her. She's a child, can't be much more than three and ten, the age girls usually ripen. Perhaps the alienists were right about hard work: the laundry rooms, washing and scrubbing, turning the mangle, anger spent out in suds. It was a distraction and Betty needs a distraction.

Molly turns. That sound again. The trickle of water.

'Can you hear that?' Molly asks the silent girl, cupping her hand over her ear, even though she knows the girl can hear perfectly well, better than most.

The girl points beyond the large tree, her slender hand indicating right. She taps her chest.

'Yes. I'll come with you,' Molly whispers, glancing behind her at the other women grouped in the sparse shade of the clearing. Many of them are asleep. Should she say something?

Sarah is sitting on a jagged black rock, legs spread apart, ignoring the cloud of flies that flit around her. She has Ada's baby in her arms, and her own baby resting in the hammock of her petticoats. Earlier, Molly watched the women take Sarah's cue, collapsing on the damp earth like fallen cards and sleeping where they fell, but they cannot stay here. It is too exposed.

'What do yer want, Miss lar-di-dah,' Sarah says as Molly approaches, her voice loud and loaded with contempt.

Molly feels the familiar snap of verbal restraints, until the silent girl appears at her side and loosens them.

'This one ain't no church bell but she got us off that ship, didn't yer, Newt? Saved our Ada's bairn. What do *yer* want duckie?' Sarah asks.

Molly's skin prickles as the silent girl turns to appraise her, reading her like one of the books she had access to in Dr Johnston's office. Then the girl turns back to Sarah and mimes walking and taking a drink, indicating the direction of the large tree, before finally unstrapping her baby.

'Got me daddles full duckie,' Sarah says. 'Tattio!' she yells.

Molly winces at the volume of Sarah's voice. Has she learned nothing from Ada's death? Tattio saunters over to them, her skin glistening in the heat.

'I will care for e,' Tattio says softly, taking Newt's baby in her long dark arms. She sits down next to Sarah, mirroring her, her petticoats tight over spread legs. She places Newt's baby there, jiggling her own baby in the sling when it whimpers.

Molly stands still, unsure what to do. She's never been comfortable with power games, prefers straight talking, but women aren't supposed to speak their mind, even here it seems.

The other women look at Sarah as if they are waiting for her instruction, as if she has some kind of hold over them, even though she did nothing to help them on the ship except bark orders. Finally, Sarah nods and Rosie steps forward – the slight girl with red hair who was praying with Betty before. Molly unstraps her child and kisses it on the forehead under its thick mop of fair hair. It cries, one sharp stab. Molly freezes, expecting something awful to happen.

'Be safe with mine,' Rosie promises, holding out her bare arms. They're covered with fine blonde hairs and freckles, but her hands are calloused, rough when they brush against Molly's skin. Molly recognises the hard skin; hours in the laundry or scrubbing floors. 'God helps 'em that help each other.'

Rosie's right. It'll be safer for the baby here. They have no idea what they'll find and Molly fears that sand that sucks the life from you won't be the only danger in this new place.

NEWT

Newt's been called worse: baggage, blowse, savage, half-caste bitch, but names don't mean nothing, they're just a sound that trumpets out of people's mouths. Her name is not for them to speak, it died on her tongue when her Ma was taken from her.

Newt's not scared of women like Sarah, and she'll not be bit. They don't do nothing except shove people around with their hateful words, but they're not in the pan now. Others will soon see that Sarah's weak. Anyway, she's made a friend of Sarah as best she can, and she won't rock that boat: don't need the kicking. Let her use one of the others as a punch bag. Her baby will be safe with Tattio, and she'll teach her child to fight its corner when the time comes.

Newt scratches her leg and glances at Molly, who's looking ahead, past the trees and towards a large rock. Clearly, she thinks there's something there.

Newt's good at reading people. It's how she stayed safe on the streets. Take Molly: she's older than most others but you can tell she's always slept in a comfortable bed, never an alleyway or under the bridge, on hard cobbles that dig into yer back. She ain't never slept in the slums with one eye open and a knife by her petticoats. Never had to take a coin for her quim or beg for the rotten vegetables in the market. But Molly knows things, and Newt can hear the words she wants to say, even when she swallows them down like a glob of phlegm.

Newt knows how that feels—when too much needs to be said that nothing is said at all.

Molly is of use, even though she sometimes sounds like one of them women that walks arm in arm with their fella at night, in their fancy feathered hats and shiny shoes, flashing off their ivories. They're blind to their men, who'll be out on the streets later, stabbing Newt or another gel with their hornpipes.

Newt watches Molly drag Betty from the rock she's been sitting on.

'Bring the bucket,' Molly says.

It's like she's her Ma or something.

Newt don't mind Betty neither, even with her blabbing and blubbering; she's just a stupid kid. It ain't Newt's business if she wants to waste her breath praying. Words don't bring nothing; not food, nor water, and definitely not safety from monsters hiding in frockcoats. Anyway, ain't no one coming for Newt, but that's okay. For the first time since her Ma died, Newt is safe from the black-eyed gratitude of men.

Newt spits onto the ground and wipes her trap. Sees Betty wince.

Newt knows better than anyone how to find food and water and when she gets a bit of time, she'll fashion herself a spear from the hard wood trees they passed on the way to this clearing, using the knife tucked in her drawers. The same knife Molly used on the ship to cut the cords. She won't use it on the other women though, unless they give her cause.

BETTY

Molly's grip on her arm is tight, and Betty shakes it off. She don't want to think about touch; of Master Henry's hands shackling her ankles, and the straw scratching her back in fingernails as he pulled her towards him, her heavy skirts riding up in the dust. Don't want to think of her burning shame, raw and stinging when she toileted. She wants to remember afternoons at the kitchen table, eating thick slices of warm, buttered bread, and Master Henry teaching her to read the scientific stories he liked so much, even though they sometimes frightened her. It were hard to forget the strange peoples and worlds described in them pages.

At least carrying the metal bucket is easier than the babby, which did nowt but scream at her.

Betty trails behind Molly and Newt, picking her way between the scratchy dead bushes, which shred the bottom of her skirts to tatters. The wood has changed from the thick trees with glossy leaves and heavy red fruit that lined the weird white path, to thin, tall trees with bleached bark that reach to the heavens, with sticky stuff like jam that oozes from their trunks. Betty can barely see the leaves of these ones; they are so spindly, reminding her of the sweep's brush. The birds like them, and they sit up high on the branches, wings coloured bright like rainbows. They don't sing like she expects though.

Betty looks around, decides she could get lost here. Who would miss her? But what if while she was walking there was an earthquake, or a storm and she got buried? She could be trapped for three hundred years in the same dress and wet shoes.

She's quite panicked by the time they reach the curved opening in the huge grey rock. It towers above them, taller than the trees. When Betty squints, she can just see that it ends in a point, like the iron Cook heated in the coals.

Now she can hear water: the sound of rain dripping from sills. One of her jobs at the Manor had been to scrub the windows with scrunched up paper: pamphlets Master Henry had no use for, vile protestations he called them. Them windows had been spotless.

Betty ploughs into Molly, nearly knocking her over.

'A cave,' Molly says.

The word, spoken aloud, sends a shiver down Betty's spine. In Master's scientific stories, they drowned babbies in places like this.

It's dark and damp inside the cave. Betty hangs back behind Molly and Newt, who seem to have no fear of the secrets held within the dark, pitted walls. The drip of water gets louder and the air cooler and damp. Betty shivers, another reason to be glad she didn't discard her dress like so many of the others.

They are so far in now that Betty can no longer see Newt; she's camouflaged like one of them strange creatures the size of mice that ran across their shoes on the walk here. Newt had caught one of the scaly bodies in the clearing and looked in its beady, unblinking eye. It were not one of God's creatures, of that Betty's sure.

A drop of icy water lands on Betty's shoulder. She gasps, turning, frantic, not sure which way is out. Feeling for the wall, slimy like the trails of slugs on stone paths, Betty slides down until seated, dropping the bucket with a clang. She starts to sob. She wants to go home. Nowt here is as it should be.

A cool hand on her shoulder causes Betty to remove hers from her wet face and look up. Beads of light, the same shape as the drops on Master Henry's chandelier, flicker on the walls. Betty rises, leaning on Molly's arm. What is this strange blue light?

Newt has her hand in a shallow pool and as she moves it, the water glistens as if there is crystal floating there or a hundred nubs of candles flickering. Is this some devilish magic?

'We should not drink this,' Molly says. 'It does not smell right. There might be better water further in, a spring or an underground well.'

Now Newt's doing summat with her face, and Betty realises she's laughing, but it looks odd because there's no sound coming out—like she's in pain. She's holding a vessel in her hand, a jar of some sort, like Cook used to store pickles. When she taps the glass, it glows like an oil lamp.

'Where'd you get that from?' Betty asks, frowning.

Newt points down at the pool.

Betty shudders. Water that is also light? Something else that could be found in Master's scientific stories.

Newt beckons to them. Betty follows, clutching Molly's petticoat, carefully, step by step, over the hard, uneven, slippery ground. As they get closer Betty sees several of the jars lined up against the wall and, above them, faint drawings on the wall. Dark red ink; beasts of some kind.

Newt fills three jars with the strange glowing stuff from the pool and passes one to Betty. When she shakes the jar, it gives enough light that she can see the cave properly. In the main section, which is bigger than Master's drawing room, there are two shallow pools within the rocks. There's also a small opening in the curved back wall, with barely room for two persons to pass through. Lifting the jar high, Betty can see there's summat beyond.

Betty don't follow Newt but stays behind the rock partition with Molly. There is a small, raised pool inside, which looks deeper than the ones in the big cave, the water still and black. Newt drops a rock into the centre. After the first splash, it makes no sound.

Betty swallows, steps back, half expecting a creature to emerge from the water or for Newt to be dragged under.

'Can we drink it?' Molly asks, leaving Betty's side.

Betty cannot see Newt's answer, but she hears Molly laugh, and when Molly steps back through the gap, her face is wet.

'It does not smell, and the taste is clean, like water from a well. Where is the bucket? We must take some back for the others.'

Betty retrieves the bucket from where she dropped it. As she hands it to Molly, her gaze fixes on the walls of the main cave.

'We should look for the people that drew them pictures on the wall and were clever enough to use them jars,' Betty says, thinking of Master's stories, and how they always came good in the end. 'There must be men here who can protect us.'

MASTER'S BOOK OF SCIENTIFIC STORIES

Lagoon Island: a commune under the sea.

I do not know what possessed me to voyage in the small vessel entitled: 'The Adonis'. It was neither stately nor majestic, a simple wooden affair, but I suspect I had always fancied myself a romantic man and an adventurer.

On our departure, the sea was as docile as a sleeping infant, the wind a mere breath on the sail, but even before one hand of my pocket watch had completed its cycle, the sky had become dark and brooding; the sea unquenchable in its fury, howling and sending us spinning into monstrous waves.

I do not recall what happened next except I was tossed about like a shilling, flung into the pockets of the abyss. I awoke cold and with a deep hunger, my woollen suit heavy with water. I was in a tunnel, which I perceived to be somewhat pocked in texture, much like descriptions I had read of volcanic rocks. I was surprised to discover I could breathe, as if I were upon the land and not under the weight of the turbulent sea which had thrown me here. Behind me, at the entrance to the tunnel, hanging in a thick drape, was the sea itself.

Inside the tunnel the walls were certainly worthy of attention, executed with marvellous nicety, smooth, almost marble in surface, and festooned with something like diamonds, twinkling like many hundred stars and of a spiritual quality. It appeared to my untrained eye that they were nature's own designs.

My eyes adjusted to the light and I turned to observe a man standing next to me. He was tall, much taller than me, lithe and with large hands. I perceived web-like structures stretched between his long fingers, a similar greenish tint to the sea plants which grew on the substrate where I lay. The man's hair was white and scanty but the length of it was that of a woman. His decency was maintained by a skin of some unknown animal tied around his waist below a chest and shoulders of Herculean proportions.

The Fisherman, or at least that is what he named himself, seemed ill at ease with the few words he knew of the English language. His speech largely consisted of utterings not dissimilar to the bark of the porpoise, a few of which I had witnessed before the storm and my tumultuous journey.

The Fisherman took my arm as one would a lady on an evening promenade and, after some considerable walk where I struggled to match his vast stride, he led me through the tunnel to a chamber with a high-pitched cupola of transparent material not unlike the glass of home. I was surprised to see the azure sky bearing down. It was as if I were outside and not beneath the sea at all. Was this the high point of the atoll the captain of the Adonis had pointed to, in the distance, before the storm?

We were not alone in the chamber. Seated on a platform of black pitted rock, was a group of men with high, intellectual foreheads. When they spoke, their voices smote my ear, high pitched, words as prolonged as the demonic shriek of a woman. The Fisherman must have witnessed my discomfort because he held out a strange violet shell-like cone to me, indicating I should press it firmly to my ear. As if by some conjurer's magic, I could suddenly understand the men. It must have been some sort of parlour trick that I cannot properly explain.

The Fisherman informed me that these were the Elders of the Commune, the wisest in the community, gathered to decide my fate. I was astounded that their faces were smooth, tinged blue and with no evidence of wrinkles. Neither did they seem to have disease or affliction but full enjoyment of their youthful faculties. When I asked the Fisherman their age, suspecting they were considerably more than five and sixty he merely shrugged and said: 'as old as the sea.' I was at a loss as to his meaning.

After some parlay, the Elders focused their attention on me.

'What is it you want?' they asked, their voices a strange harmony, as if they spoke as one.

Of course, I could not respond in a sufficient manner because I did not comprehend what had brought me here at all.

'His carriage was claimed by the Creator,' the Fisherman said on my account.

I had many questions, but this was not the time to indulge. I had been saved from the soulless depths by these strange peoples. I prostrated myself on my knees and poured forth my praise to this Creator the Fisherman had spoken about.

The Elders watched with a seemingly keen interest.

'What is it you want?' they asked again. The harmony caused me great anxiety, so alien was it to my ears.

'To...to understand.' I could not help but stumble over my words, as if I were pigeon-livered, not a man at all.

The Fisherman approached the platform. The Elders parlayed for some time before he returned to my side, helping me once again from my knees.

'First we eat.' He never seemed to use more than the minimum of sounds to convey his intentions.

The Fisherman led me through another tunnel lit by the same sparkling stones and into a vast cave-like room. The air was damp and cold, and there was a vegetable smell which at times assaulted my nostrils. I became quickly accustomed to it. It was no more displeasing than Cook's day-old cabbage stew.

There were many men in the room, varying in height and girth but I perceived all of them had silver-grey eyes, the colour of the small fish I had observed hauled onto the shore before the voyage that brought me to this unknown place. The Fisherman informed me that the Commune always ate together and shortly the Elders would join us.

It appeared I was expected to serve myself. There were shells filled with handfuls of a dark green vegetable, which tasted of salt and small molluscs, not unlike the cockles Cockneys seem to enjoy, but flatter and with a bleached white hue. I perceived that the men ate little for their size and I was certainly not satiated.

'Eat little, live long,' the Fisherman explained.

My previous question as to exactly how long had not yet been answered.

After the meal, the Fisherman took me to the Nursery, explaining that all children in the Commune were brought up alike, children of one universal parent. I did not, of course, comprehend this.

'Where are the girls?' I asked.

The Fisherman frowned at me as if he did not understand my question. So displeased did he appear, that I decided it best to defer from that line of questioning.

The children, of all sizes, from baby to almost-man, wore the same skin-like tunic. Their appearance too was identical, with broad chests and the same silver-grey eyes. As for their amusements: shells of a structure and range of such diverse colours as I have not observed before.

The Fisherman explained that the Commune were schooled in the ways of the sea until they were grown, when they chose their futures either as parent, educator or fishermen. Only educators became elders he explained, and it was a lifelong achievement. He also confided that they had little by way of possessions, but that the hard life harnessed the spirit.

When I asked him about crime, he informed me the word did not exist in his language. I supposed that one cannot steal that which another does not have.

During my tour I did not witness any child or person deformed or monstrous in any way. There seemed no sickness and no warring. It appeared nothing if not harmonious and I began to conceive that perhaps the Commune might be something to aspire to.

Next to the Nursery was another room within which lay a large icy pool. I perceived it must be close to the outside world because I could feel a chilled breath brush my face. The Fisherman motioned for me to wait and within minutes (though it could have been considerably more——I was cold and I am unsure how time worked under the sea) a man with a babe in arms entered the room. The babe was thrown into the water without so much as a by-your-leave. It seemed an atrocity to me and I felt obliged to dive in and rescue the innocent. The Fisherman stopped me, wrapping his strong arms around my waist.

'Nature's selection,' said he.

The child did not emerge from the water. I felt a deadening of my heart.

The Fisherman explained that resources were few and members of the Commune were only too pleased to pass through the water when their time was near, embracing their union with the Creator. All children were tested this way.

'We must be whole to serve the Creator,' he said.

At that, a carriage of gold appeared from beneath the lake. It was resplendent, studded with rubies and other jewels. The child was laid within. Reined to the vessel were two handsome animals, resembling the porpoise in shape and size, but clad in a leathery grey hide. The creatures seemed docile, perfectly capable of carrying the burden of the child.

The man who had tossed the child seemingly so carelessly into the pool, now embraced the child in his arms, and as I raised the cone to my ear, I thought I witnessed a blessing of some description.

'What will happen to the child?' I asked.

'It will be returned to the sea, once we have mourned, for even the beasts must be fed,' the Fisherman told me.

I must admit, that although witnessing the child's demise appalled me, when I saw the peaceful, sleeping face of the child, now swaddled in a cloth somewhat akin to the petticoats of the fairer sex, and noticed his missing limb, I wondered if this was, perhaps, a sensible solution.

'Passing is painless,' said the Fisherman, as if to allay my fears.

'This Creator,' began I.

'The only One we serve.'

'Yes,' agreed I. 'What exactly is he? A god?'

'He is nature and the sea,' the Fisherman explained, leaving me no better informed. Yet I was struck by the fact it was a simple and peaceful life in the Commune, one not plagued by sickness or injury.

The fisherman frowned. 'They search for you. It is time to go,' he said.

I was disinclined to take my leave. I still had so many questions and, of course, I was uncertain as to his meaning.

The porpoises, if that is what they were, drew the carriage to my side. The Fisherman motioned for me to enter, with a flap of his fin-like hands. In a flurry of activity, one I can barely recall, I believe I observed the Fisherman enter the lake and take hold of the creature's reins.

The next thing I recall, I was face down in the water, drifting near the shore where we had begun our voyage, amid cries of my fellow men, who informed me they had been searching for me all night.

Later, when I removed the cone-like shell from my jacket pocket, I was surely not mistaken when I heard the cries of a child.

MOLLY

Molly awakens with the heat from the sun, which powers through the cave where they slept last night, their backs against the damp walls. Her legs are stiff from sleeping so awkwardly. There's not enough room inside to contain thirty of them comfortably. The saltwater stings as she splashes it onto her skin from the shallow pool at her feet, entering the cuts and scrapes made by the sand and the ship, when the storm wrecked it. She runs her finger over them. They are healing quickly; less angry this morning than she expected.

She glances across at Sarah and Rosie, still sleeping, their warm breath adding droplets to the dank air. Some of the women's chests crackle like crumpled paper when they exhale, reminding Molly of the spores that grew on the Asylum windowsills and how difficult it was to breathe sometimes. It is too damp to stay here, even though it's cooler and the babies are safe, snuggled in the hammocks of petticoats.

Molly's gaze lifts. There might be something in what Betty said about the simple line drawings on the cave wall: some kind of animal? Perhaps they once roamed this land. They are certainly evidence of another people, here before them, marking their territory. She'd meant to look at them more closely last night, but the women were packed in too tight, and then the sun sunk without warning, pitching them into a darkness Molly had never experienced before. The jars didn't seem to hold light for long without constant shaking and no one had the energy for that.

They must search for the other people today but also be cautious. Sometimes those who are charged to protect you, who appear honourable, cause the most harm.

Careful not to wake the others, Molly steps out into the forest, her baby strapped tight to her chest, its face resting on her bosom. Last night she rinsed the thin strips of woollen cloth used to bind them together in one of the salt pools, and it no longer smells of the sweat of the woman that once wore it, or her baby's waste.

Molly blinks, not yet accustomed to the intensity of light. Crouching, she removes the cloth cover from the bucket they refilled last night, cups her hands, and takes a drink.

Newt and Tattio are already waiting outside. Molly isn't sure if they rose early or slept there. The exhaustion from spending the last few weeks fully awake on the ship, her hands busy with birth, has fair knocked her sideways.

She takes in a breath of hot air. They have survived the voyage, the wreck, and the night. It is a start.

'Us should follow de track.' Tattio indicates a strip of dusty, crushed undergrowth leading away from the cave and further inland.

The path Tattio points to has been flattened down, tracing the grey rock which rises to the right of them, reaching a point in the heavens.

It is further evidence of other people.

'We should be careful,' Molly says.

Newt nods and passes Molly a broken branch from a stack, propped up against the cave wall. It will not protect them much, but it is better than nothing.

It's hard keeping up with Tattio's long strides, one to every two of Molly's in her salt-crusted shoes, which dig into her feet since they dried out and shrank. The ground beneath them is hard and the plants spiky. The seeds lodge in skin, adding to the red ribbons already marking Molly's legs.

Molly has her pinkie ready to thrust into her baby's mouth in case it wakes, for they must tread silently, find food and better shelter until rescue comes.

Her stomach complains. The snails, which fair wore out her teeth chewing them, have made her feel sick. They need more than a bit of flesh and fresh water to keep their milk from drying up.

Within minutes sweat runs down Molly's back, pooling between her shoulder blades. She has never felt heat like this. The trees with their skinny trunks and high branches provide little shade.

Tattio stops suddenly, her finger to her lips. Molly listens. There is an absence of sound, more frightening than if there were a dozen voices. It's as if they have happened upon a graveyard.

Molly's head is full of what-ifs. What if the people eat human flesh to survive? What if they are enslaved or sacrificed?

They move carefully forward, conscious of every footstep, every crunch of dry vegetation and murmur, until they circumvent the corner of the rock. Here, the sound amplifies as if a gag has suddenly been removed and the island has found its voice.

There are six round huts, packed with earth and set in the shade, and other damaged structures which might be mended. Some distance beyond, over barren rock, is the sea. They have reached the other side of the island.

NEWT

There's so much on the island still to explore but the others, when not watching for ships, have seemed content to sleep all day for the last week, like fuzzocks. Newt don't know how they bear being stuck, snuffling and snorting like pigs in the small grass huts together that stink of smoke. The nights is so close, like rancid breath on yer mug, but a storm don't come. The huge ink sky makes a better roof than them bark strips they use to keep the bugs out, even if you can't see yer daddles in front of yer mug when the sun disappears.

Newt's never liked being confined. Here she's a dew beater, rising with the heat. Collecting the tin buckets, she quietly traces the flattened path to the grey rock. She likes the silence here, is no longer concerned with the thud of hooves, the clatter of carriage wheels and the half-hour gentlemen, bung-eyed, leaving the public houses, looking for a trull to turn a trick.

Picking up one of the white shells, which seem to erupt like pox on the sand when the tide recedes, Newt scores another line on the cave wall, careful not to draw over the pictures of the strange red-brown animals. What do they mean?

Newt turns away, ain't got time for wondering. Leaving the buckets in the cave, she cat-foots it towards the beach. She passes the half-buried ship. Even when the sea comes in and floods, it never move with the swell. It's like one of them statues of haughty rich men meant to remind you of yer place in the world.

Breathing in the salt-air Newt looks out to the horizon. As usual there ain't nothing but the sun, fiery and orange, rising slowly above the thick green sea. Before Newt boarded the ship, she ain't never seen water this size, the way it stretches out. She was used to the Thames, the noise of the barges and the stink of shit.

Some of the rednuts have dropped onto the earth overnight. Newt picks them up, peeling off the outer flesh before washing the husk and her hands in salt water. The red coating brings yer hands up in welts, like you been whipped, if yer not careful. Newt is very careful. Thirsty, she takes one of the cleaned husks and slams it repeatedly against the hard wood trunk of the nearest tree. It helps to think of his gibface when she smashes it. The reason for her incident; the reason she's here.

The sound of the thudding dies as it hits the dense vegetation. The husk splits and Newt draws the nut to her trap, drinking the cloudy milk before it spills. She never thought she'd ever be in a place where fruit was there for the taking. Smashing the nut further, she ties the small shards of white meat up in rags, threading them into the hem of her petticoat. She's collected enough to survive a few days if need be. She's managed on less. She'll put them under the rock in the cave, with the other things she's found. The remaining rednuts she folds into a square of woollen cloth which she hooks over her shoulder.

There's a sound on the path behind her: a crunch of shells. Newt glances back, mindful she has yet to explore the whole island, but it's only Betty, sitting alone on the shore, as she has been the last few days since the community decided time were better spent with the children than waiting for rescue. Betty's lost weight. Her dress hangs from her bony frame, her plump cheeks are sunken. She looks the grey of dirty linen hung between houses, despite how her skin has been smacked red by the sun.

Betty needs to look after herself better.

You can't rely on no one but yerself.

MOLLY

Molly doesn't sleep well. The heat, her full breasts, and the thin bark matting, part of the industry left by whoever lived here before, all keep her awake. The mats are the only thing that separates Molly from the hard dust floor and the chirping insects, scuttling and jumping around the circular dry-grass hut like circus performers. Still, it is better than the damp cave where they spent that first night.

Careful not to wake the other women who share the tight space, Molly steps between their relaxed, tangled limbs, and pushes aside the woven grass panel, which serves as a door. Stretching, she lifts her face to the light and enjoys the warmth on her bare shoulders. She likes the early morning, before most of the community rises. Everything sleeps: the bright birds roosting in the highest branches of the trees, which shed their brown needles on the forest floor; the violet snails on the trunks near the cave; the furred creatures with bushy tails, reminding her of squirrels except their coats are ebony and their teeth prominent and sharp like daggers, and the dark sea, calm, silent, lapping close to the white path, obscuring the black sand, making her sometimes forget what lies beneath.

Molly walks the few steps to the nursery hut and pushes aside the screen. She's greeted by the stuttered breath of two dozen infants and the snorts of Sarah and Rosie, who have slept here since that first night. The nursery seemed the best solution to keeping the children safe and fed, what with so many women needing their strength to mend the damaged huts and forage, and food not being plentiful.

Inside the mud-packed walls, the babies sleep in hammocks made from discarded dresses, stretched and knotted over branches. Molly glances around to find any child that's awake and needs feeding. She cannot wait. It is too painful, and milk must not be wasted.

Her own child is snuggled up tight next to Ada's baby, fist in mouth, but Newt's is stirring in the end hammock, not ever one to sleep long and always hungry. Molly takes the child from the hut and sits quietly outside, cradling it, mindful not to disturb the others. Its brown eyes are bright and beady, staring up at her as it feeds, as if it is eager to know this world. She loves this child as if it were her own and plants a kiss on its hot forehead as she burps it. The children are growing quicker than expected with some already strong enough to hold their heads steady. The days feel longer here. Perhaps it is simply the heat. Or possibly the women are more relaxed, no longer shepherded by men.

The baby satiated and Molly more comfortable, she returns the child to their bed and prepares for the day ahead. Removing the glossy leaves from the entrance of the food hut, Molly ducks in and grabs the broom, a dry, spiked branch. She sweeps out the strange, coloured creatures seeking shade inside. Looking up, at the sharp crack of a twig, she sees Newt weave her way towards her. She's carrying one of the three metal buckets that washed in from the ship. It's brim full of water. Tattio is behind Newt, a wooden spike in her hand and a woollen bag slung over her shoulder. Tattio's probably been out collecting plants, and weeds from the sea. She says everything looks different here from the ones she used before to make tinctures, but they smell the same if you know what you need. Except for the purple leaves that smell like mint. They make you sick as a dog.

Molly nods and carries on sweeping, as they busy themselves preparing food outside the hut. They all have their jobs to do: ones they have chosen.

As the sun reaches above the top of the big grey rock, which shades the huts, the camp comes to life. Molly rests the broom against the side of the hut and helps Tattio gut the fish, hanging the thin strips of meat on a line to dry. The task complete, Tattio leaves her to walk over to the nursery hut, joining the queue to be given one of the babies to feed.

The babies tended to, and the community seated in the meeting place, Molly spoons the meal into the shallow brown cups, made from the hard shell of the rednuts, and places them in front of each of the women, who are ravenous, as is usual after nursing.

Molly frowns, a spare cup in her hand. Betty's missing from the circle again. Her mood has been getting worse, changing as many times as the scaly creatures, which shed skin daily as they sunbathe in the grey dust. Molly's run out of words to try to convince Betty that there are no miracles, that no one is coming to rescue them—they must make the best of it. She's not the only one who has tried: Sarah, with her harsh words designed to spark Betty to anger, has failed to rouse even a frown on Betty's young face, and Betty has brushed off Tattio's gentle touch as if she cannot feel it.

They need to move forward; focus on this new life they have been saved for. The island is already giving them more than Molly hoped on that first day.

She glances round the circle, before taking her place. Now is not the time to mention Betty's absence, especially as Sarah thinks Betty's got the morbs and shouldn't be near the children.

Linking hands, the women voice together:

For what we are about to receive may we be truly thankful.

Molly is thankful, but not to any God, rather for their own endeavours and hard work. Saying grace is a habit the group have not yet broken—the other women seem to need it, especially Rosie and Flora.

Pushing the fibrous root into her mouth with her fingers, Molly chews. It's been steeped in the pale milk drained from the rednuts that fall from the trees by the beach, and is creamy and filling, with a taste like marzipan. It's not so different to the breakfast porridge at the Asylum but here at least, Molly can choose not to finish her meal, without it being noted down in a journal. Not that she ever leaves anything. Here you must eat every mouthful.

One of the other women collects the empty cups, rinses and refills them with water from the cave, then collects them again. It is a routine that works, born out of necessity rather than any planning, but soon they will need to think further ahead.

Molly sometimes wonders what her life might have been like if she'd stayed in London, whether Dr Johnston might have been able to bend the rules for her. It is an unrealistic dream. Molly would have been deemed an unfit mother, and her child, like the others, would have been taken from her. At least here she can be part of her baby's life and witness them grow—have her say in how that is done.

Molly readies herself to start repairs. It's hard, heavy work but there is something to be said for having purpose. Today a group of them will tackle the walls of the far hut, which needs re-packing with the wet grey earth. There's a big black hole in one side, as if something hot rolled through and scorched it. It will need several layers and drying time in between. Not that they have to worry about the weather. The sun rises every morning without fail and hangs heavy in the sky until late at night.

'I'll collect the bark,' Molly says, keen to put distance between herself and Sarah, who is already snapping out orders.

A group of them will strip bark from the tall, thin trees near the cave, remove the outer husk and then bash the soft inner flesh flat with a rock until the surface is double in size. Once steeped in water they will then weave it in layers, not unlike the willow baskets they were instructed to make at the Asylum. This bark has a more papery texture than willow but holds well enough and dries tight.

Molly wipes her hands on her petticoat, caring nothing for the callouses marking the base of her fingers, or the deep scratches on her skin from weaving. The work is for the community: to keep the children safe.

NEWT

Newt walks barefoot along the shell path, past the ship sunk in the sand, and along to the rocks to do her ablutions. She don't like shoes, always too tight and with stitches that dig in yer flesh. Here, there ain't shit, other than what you bury, so you don't need nothing on yer feet if yer careful, and the dark green seawater heals skin quick.

The rock pools, which start where the path ends, is too far for most to walk on a hot day; the others seem to prefer to stay close to the children. They have enough milk without Newt always being there.

They ain't missing much. Newt's done the whole island now, and it ain't that big, no more than a day and some of walking each ways from the ship. There ain't nothing much to see, just the thick-trunked rednut trees on one side and thinner ones, packed tight like the women who choose to sleep in the huts. The far side don't have nothing that grow. The big rock is all that's in the middle.

There ain't much growing anywhere if truth be told, 'cept the bushes and the berries which stain yer daddles when you pop them hard like a blister, and the pale roots that don't seem to care if they've only dust to live in.

Newt don't much like the woods just off from the end of the beach, close to where the fishing is best, where the black sand gives way to sharp rock and where she is now. Instead of shade it gives you hot breath, and it's full to brimming with biting insects. It ain't just the air that causes her discomfort. Newt ain't shown no one the cracked, pitted, grey rock she found there, half buried in the brush. It had a child's mug on it, like there were a small skull stuck inside. It don't make no sense that a stone would eat a person, but there ain't no other way to explain it.

Newt spears the few silver fish brought in by the tide and trapped in the rock pools. They is easy pickings, not like the jumping creatures which don't go near no traps. There ain't no point trying for food further out from the camp neither, for the rock is too high to cast her net and the sea below so deep and dark it have no end.

Newt looks up as the sand ripples, a warning that someone's coming, no doubt yabbering too loud, and forgetting they make waves. Sometimes when the sand answers, Newt imagines Ada pushed back out, arms raised, like nothing happened.

Too long in the sun makes yer head go funny.

Newt washes herself, plucking out the thorns, which stick in her skin like spines. Then she dampens her hair, shrinking it to tight black ringlets. It's the best way to keep cool.

Collecting up her spoils, Newt slings her woollen bag over her shoulder and heads back to camp, stopping to score another mark on the cave wall. There are already too many to count.

BETTY

Betty clutches the branch close to her chest, watching for passing ships. She's knotted a scrap of sail to it, like a flag, to draw their attention. But rescue's not the only reason she keeps coming back to the beach.

She bites back tears as another warm, sticky, trickle of blood runs down her thigh. She's tried washing herself with the salt water, but it's done nowt to cure her of her affliction. She's fearful that she's going to end up like Master Henry's wife, hysterical with the curse. Betty never met her. She'd already been taken to the place for women like her by the time Betty arrived at the Manor House, but Cook told her that Lady Harrington were always angry and her manner most unladylike: screaming and cursing and whatnot.

Betty unwraps the small gift that Newt dropped into her lap. Earlier, Newt didn't say nowt, not even with her hands, didn't even wait for thanks. Discarding the shard of brown husk for the moment leaves Betty with the scrap of cotton sail cloth. She dips it in the sea and then wipes herself underneath her skirt, so she don't have to look at the mess. She knows it's wrong to toss the stained cloth into the water, they need every piece of cloth for the community, but she can't bear to look at it, red with her shame.

Clean for the moment, she picks up the brown husk she discarded and starts to chew on the pale flesh on its underside. She don't much like the taste of the rednut flesh. It sticks in her teeth, but if she eats enough of it, and don't move too much today, maybe her body will cleanse itself. The thought of squatting in the bushes fills Betty with disgust but she supposes it's better than being diseased.

Betty hates this place. The dirt, the biting creatures and the flies, but mostly she can't get used to the sweaty smells of the other women who sleep half-naked, close to each other. Betty misses her mattress on the floor in Master Henry's attic and Cook's soft snores from the bed beside. She misses the smell of the orange soap that Cook bought from the oil shop and Cook's rough hands scrubbing her skin until it were raw. Cook would know what to do to keep Betty from being unclean.

Tossing the empty husk into the sea, Betty rises, jamming her flag into the earth behind the shell path. She must have faith. It don't matter how many marks are on the cave wall, they will be rescued, and things will be exactly as they were before. In the meantime, she'll keep her promise and help organise the baptism for the community, or 'mune as they are starting to call themselves, so that when the ship comes, the men will know they never strayed from God's path and that her conduct, at least, was befitting a lady.

Betty follows the white shell path to the cave where she finds Molly collecting bark with Newt and the others, stripping it in thin layers from the trees that the violet snails seem to like. Chewing on their raw flesh in the damp cave had made her feel sick in those first few days before Tattio had made fire using one of the broken glass jars and the dried husks of the rednut.

'I missed you at breakfast,' Molly says. 'I've saved a bowl for you.'

Betty feels herself get hot in the face. 'I'm not hungry.'

'You must eat.' Molly's face is lined with worry.

Betty don't mention she saw Newt earlier, or the gift of the flesh of the rednut in the cotton rag. It's no one's business what she were doing on the path. She's glad Newt do not speak.

'It's the Baptism soon,' Molly continues. 'You must be excited.'

Betty nods, her face serious. 'We must bring the children up as one,' she says.

'One?' Molly asks.

'With one universal parent. So, they are created equally in God's eyes as man was.'

Molly frowns. 'Universal? I don't remember that in the scriptures?'

Betty sighs, not sure why it's so hard to understand. She thinks about the underwater men in Master Henry's story, how different it would have been for her if she'd been in a place like that when her ma died of consumption.

'If everyone looks after everyone, Ada's babby will be the same as the others, it won't matter that their ma died,' Betty explains, also not wanting responsibility for any child.

'The children have enough parents. They need names, they cannot continue all to be called child,' Molly says.

Molly don't seem to be listening properly to what Betty's saying.

'Are you truly fine?' Molly asks, touching her arm.

Betty flinches. 'Yes, I'm fine.'

Realising her words were said hard, and that Molly were just trying to be nice, Betty smiles; a small curl of her lip that takes immense effort.

'Thank you for asking,' she says, scurrying on.

MOLLY

The camp is quiet after another lunch of stew: dried silver fish, snails, fresh seaweed and root.

Molly watches the children as they leave the meeting place in the same order they came in, smallest first and in one long ordered line. They crawl, stumble and toddle and seem to be flourishing. There is still a sinking feeling in her stomach, even though she understands why the childcare must be managed like this; there are not enough of them to do the work.

Her own child is hard to miss, staggering like they're pickled, the makeshift tunic billowing over bowed legs. Rosie's a skilled needlewoman, even when using a spine as a needle, and has turned the scraps of sail from the ship into uniforms, which are whitened by the sun. Rosie likes to think of them as tiny angels, but to Molly they look more like puffed-up bells of lily-of-the-valley.

The children are obedient, waiting for their hands to be rinsed before entering the nursery hut at Sarah's command; a single sweep of her hand. Sarah does not need a whip. The lash of her tongue is enough.

Once the children are settled for the afternoon, the bowls are cleared and water is boiled in the bucket for the herb tea, which seems to improve everyone's mood. The women who do not choose to partake in an afternoon sleep gather in a circle in the shade of the grey rock.

Betty is the first to raise her arm to speak.

'It's been agreed that the children are to be baptised soon and we can't baptise a child without no name.'

She glances across at Flora.

'Agreed,' Flora acknowledges.

'They're dandy as they is.'

It's Sarah, never missing an opportunity to voice her opinion.

'Can't baptise without no name.' Betty shrugs.

'There is no family name I wish to pass on,' Molly says, thinking of Edward and her family and how quick they were to send her to the Asylum. Anyhow, this child was not of her husband's seed, and neither was her child conceived in pain like some of the others.

There is a murmur of agreement among the few women seated in the dust.

'But that is the proper way,' Betty frowns. 'The father's name must be acknowledged.'

Sometimes Betty shows her inexperience and her youth. The children are all bastards and will never be offered an inheritance from their fathers, or the family name, but Molly keeps quiet and wills someone else to offer a solution.

Rosie raises her hand tentatively. 'We could give 'em numbers,' she offers, 'like the scriptures?'

'Didn't think yer could count past a bunch of fives,' Sarah laughs.

Tattio's hand shoots up in the air, stiff and insistent. 'I want no branding for my chillun.'

'*Our* chillun, I mean children,' Betty says. 'They are all *our* children.'

'Mad as hops,' Sarah mutters, but doesn't set against Betty.

'The names of saints is fitting,' Flora says. 'As God rescued us.'

'Or flowers?' Rosie suggests. 'Done you and me no 'arm.'

'What about the boys?' Betty frowns.

'Children is children,' Sarah says. 'Ain't no difference.'

Tattio nods. 'Hornpipes dun mean notin here. Dun make no one better dan anudduh.'

THE MUNE 51

'We should cast the shells.' Betty puffs out her chest. 'Boys need fitting names.'

'We shouldn't dwell on what's under the children's tunics,' Molly says, picking up a shell and starting the process by throwing it into the basket marked 'N'.

Even those women that don't read know what the letters Y and N mean now.

It is obvious from the first few shells that are cast, that the community wish to move on from the old ways.

Molly takes a deep breath. 'We could use something from the island to name them?'

It's neutral: a break from the past and that is what they all seem to want. Except maybe Betty and Flora.

'Name yers Dirt then, always face down in it.' Sarah laughs. 'Pins like jelly.'

Molly clamps her jaw tight, holding in the words she really wants to say. All the children are just beginning to find their feet, hers is not alone in that. She raises her hand again.

'So, a word which describes each child, like Sarah said?' Molly suggests, adding, 'But not cruel.'

Surely Sarah won't argue her own point?

'Ada's bairn likes to sing like 'em coloured birds when they fly past the rock in the morning,' Rosie pipes up, 'but me head's not clever enough to think more 'an that.'

'Rainbow,' Betty says. 'Like the wings.'

'That's lovely, duck,' Rosie says, softly. 'Another of God's miracles.'

Betty looks pleased with herself and even Sarah nods, looking down, her face pinched but not with malice for once. 'Ada would like that.'

'And Tattio's is fast, like her,' Rosie continues, laughing.

'Lightning,' Betty says.

'And Sarah's is always crying.'

'Rain,' Betty says.

'Won't always be like that,' Sarah snaps, her face darkening.

'Without rain, notin grow,' Tattio says, which placates Sarah.

'Newt's is loud,' Rosie continues, 'making up for their ma.'

'Storm or thunder,' Betty suggests, smiling properly for once.

Molly raises her hand again. 'Maybe Rosie can help Betty choose the names for all of the children? Rosie knows the children and Betty is good with words and she's kind, helped them into the world.'

Molly smiles at Betty. The women are all nodding.

'We should cast the shells again,' Sarah says.

Sarah, always stamping on the bugs of ideas that she's not thought of, but she's right, it must be done properly, so there's no argument later. It's what's been agreed.

Molly stands first, brushing the needles from her hardened feet. Newt empties the baskets and passes her a second shell, which Molly tosses into the woven basket marked Y.

Dear God, Molly thinks, don't let Betty choose Dirt as a name. It's cruel and her child's done nothing to deserve it.

MOLLY

The mood in the camp is high. The children are back from the sacred well, their foreheads wet with Betty and Flora's ministrations, and tonight, they will eat turtle meat, scooped from the shell and cooked in brine. The brown shells make useful toys for the children.

Molly is eager to know the name of her child and Newt, one of the few women who attended the ceremony, must notice her anxiety because she takes Molly to one side and draws a star in the dust. Molly puts her hand on her heart. It sums up her child perfectly, always looking up at the heavens instead of the floor, where they might trip.

'And Sarah's?' she asks quietly, wondering if she made a fuss when she was waiting with the children outside the cave. 'Did they pick Rain?'

Newt shakes her head and draws a tree in the dust with some lines below it.

'Wood?' Molly asks.

Newt shakes her head again and scores the lines beneath the tree with more fervour.

'Earth?' Molly asks.

Newt shakes her head, points to the lines underneath and then draws an arrow and a vase shape.

'Clay?' she asks.

Newt nods.

Molly frowns but then thinks about the slender, quiet child, so different from Sarah, who loves to sit in the dirt and shape wet earth into piles. It makes sense and it's a solid name. Whether Sarah likes it or not, is another matter, but she's sure Sarah won't be slow in criticising Betty if she doesn't, no matter what was agreed.

'I should do something for Betty,' Molly says, more to herself than anyone else but as usual, Newt is listening. The girl's so quiet, sometimes Molly forgets she's there.

Newt picks up an empty bucket and beckons Molly to follow her and she looks serious, which is unusual. She doesn't often show her emotion.

No one notices them pass by, but then, this time between meeting and sleeping is their own, but even in her free time, Molly sees Rosie using charcoal on scraps of bark to draw shapes for the children.

'What's your child's name?' Molly asks.

Newt smiles, points up to the sky and then claps her hands.

'Thunder,' Molly laughs.

Newt nods.

It's appropriate. No one will ever need an ear trumpet to hear them.

They trace the path round the grey rock, but Newt doesn't stop at the cave entrance. She continues to the shore, to the ship and crouches down on the white shells, pointing.

There are spots of blood on the path.

Molly frowns. 'Betty?'

Newt nods and acts out washing her privates. She runs her fingers down her cheeks.

'The poor child. She's told no one?'

Newt shrugs.

'She must be terrified.'

Molly stands up and looks beyond the ship, where the sea is starting to wash back. Is there something there? Or is it a trick of the sun glancing off the dark sea?

'Do you see that?' Molly asks, shading her eyes.

Newt frowns, looks to her right and then beckons Molly, continuing along the path, her pace so fast that Molly struggles to keep up.

Molly's not been back to this part of the shore since she was washed up. She's avoided it and the memory of her baby sinking in the black sand. But now it comes back: the panic, the horror, not knowing if Star was dead.

She swallows hard, focuses back on Newt who's pointing to something sodden, laid close to the path ahead. Molly crouches down to get a better look, careful not to spill any part of herself onto the sand, or to anger it with her voice. It's the body of one, or maybe two of the squirrel creatures she's seen on the island, but they've been ripped apart and only sections of their pelt are left.

How has this happened when the creatures are so fast? Too fast for them to catch, even with Newt's traps.

'What has done this?' Molly asks quietly, tossing the remains onto the sand, clapping twice, and watching the sand ripple and draw the pelts down.

Newt points back to the movement in the sea.

'For how long?'

Newt shrugs, but that might be because they stopped counting the days. There seemed little point.

'We should take note but say nothing.' Molly's stomach sinks.

There's no point causing panic amongst the community until they are certain there is a threat. She does not want to ruin the mood in the camp or restrict the freedom they have enjoyed these past months, but when something seems too good to be true, in her experience, it usually is.

NEWT

Newt looks up at the sky, at the stars and the moon, which is huge and round, bigger than it seemed in London. Tattio says each star is a soul of a dear departed, taken too soon and when they is twinkling, it's their heart still beating. There is thousands of them hanging there.

Maybe her ma is one of them?

Newt thinks of her ma a lot when she's on her tod. How sick she were at the end, stinking of gin and Newt barely tall enough to reach the door handle in the room they lived in with the other folk. It were noisy and damp but they had a mattress in the corner where she slept curled up in her ma's petticoats. They was the good times.

She gulps in a breath of salt air. She likes the hush of the night, away from the women in the camp that do nothing but gab. A place like this might have kept her ma from expiring.

Newt ain't no Charley, hates to be still. Sitting here forever, looking and waiting to see if the beasts in the water is a danger to them, and not only to the creatures they tear apart on the shore, is making her feel like she did on the streets amongst the drunks and mutton mongers. Like her life is a bubble of spit that can be burst with a flick of the tongue.

As the sun shows its mug above the sea, Newt starts the walk back along the shell path to the 'mune. On the sand near the rock pools, where the sea has withdrawn, is another dead jump, one of the squirrel-like creatures that live in the trees. Reaching across, Newt uses her spear to drag the carcass towards her. It don't look like it's been eaten. Pulled apart, like a cat with a mouse, no purpose 'cept spite.

A shuffling sound gets her attention. There's a beast a dozen feet away from her, blocking her route back to camp.

It must have used the high tide to reach the path. What do it want?

The beast raises its head and sniffs, then turns in her direction. Can it see her? Newt steps back onto the claggy mud that forms the forest floor, hoping the scent of rotting leaves will confuse it. She don't like the look of its ivories, two sharp spikes at the front of its open trap, or its goggles, black lumps of coal, dead and unblinking on the side of its leathery gib-face. It's big too, bigger than one of the childs and they ain't like babes no more.

Newt's good with a spear but she'll not manage to kill it on her tod.

The beast sniffs the air again, then lets out a high-pitched wail that cuts through Newt's bonce, worse than any child. Newt fights the instinct to drop her spear and clamp her hands over her jugs. She grits her ivories instead, until her mug aches.

The beast turns away as suddenly as it appeared, lurching backwards, using its tail like a paddle, in water shallow as puddles on the street. It's quick, back in deep water before Newt can draw breath. It reaches the others, swimming in and out of the remains of the ship, like they is all playing a game of follow the leader.

Newt picks up the jump carcass. She don't frighten easily, but this beast ain't like nothing she's seen before. She might not want to be close to the others in the camp, have them know all her business, but neither do she want to be alone. She's had too much of that.

MOLLY

Molly pushes the earth back into the hole she's dug, smoothing it over with her hands, trying not to breathe too deeply. The stench is ripe. She's buried the squirrel creature that Newt slapped down in the dirt in front of the food hut this morning. She understands why Newt did it. With no words at her disposal, it's the only way she can show Molly how serious she thinks the danger is. Letting the sand claim it would have been a better solution because what if someone should see?

She's glad it was too early for the others because this isn't the way to introduce the subject. A half-ripped carcass will cause panic and they must be logical.

Turning away from the small grave, Molly wipes the sweat from her forehead. It's already too hot to be exerting herself like this. She takes a cup of water from the metal bucket and sips slowly. It's enough for now, and breakfast will be ready soon because the sun has nearly reached the top of the grey rock. Molly's getting used to the heat, even though it barely dips during the night when the sun finally sinks. There's no breeze, no season, no clouds. She never thought she'd miss the cold breath of winter on her small window or the April showers that lashed against the glass. The only things that change here are the moon, when it appears, shrinking and expanding rapidly, and the tide, which washes over the path almost to the cave when it is whole.

There's the crunch of dry leaves and Molly looks up to see Tattio in the distance, limping towards the camp. Has she stepped on one of the spiked leaves the trees shed and injured herself? It's easy enough to do and the pines are like daggers. Then Molly sees the cloth, soaked red and wrapped around Tattio's ankle. Her stomach flips.

She puts down the cup and rushes to the path where the huts begin, not caring about her own feet, though they will be fine what with their hard crust of skin.

'What happened?' she asks.

Tattio grimaces as she sits down on one of the pitted black rocks which litter the camp, like someone's rolled them there in a giant's game of marbles. She unwraps the cloth to reveal two deep marks above her ankle.

Newt appears in the dust and stands behind Molly, her arms crossed tight over her chest. She doesn't need to say: *told you*. It's written into every taut muscle of her body.

First things first. They need to clean the wound and re-dress it.

'Let me see,' Molly says, reaching forward to press the skin around the incision, to see if the bite looks clean. Grains of salt are forming a crust.

'For me to do,' Tattio says, shifting away.

Molly hands her the strip of bleached sail cloth and the hush-hush leaves, and watches as Tattio dresses it. They use the hush-hush leaves, similar to dock leaves, when the children scrape their knees.

'Creetuhs in de water,' Tattio says, hands shaking.

Newt is staring holes into Molly that are deeper than the beast's bite.

She feels Tattio's eyes on her too.

'You knew dey were dangerous?' Tattio asks.

'We didn't want to frighten anyone. It's been so peaceful, living here. Why risk it?' Molly sits back on her haunches, biting her lip. 'And they didn't seem to be interested in us, only the jumps.'

'What de damfino are dey?' Tattio asks.

'Some kind of fish,' Molly says.

'Shark? Fish dun normally take chunks out of you.'

Molly shrugs. 'Where were you?'

'Bin near de ship. Bigguh spoils to be found when de sea covers sand.'

'I didn't know you went into the water.'

'Dun need permission,' Tattio says.

Tattio is right. That's what makes the community work. No one tells anyone else what they can do. It's no excuse, but maybe the beasts aren't back near the shore after all but staying in deep water. Molly should have said something about them though, and Newt, who is busy drawing something in the dust, clearly thinks so too.

BETTY

Betty can't go to the shore to check on her flags because they've been summoned to the meeting area. Her flags might have been knocked over again, like the other day. Cook's scrubbed sheets used to tear like that on the line, when the wind were blowing a gale, except there's nowt in the way of wind here. Betty wonders if one of the other women did it, trying to stop her immense efforts for rescue. She's seen their faces when they think she's not looking—pinched and unkind. They are stupid. It is obvious rescue will come. Someone built the huts and made pictures in the cave. They are not the first here.

She rubs her eyes and slumps down in the dirt with the others, annoyed that her routine has been interrupted. Looking around, she sees Tattio sitting next to Molly, which is odd. Normally she's at Sarah's side, like she's her kitchen hand or summat, ready for her beckoning. Betty shudders, tries not to think about the other day when she saw Sarah touch Tattio, and not in the way God intended. Flora agreed it were a sin. They'll be punished soon enough, of that she's certain.

There's silence as Molly raises her hand and clears her throat, like she's got summat stuck in it. Betty can see she's struggling to speak, which is not like her at all. Must be proper important. Has she seen a ship?

'We're in danger,' Molly says, her voice cracking like an old chamber pot.

Were it a ghost ship? Like the one in Master Henry's scientific stories, that takes people to their death? Betty crosses herself and mutters a quick prayer.

'Danger from you...' Sarah laughs, but the sound dies as Tattio unwinds the bandage from around her ankle and points at two marks, deep in her flesh.

'Dem creetuh on de side of de cave is real,' Tattio says.

Tattio could have cut herself for attention. Master said his wife did that, caused herself injury to make trouble for him. Betty glances at Flora, to see if she's thinking the same.

Now Newt is drawing summat in the dirt, some kind of round shape with spiked teeth. Betty leans forward.

'They come from the sea,' Molly continues. 'We don't know why. Newt's seen them on the path.'

'Fish don't have no legs,' Sarah snorts. ''Tis flapdoodle.'

Betty sees Molly stiffen and look at Newt, like she's hiding summat. It makes Betty think about the creatures in Master Henry's stories that changed, so they could keep living. Adapting, the Master said. But fish walking? It's proof that this is a bad place, like she keeps telling the others.

'Bit o jams on the shore all days,' Sarah says, turning to Betty. 'If Betty ain't seen nothin', there's nothin' to be seen.'

'I've not seen aught,' Betty says, not wanting to lie.

Sarah nods at Betty like she's pleased with her for summat.

Molly gets up from the circle and walks quickly to the food hut, disappearing round the side. Betty can see bits of dirt flying up from behind it. Then Molly's back, dusty, carrying summat that stinks like the rats that Cook used to poison and then beat to death, piling up their bodies in the yard to frighten others away.

Molly flings the thing into the centre of the circle, and it slaps down in the earth, bits of it breaking off.

Betty's not the only one that gags.

'Newt found it this morning. On the shore.'

It's one of them brown fur animals they sometimes see jumping between the high trees but there's a huge tear in its flesh.

'Dey is fast,' Tattio mumbles, prodding the carcass with a stick, glancing up at the canopy beyond.

'It snuffed it and 'em crabs have had a bellygut,' Sarah says.

Betty thinks Sarah's probably right. They do find dead creatures here sometimes, mostly shrivelled up. Yesterday she had to prise one of the scaly animals off Clay, who tastes everything like it will offer answers. That child is not right in the head.

'Us must watch de shore,' Tattio says, tossing the bloody stick away. She rubs her wound. 'Anudduh dun need to get hurt.'

'I agree with Tattio. I don't think we should just sit and wait. We must protect ourselves,' Molly finishes.

MASTER'S BOOK OF SCIENTIFIC STORIES

The Phantom Boat

I tell my story with some reluctance, though there is absolute truth in the circumstances I found myself in.

It was some years ago, the end of the hunting season, and I had been out all day with my gun, yet without a sniff of a pheasant or grouse. The weather was turning, the month December, and the drab and foggy cliffs on the coast of North Yorkshire were not an agreeable place to lose one's way. But lost I was.

Ahead of me, in the gathering darkness, I saw nothing but bare earth, the ragged coastline, and an ever-increasing flurry of snow, which whipped around me in a blanket of iciness.

There was nothing for it but to march on and take my chance wherever I may of finding some shelter, a cave or barn. I pushed resignedly forward, my gun kept dry beneath my coat now weighed down by the elements.

My prospects blackened with the deepening sky, and my heart grew heavy as I thought of my new wife, waiting for me in our simple parlour, which would have a fire roaring in the grate and a warm beverage on the simple oak table. I had promised before leaving that I would be home by dusk and I had failed to keep my word! She would be worried, what with the sudden turn of the skies.

I stopped and halloed for help every now and then, but my pleas seemed to make the silence deeper. My unease grew with remembered tales of travellers who had wearied, lain down in the snow and were covered, their lives lost in sleep. My resolution must not give way!

In the distance, in the direction of the sea, I saw a wavering speck of light appear from out of the dark. Running with as much speed as I could muster toward that shifting flicker, I found myself face to face with an old man, holding a lantern.

'Thank the Lord!' was the exclamation that burst from my lips.

The old man lifted the lantern, better to see my face.

'What for?' he growled, seemingly annoyed.

'I feared I should forever be lost in the snow. How far away is Saltburn-by-the-sea?'

'A gude ten mile,' said he.

'And the nearest hostelry?'

'Six mile t'other side.' He jerked the lantern in the direction from whence I'd lately come.

'Where do you reside?' asked I.

'Yonder,' said he.

'Perhaps I could avail myself of your hospitality?' asked I.

'Master won't let you in,' said he, in a mysterious manner.

'Who is your master?' I enquired. Perhaps I had happened upon him in the course of my work?

'Nowt to do with you,' said he, unceremoniously.

I ignored his words, deciding to follow the wizened man as he shuffled through the treacherous snow. I had no choice but to engage directly with his master, and request shelter and some respite from the cold if I was to survive this bitter night.

A dark mass loomed up presently, and the old man fumbled for his key. I drew up close behind him so as not to lose chance of entry. From my position close to the heavy studded door, I could smell the saltiness of the sea and hear the waves crash viciously against the rocks nearby.

I pushed past him into the hallway, a surprisingly auspicious raftered affair, serving a multitude of purposes. One end was piled high with supplies, sacks of grain and the like, the other with all kinds of miscellaneous timber.

A bell rang: a sharp sound in the cavernous room.

'That's for you,' the old man said, in a less than pleasant manner. He pointed to a black door.

I rapped, loudly, and did not wait to be invited in.

A white-haired man rose from a comfortable chair, which barely contained his girth.

'Who are you?' he demanded.

'Thomas Southwick, barrister-at-law. Lost on foot. Beseeching you for sustenance and shelter.'

'Mine home is not a hostelry,' said he rather conceitedly, before turning to my guide. 'How dare you permit this fool to enter my house!'

The old man grumbled, explaining I had forced his hand.

'I seek only self-preservation,' said I. 'The snow is more than five foot deep: enough to bury a man.'

The white-haired man shuffled over to the window and pulled back a thick velvet curtain.

'It is true,' said he, with the flick of one meaty hand. 'Serve the man supper, Albert.'

I placed my gun in the corner next to the book-laden table, and took the proffered seat, a fancy tapestry affair with winged arms. The man had by then become absorbed in his papers, my presence an irritation to be ignored.

There was much to witness in the room: jars of chemicals, some peculiar painted wall hangings of a paper-like fabric, tattered maps, an array of specimen rocks, which looked volcanic in nature, and some kind of grey animal skin stretched across a wooden frame. So strange a room I had never witnessed before. Who was this man before me? His forehead under the white hair was broad with intelligence, and with a stern furrow of the brow, his concentration palpable, but he was clothed in attire more suited to a poet.

The serving man, Albert, presently furnished me with a dish of ham and eggs, and a side of bread coupled with a jar of some sort of berry preserve. I had never eaten anything quite so simple yet delicious and savoured every mouthful in silence, before joining my host near the fireside.

I was surprised when he began to interrogate me: a scientific rather than pleasant discussion of my accomplishments. He seemed familiar with all the topics of mathematics, philosophy and practical sciences but somewhat lost me when he began to speak of shifts in time, and islands that exist beyond maps.

'This world,' said he, 'places all its value in physical science. It rejects as false all that cannot withstand tests of the laboratory. They treat apparitions and alternate worlds as nursery tales.'

He spoke with a surprising sourness. 'I was ridiculed by my contemporaries for my visionary convictions. No man wishes to hear of my discoveries. Since returning to this godforsaken land, I have been living as you find me now, unable to return to my studies.'

Exhausted from his conversing, he took to his feet and went over to the window, parting the curtains once more. 'It has ceased snowing,' said he, clearly desirous I should leave.

'I must return home to my wife,' said I. 'But how shall I get there? I have not the reserves to walk to Saltburn tonight.'

'There is a boat,' says he, 'which takes supplies to the villages. It is not far from this house by foot, less than a mile, give or take. Albert can lead the way.'

'Most agreeable,' said I, eager to be reunited with my dearest wife who must be worn out with worry.

He rang the bell and Albert appeared with a bottle of liquid.

'It is best to take a glass of tea before the journey. The snow is deep, and this will warm you well enough,' said my host.

'It is strong,' said I, drinking it quickly, for it was bitter but it did indeed make me feel warmed.

I was about to thank him for his hospitality, but he had turned away.

Although it was no longer snowing, the wind was brisk and bitterly cold as we left the house, and the sky was a blanket of black unsullied by stars. There was not a sound, save Albert's crackling breath as we made our way along the cliff.

'Yon's the spot,' Albert said, waving the lantern in front of me.

'How do I reach it?' asked I.

'There is a path down to the shore yonder.'

I reached in my pocket for my wallet, a gesture of appreciation.

Albert warmed to me once he had hold of my half-crown. 'Mind your step, lad. Sea's a dangerous beast. Been unexplained happenings in these parts.'

'What happenings?' asked I.

'Gude night sir,' said he, turning.

He pocketed the half-crown and trudged back the way we had come.

I watched the lantern sway till it was disappeared, and then continued forth, reaching for the wooden railing that marked the cliff edge. It was difficult to see anything, and the night air appeared colder than ever: a veritable chill.

At last I happened upon a gap in the rail. I could barely see the steps carved into the cliff leading down to the shore. I descended, careful with my footing. When I reached the bottom, the shore was stony under my feet, by now certainly turned to ice.

The night boat was approaching at speed, sooner than I had been led to believe and looked strangely lofty. A lantern blinked. I rushed forward, almost losing my footing on the narrow jetty, and waved. I would be home and dry presently.

The vessel was barely perceptible in the dim light of the lantern. All I could witness as it drew alongside, was the captain, muffled to the eyes in a thick sailor's cape, and three passengers of the fairer sex, seemingly asleep. When it was close enough, I clambered aboard. It would not be long until I was in my fair wife's sweet embrace.

If anything, it was colder on the sea than on the land and there was a damp and unpleasant smell. I looked around at the crates of goods.

'How long before we reach Saltburn?' asked I.

One of the passengers lifted her head but did not respond, merely looked at me, though I could not make out her exact features above her laced bodice: just the twist of her fair hair, escaping her bonnet.

I was chilled and anxious for distraction, so I leaned forward to get a closer look at the vessel. It was covered with a thick coat of limpets, the wood broken in places. I examined it more closely and saw it was in the last stage of decrepitude.

I turned to the captain and attempted one more conversation.

'This boat is in a state of disrepair beyond belief. How does it stay afloat?'

He moved his head slowly and looked me in the face. I turned cold at the sight. His eyes were a flaming, peculiar colour and one of his eyeballs hung on his cheek on a sinewy thread. His face was paler than the snow and his bloodless lips were drawn back as if in the last throes of an agonising death.

My sight by this time had become accustomed to the gloom and I could see now, with intolerable clarity, that this was no ordinary boat. Everything had a layer of rot, the wood mouldering and damp. Even the maiden's clothes were white with spores.

Crying in horror, I flung myself from the vessel into the icy water and with my last vestige of strength swam towards the shore. From the shallows, I watched lightning strike the stern and the boat flip over, its passengers thrown forth as if they weighed no more than pebbles tossed into the sea.

It seemed like years had passed when I awoke, with my dear wife's hand upon my fevered brow. Said she, through her bouts of tears, that I had been discovered on the shore of Staithes, a village just beyond our own, by a fishing boat. I was soaked and icy cold and doubtless saved from certain death.

I never told her the circumstances of that night, but I told the doctor who treated me. He supposed the whole adventure was a dream, born of my fever and near death from drowning, but I know, that night, I was a fourth passenger on that fateful vessel.

BETTY

The children are seated around the fire, sipping liquid from the brown cups, which sends them into a deep slumber despite the light. It barely fades until the dark descends: a coal-black curtain, thicker than the velvet hangings in Master's drawing room.

Betty takes a draught of the drink they call tea, aught to lessen her time here, awake. Her father used to do that, but with a drop of liquor added to the evening brew. It were hard, he said, without her ma to help. In this place, there is no shortage of mothers.

She scowls. The tea is barely warm and nowt better than dishwater.

It has fallen to Betty to prepare the children for bed because the other women are too stupid to speak more than a sentence, and even then it is only ever their thoughts about the weather and how lucky they is. Only Rosie and Flora seem to care that the children pray.

If the children still needed help to wash, feed or dress, Betty would not be here with them and she will not, like Molly, be filling the children's heads with sweet tales. The children must be taught the truth of the island and place their trust in the past. They must know where they came from and where they must return and learn to recite the scriptures as Betty were taught.

'I'm going to tell you a true story,' Betty says, feeling the children's eyes on her: their sole focus. It is unsurprising, for there is little else here to fill the interminable hours before dark. The days stretch out longer than before they boarded the ship but perhaps that's because Betty had purpose then: a reason to rise every morning back home. A reason for being.

'The Elders,' she begins, because that is what the women have started calling themselves, since the children started to speak, 'used to live in a place very far away from here.'

'How far?' Clay asks.

'It's bad manners to interrupt,' Betty snaps at Clay, before continuing. 'They came here by boat across the big ocean. Do you know what a boat is?'

The children look empty-headed as usual. Sarah should not be in charge of their days.

'It is like the cup you hold, but bigger and filled with people,' Betty explains. 'And it floats on water.'

Master always used to check Betty understood the scientific stories they read together, though often Betty still could not grasp what were meant. Master said there were no point reading words if one didn't understand their significance but it were hard when she saw nowt she recognised in them. There were also some stories, Master said, that were untruths, like those written by women about rights, who twisted words to suit themselves. You had to know which ones to believe.

Betty watches Star turn the empty cup over and frown. Star is clearly listening at least and thinking about boats, so perhaps all is not yet lost and there may be some hope when rescue comes. Unlike Star, Clay's hands are in the dirt, sifting it through fingers, and Lightning is barely able to keep still, knees jittering like bugs in dry grass.

'This place from whence we came is civilised and full of riches. People live in big houses made of brick, sleep on feather mattresses, and always have enough food.'

'Feathers is spiky,' Star says, pulling out a small red and green feather from the folds of their white tunic.

'In England, feathers are soft and very comfortable.' Betty swats away a black bug that has landed on her ankle, the only skin she willingly exposes. 'But one day, when we were on the boat, the sky changed: thunder roared, lightning struck, and the boat filled with water.'

The children giggle, which were not her intention.

'Me?' Lightning asks.

'Nowt like you,' Betty snaps. 'You are named after summat the sky does in a storm.'

She's trying to be patient, but all these questions are starting to irritate her. The children know nowt, stuck here with just the sun burning a red hole in the sky and Rosie, who although godly, wouldn't know the correct end of a gentleman's cane.

'What is storm?' Star asks, eyes raised to the cloudless sheet of blue which hangs close around them.

'Lightning is like white fire that breaks up black sky and thunder is a sound, a loud bang.' Betty claps her hands to demonstrate. 'They come together.'

'I'd like to see that,' Star says.

'And you will,' Betty says. 'When we are rescued.'

'A boat will come?' Clay asks.

'That's enough for today.' Betty bangs down her bowl and gets to her feet, glancing up at the sky, willing the dark curtains to close and release her from another day. 'Tomorrow, I'll tell you how we made bread. Prayers and then straight to sleep.'

She walks away before the children can ask her what bread is, her skirts brushing the dirt.

MOLLY

The salt water feels cool against her hot legs as she rinses her feet, one at a time, careful to keep her weight on the white shells and not forget what's hiding underneath the sea; the sand that claims life, if you let it.

Since the vote, which was won by a small margin, there have been no reports of the beasts in the shallows, even with a constant guard on the shore. So many days have passed since, that Molly's starting to doubt herself. Whilst she's grateful that life here passes without pain or humiliation, that the women care for each other and share common goals, there's a nagging doubt in the back of her mind that she can't seem to shake, that something's coming. That it's too easy. Perhaps it is because she has always been told that women like her don't deserve to be happy.

'What do they look like?' Rosie asks, her voice a whisper.

Molly was surprised when Rosie volunteered to keep watch with her. She's usually focused on the children and she's good with them, knows what to do to make them laugh.

'I only saw the creatures in the water by the ship,' Molly says. 'I thought they were big fish, maybe sharks because they're so far out.'

'Never seen none of 'em neither,' Rosie mutters.

'I've only seen them drawn in books.'

'You can read, then?' Rosie asks.

Molly nods. 'I was allowed access in the…' She stops for a second, doesn't tell Rosie about Dr Johnston's library, doesn't want to say too much about her past, especially with Rosie so close with Sarah. 'Not that it does much good here.'

'Ma didn't 'ave no money to send us to school,' Rosie shrugs. 'Made sure we learned the scriptures, even when we 'ad no Sunday best.'

'You were in the workhouse with Sarah?'

Rosie nods. 'The same pan. Me ma took sick. Not a bob and no place else to go.'

'Was Sarah always…difficult?'

Rosie laughs. 'Only when she'd make the young 'uns empty the pail.'

'Pail?'

'We was all in one room see. One pot to piss in. Proper dirty. Don't expect you ever 'ad that. Sarah kept us all goin'.'

'I was lucky,' Molly agrees. She says it to herself more than anything, as if she's trying to convince herself. A proper place to piss in doesn't open the door to free you, but maybe she's misjudged Sarah.

'Ain't got to fight no one for nothin' 'ere, don't need Sarah to keep us safe no more,' Rosie says, with a small smile. 'No one whips us, and food ain't bad neither. God took good care of us, leaving us 'ere.'

Molly smiles at Rosie. She must try to be more like Rosie and focus on each day, what they have, not what might happen. They survived a shipwreck; they have the freedom here to do as they choose, no matter the mistakes made; they have made lasting friendships; the children are thriving and still in their care, and they have shelter and sufficient food and water to sustain them. It's more than enough. Yet, when Molly looks out over the water, the questions still come: is the ship lower in the sand than yesterday, or is the water higher; where exactly are they in the world, and how will they protect themselves if the beasts attack?

BETTY

You'd have to be deaf not to hear the child screaming. Betty sighs and walks away from her vigil on the path and towards the sound, which bounces off the tree trunks, doubling in volume.

'Shut your cake hole, will you,' she mutters to herself.

It's Clay. It's always Clay. Clumsy, getting into scrapes. The child's got two left feet. Clay's had more hush-hush leaves wrapped around wounds than the rest of the children lumped together. Children should be seen and not heard, that is what she were always told.

She leaves the shell path and heads left to the Cinder field, the clearing where they first rested when they arrived on the island, and on towards the cave. Clay's lying in a heap outside the entrance, like a pile of old rags, but for once the screaming might be for good reason. One thin, twig-leg is bent out at an unnatural angle under the smock. Betty stares at it but not for too long. The children, like the women, don't seem to care about showing their flesh and she has no desire to see parts which should be kept private.

'What has gone on?' she asks, maintaining her distance, a good foot away.

God knows what other deformities the child has.

'Hurts.' Clay's pale face is streaked with spent tears.

'You're too big to carry,' Betty says.

Clay is not much smaller than her now, their head level with her shoulder and some of the children are starting with body hair she'd rather not witness. It is a reminder of how long they have been stranded on this dreadful island.

'I'll fetch help,' she says.

The child is always all over her, like a rash she can't get rid of. Probably why they're here alone in the first place.

'The hurt will pass,' she adds, leaving.

Betty rounds the corner of the grey rock and sees Molly mending the first hut, pushing wet mud into the spaces between the hardened weaves. She looks wild: hair crusted, skin an earthy brown, and limbs barely covered by the stiff tunics they all insist on wearing now. Some of them even decorate the material with charcoal like some tribe of savages.

'Clay's hurt,' Betty says, approaching Molly, averting her gaze from Molly's glistening skin.

Molly sighs.

Clearly, it's not just her then, others have noticed the child has their hands and beak in everything. Betty should have insisted on the children being educated proper, not allowed to run around like wild animals.

'Tattio's back.' Molly indicates the food hut.

Betty walks past the meeting place, enjoying the cool shade of the grey rock. There's no point rushing, the child's not going anywhere, and anyway, it's too hot, worse than working by the Aga in the summer with the stable door shut.

Tattio's sitting in the dirt outside the hut, her long legs stretched out in front of her. She's grinding summat in one of the nut bowls, with a smooth black stone.

'Clay needs help,' Betty says.

'Eaten summin or fell over again?' Tattio asks, one thick eyebrow raised.

'By the cave—don't look right,' Betty indicates her leg. 'Were screaming.'

'Dun hear notin back here,' Tattio frowns, putting the bowl to one side. 'It were easier when e just played with dirt.'

Ducking into the food hut, Tattio emerges with a handful of leaves, strips of frayed cotton and twine, tied in a bag made of an old sack.

'I'll tend to e,' Tattio says.

Betty don't offer to follow, don't want to encourage the child. Instead, she sits down and helps herself to a cup of water. She'll head back to the shore later.

MOLLY

Tattio's carrying one of the children on her back. Molly squints to get a better look as they approach the hut she's been working on, a seemingly never-ending job. It's Clay, hands tight around Tattio's neck in a stranglehold. Where's Betty? Didn't she find the child ailing?

Molly wipes her mud-crusted hands on her short tunic, which is cool, skimming her body, allowing the air to circulate. Rosie's done a good job with the bark fabric they've been making, managing to press the sheets together and stitch them with the threads from the clothes the children have outgrown. It's a long process, especially with only thorns and spines to use as pins and needles, but it's a valuable skill to be able to create something from nothing.

Molly lifts Clay from Tattio's back, which is slick with sweat, and lays them gently on the ground.

'E's hurt,' Tattio says, indicating the leg which sticks out in an unnatural arc. 'I need help to keep e still.'

Molly pulls Clay towards her, clasping tight while Tattio folds up a strip of cloth. It's the same method Molly used to help the women during birthing: to give them something to bite down on to stem the screams.

Tattio nods to Molly and puts the gag in. Molly strengthens her hold on Clay, feeling the clammy body shiver against hers, nothing more than skin and bones and clearly in shock.

'You good?' Tattio asks.

Molly nods, clutching tighter, her hand over Clay's eyes. Maybe being in shock will lessen the pain? She turns away; can't bear to watch what must be done to such a fragile body.

There's a grinding sound and a sharp scream as Tattio pulls. Clay collapses against Molly's chest. She strokes Clay's long sun-bleached hair, murmuring words of comfort that probably can't be heard. She continues to hold tight while Tattio ties a branch tight along the length of the now straight leg, with strips of sail cloth.

'Will Clay be all right?' Molly asks, her voice faltering, still holding the limp body tight to her. It hurts as badly as if her own child were held in her arms.

Tattio shrugs. 'Seen dem do it in de infirmary.'

'Is that where you learned about all the medicine?' Molly asks. Anything to take her mind from Clay's shallow breath.

'Me ma bin a root doctor, learnt it from their ma.'

'Root doctor?' Molly asks.

'Roots and 'erbs.'

Molly nods. Another skill they could not survive without.

'We all need a purpose,' Molly says.

It seems that everyone on the island has discovered strengths to help the community: Rosie and Sarah with the children, Newt with hunting, and Flora with organising the stores. Molly has discovered the joy in fixing things—men's work that she would never have had the opportunity to try elsewhere. They are flourishing. Except for Betty, whose focus remains on the possibility of passing ships.

Still, at least she found Clay.

BETTY

The incident don't seem to have done the child no harm, and at least now Betty can hear the tap-tap of Clay's stick when they is following her. It gives her a chance to double back and lose sight of them, which is not hard in this place with so many trees close together to disguise oneself behind. Flora agrees that it were Clay's doing. Accidents happen when you don't follow the rules, and anyway, there is plenty of children to help. Star's glued to Clay's side like a piece of overcooked pigeon pie stuck to a dish.

Betty used to hate scraping the dishes when Master were entertaining, all them men seated round the polished table, in fancy neckties and waistcoats and hats that stank of sweat and snuff. She got nowt in the way of time to read the scientific stories on them days, banished to the servant's quarters to help Cook make special dishes, like she were any old servant. The pans were filthy after they'd stuffed their fat faces.

Angry, though not sure why, Betty stamps along the white shell path until she reaches the shore where she's staked her row of flags. Newt is in the distance, collecting the rednuts. That girl don't know how to stay still, forever doing summat, and Betty's never seen her kneel to pray. Lord knows what life she led before this. Certainly not a blessed life like Betty's, in such a grand house.

Lifting her skirts, Betty moves to sit down to begin the day's watch for ships but is distraught to find she's bleeding again. It's soaked into her petticoats in a thick red tide. She gasps, tries to rub it out, but her effort only serves to spread the stain. She's been so careful, wearing her second-best dress, the one Newt discarded, when she thinks the curse might be coming, but recently it's been patchy. She hoped it were gone, that the false-mint she's been chewing, that make her so sick, made a difference. Cook always said that the medicine is often worse than the disease.

Tattio is no help—said it were natural, a woman's lot, but Betty don't see why she should put up with the pain and humiliation. It would never have happened at home. She's sure that Cook would have given her summat to rid herself of it.

It were Cook that heard about the ship: 'A new beginning for Surplus women.' Cook said that someone in Betty's predicament, with a bastard child from the Master's seed, would be best off elsewhere. Even though she agreed that Master must love Betty to share himself as he did, she said it were safer that Betty go now she were starting to show. It were her duty to protect Master who would not want aspersions cast in his direction. Cook's face had gone quite red with her speech, and it weren't that hot in the kitchen.

When Betty boarded Master's carriage to begin the journey to the docks, she'd spied a new girl arriving from the village. Fresh faced. Made Betty feel old and fat.

Well, she won't let herself be unworthy here. Sitting close to the shore, Betty drapes her stained petticoat into the sea. She starts rubbing at it, hard enough to split one of the seams, but she don't stop, her face set firm.

Her babby is dead. There is no bastard child. She will make herself clean.

NEWT

Newt tries to holler, but no sound comes out, just a faint gurgle. She couldn't scream when the Johns pressed their fat fingers round her neck and she can't now. She touches her salt-cellar, trying to squeeze out a sound, but still nothing comes. She's as cank as the stone she dropped in the sacred well that first day on the island.

She claps instead, but Betty's goggles is on her petticoat and the water covers the sand, so that do nothing. Betty's trying to scrub the red tide from the cotton and she don't see the shapes in the water that darken the sea, like black stains, an arms-length from her chalks.

Betty's got the curse and the beasts have the scent. It don't take a high forehead to work it out.

Newt tosses a rednut at Betty and Betty scowls as the fruit hits her arm, marking it.

As she scrunches her mug up at Newt, a beast the size of a guard dog emerges from the water and drags the petticoat into the water and Betty with it. Betty don't fight: splash or kick out, but goes limp like some half-dead sow dragged to the slaughter house.

Newt runs towards the water, hurling more rednuts, but this time at the beast as it drags Betty further away, strong as an ox. More of the beasts is coming, Newt can see them circling further out, their tails beating the water, like some kind of war drum.

One of the rednuts finds its target, bouncing off the thick leathery skin of the beast and making a splash. It's enough of a distraction for Newt to grab Betty's arm, which is trailing behind her, like some piece of frayed rope. Newt pulls, hears fabric rip and frees Betty.

The beast retreats with its spoils as Newt pulls Betty onto the path, not caring that she's purpling Betty's pale arm with her grip. Once she's got her safe on the path, she clasps Betty tight, dragging her as she hoofs it into the wood, far enough away that the smell of the blood is dulled.

Betty's shaking, tearful, her petticoat ripped like bandages. There's blood everywhere, thick and dark, but even in mortal danger, Betty's focus is on pulling what's left of her garments down to cover her quim.

The water bubbles with the beast's frenzy, loud even at this distance.

'You ought to have left me,' Betty says, tugging the cloth and sobbing.

Newt drops her hold on Betty, lets her sink to the dusty floor, disgusted. The girl's a meater and an ingrate. Ain't nothing going to change that.

BETTY

The whole community are seated in the meeting place, except Tattio, Newt and Flora, who have chosen to patrol the shell path that runs parallel with the shore, armed with spears they've carved from branches, using the sharp black flint sometimes found on the island. Betty worries that Flora, so Christian before, is losing her way like the others.

Tattio means to kill one of the beasts. She said as much earlier when Betty got back to the camp, dishevelled and bloody. She says they need to know what they're fighting. It's like Master, who liked to study the dead insects he collected before he pinned them to the boards in his wooden cases. Betty knows a better way.

She shifts her position in the dust. Rosie tried to stitch her dress back together after the attack, using thin strips of cotton cloth, but it's not comfortable. The fabric is unyielding, but she supposes at least she is covered. She must keep the other dress unsullied for when they are rescued. As she raises her arm, swollen from Newt's manhandling, the murmurs in the circle die out.

'The beasts need a sacrifice,' she says.

It's a simple solution: a sacrifice for the greater good. Clay cannot run since falling, with a leg twisted like the ribbons on a Maypole, and Sun is slow witted, barely knows their own name. Master often said that weaker, smaller animals had an important part to play in keeping others strong.

'What do you mean, sacrifice?' Rosie asks.

'We must appease the beasts,' Betty continues, unperturbed. 'Nature's selection for the good of the community.'

Betty glances towards Clay and Sun and then to Sarah, expecting support, but Sarah's face is set in a hard line. She stabs her finger at Betty, her words spitting out.

'Shut yer filthy sauce box!'

'The beasts look for food, just like us. It is their nature,' Molly snaps. 'They do not desire to be worshipped.'

'Why is we parlaying like this?' Rosie's voice is shaky, tears in the corner of her eyes. 'You said we was all one family. All life is sacred.'

'She ain't got a bairn,' Sarah sneers, her face contorted. 'Thinks she can throw ours to the beasts to save he'self!'

Betty feels dangerously alone in the silence, which crackles like flames around her. Tattio is not here to calm Sarah's anger, nor Flora to explain that deformity is God's punishment for sin. Why do the others not see it is kindness to let the damaged children go? They are a burden that will only get heavier.

'Don't need no sacrifice,' Sarah says, her eyes on Betty's dress, which is a darker brown than before around the skirts. 'We got blood to give. It were that that drew 'em close. Not flesh.'

There is a murmur from the circle.

'We can wear rags, 'stead of leaves, to hold the blood better. Toss it all in the sea,' Sarah continues.

'We could use it as bait or to distract them,' Molly agrees.

Betty fiddles with the stitching on her dress. It is already starting to separate back into pieces. All this talk about what should remain private is making her feel faint.

Is she the only one left with standards?

NEWT

The beasts is too hard to catch with a spear, even with the end sharpened with the knife Newt keeps hidden in the cave. It barely grazes their devilish hide and the water acts like a scumbag: a second layer. Ain't as easy as skewering stuck pigs.

They're working on a net now, knotted lengths of fibre from the bark they rebuild the huts with, and threads of thick, dry grass. They're going to use blood-soaked leaves as bait, which some of the women have been burying, after keeping themselves dry from the curse.

Newt don't see the fuss. Who cares about a bit of blood running down yer leg? She's used to being dirty, not having nowhere to clean herself and it don't smell when it's fresh. Kept the punters away too and Lord knows she needed the rest.

Anyways, she ain't bleeding half as bad as when she were in London, or when Thunder were born. She could have filled a bucket that first day on the ship. It were like a well that never got dry—thick with dark glossy lumps the size of ha'pennies.

'Ready?' Tattio asks, checking the final knot by biting.

Unlike some of the others, Tattio's ivories is white and strong. Maybe Newt should rub her gums with salt water like she's seen Tattio do? She's got another one loose and it hurts her bonce; worse than a lashing.

Newt nods at Tattio, hopes this new plan works, that the rope is strong enough. She don't fancy bathing with the beasts for no one.

She lowers her end of the net carefully into the dark water, holding the end of the fibres tight in her fists, then pulls back, both feet behind the path, anchored in the thick damp soil where the heavy trees grow. Tattio do the same, glancing across. Newt gives another little nod.

It don't take long before the water starts swirling with dark shapes.

They only need one of the beasts to take the bait to learn what they is.

BETTY

Betty waits with the others at the edge of the path in the Cinder field. She can hear Tattio cursing and the scrape of summat heavy, dragged along the shells.

It's a beast, tangled in net, writhing like the devil itself. It's twice the size of one of Master's hunting hounds and with none of the obedience. Betty's heart thuds hard against her bodice beating a warning. She's glad she didn't get a proper look at the creature earlier.

Tattio, as always, is unbroken by the adventure, pulling on the ropes, her expression hard. She is a proud creature and, like Newt and Molly, seemingly has not learned the delicate ways of their sex. Betty thinks perhaps this is why women like these live like dogs on the street, or in asylums, and not under the patronage of a good man.

'Ketch de chillun back,' Tattio shouts, approaching. 'Dey ain't safe here.'

The beast must have smashed itself on the stones for a gash has opened up down the thick skin on its side, oozing a pungent liquid.

Betty wrinkles her nose and shudders, turning to leave with the children. She do not want to be near the creature with its flat soulless eyes and bloody teeth. What if it escapes?

Clay's at the back of the line, limping along, deliberately slow, with Star assisting him. Star is dawdling also, looking at the scene behind.

'Move,' Betty says, jabbing Star in the back with her fingers. 'There's nowt for you to see.'

'What is it?' Star asks. 'That thing that fights?'

'Not your business,' Betty says. 'Keep your beak out.'

'Is it a beast?' Star asks.

'Is they going to kill it?' Clay's voice wobbles like unset jelly.

'Act like a man for once,' Betty snaps.

Clay's too sentimental, crying over the smallest things and will never be commanding and courageous like Master. The others should have listened to her and made a sacrifice. Catching one of the grey monsters would not have been needed if they'd done that.

'What do you mean *man*?' Star asks, frowning and turning back again.

'Men look different...' Betty flushes. 'Down there,' she adds, lowering her eyes to her tattered woollen skirts as she walks on. 'Elder men.'

'I dun understand,' Star says.

'The word is *do not*,' Betty corrects, remembering how Master tried to help her say things right when she were reading.

Betty will not lower herself to talk about hornpipes or men's ways but she must make this child understand there is a difference. They all have their place in the world.

'Men are stronger, better at understanding and thinking.'

'Clay is good at thinking.' Star glances at Clay.

Betty snorts. 'A man must hunt.'

'Lightning is the strongest of us,' Star says. 'So will Lightning be a man?'

Betty purses her lips. It should not be left up to her to teach the children right from wrong but they is unruly, it will do nowt in the way of good to behave like savages when rescue comes.

Betty swats away a fly, feeling the thud of its body on her palm. She is tired of being the one that has to keep the children on the path of righteousness.

'Ask Elder Rosie,' she decides.

'But they'll tell me it *do not* mean nowt here.'

'But, but, but. Just move!' Betty snaps, keen to put distance between them and the writhing creature behind. At least the child has listened and corrected their speech.

They pass the cave, where they will imprison the beast, and follow the dust path around the grey rock. Betty's relieved, didn't realise quite how tight she'd been holding her breath in, and now she lets it escape like a whistle through a broken window.

Once the rock is skirted, the first huts come into sight. Here they are safe from the sound of the sea and whatever devilry lives beneath it.

For the first time, Betty is comforted to be amongst the 'mune, but that does not stop her wishing it were all a feverish dream.

MASTER'S BOOK OF SCIENTIFIC STORIES

The Glass Pipe

There was, until a few months ago, a small Tobacconist on Clerkenwell Green, with a fading sign which read: 'Tobacconist and purveyor of fancy goods.' The display behind the smoky window was a curious mix of wooden cigar boxes from exotic locations, glass jars of the finest tobacco, and a broad selection of wood and bone pipes. In one corner of the display, housed on a seat of blue velvet cloth, was a delicate glass pipe.

A man looked through the window: a gentleman of some standing, wearing a luxurious woollen three-piece suit. Pushing open the door of the shop, he headed towards the glass pipe which had captured his attention.

At this very moment, Mr Smyth, the owner of the small but well-stocked emporium, came through from the back of the shop, wiping the crumbs of his hastily eaten lunch of jam and bread from his full grey beard. He was a small, slight man with a large nose and a back bent like a spoon. He seemed greatly agitated by the appearance of the well-dressed gentleman in his shop.

The gentleman wasted no time in asking the price of the glass pipe, even daring to run his large fingers over the smooth transparent shank. He informed the shop-keeper that he wanted to acquire it for his collection. Mr Smyth looked nervously behind him and said five pounds, clearly very much more than what he had paid for it. The gentleman commented that it was a lot of money but wasn't perturbed. Mr Smyth, his face now a torrid white, then explained in a rushed voice that the pipe was already promised to another: a gentleman such as himself, who had visited the shop that very morning.

A woman appeared at the door behind the polished wooden counter. She had a round, pox-scarred face, and was considerably younger and larger than Mr Smyth.

'That pipe *is* for sale, husband,' she said with a look that would cut a lesser man in half.

An argument ensued between husband and wife. The gentleman observed the rising voices and harsh words with some amusement.

Finally, Mr Smyth agreed to take the gentleman's details, promising if the sale should fall through, he would contact the gentleman forthwith.

Before the gentleman had sufficient time to leave the shop, Mrs Smyth began berating her husband. Doubtless, in her own mind, she had already spent the five pounds on silken fabric for a new dress. Exhausted by the lash of his wife's tongue, Mr Smyth excused himself, no doubt full of regret that he had left the pipe in the window in the first instance.

The next day, Mrs Smyth discovered the pipe had been removed from the window display. After a furious hunt for the object, cursing Mr Smyth, she found it secreted behind the less popular tins of chewing tobacco. She placed it back in the window in a prominent position and sent word to the interested gentleman. Satisfied, she left for her afternoon stroll.

Mrs Smyth was irritated on her return to see the pipe had, once more, been removed from display, but try as she might, she was unable to unearth its hiding place in time for the gentleman's arrival. There was also a box of cigars missing.

Mrs Smyth was explaining this predicament to the gentleman when Mr Smyth returned from his deliveries. She was furious with him and accused Mr Smyth of hiding the glass pipe. He appeared much surprised, and following a thorough check of the window display, exclaimed, 'What has become of it?'

Mr Smyth was not telling the truth. That afternoon, he had pressed the pipe and the box of costly cigars on a friend for safekeeping. He told his friend he had acquired the pipe in a box of oddments, purchased from a sailor, down on his luck. Unable to sleep, and Mrs Smyth being the persistent type, he had begun to seek refuge and respite in his dark shop in the early hours. It was then he discovered the pipe was no ordinary glass object. At first, he explained, he was certain he had been mistaken, his eyes overcome with tiredness, for how could an unlit pipe glow and emit smoke? But sure enough, the following day he witnessed the same extraordinary phenomenon: a yellow light within the bowl and a slight grey plume swirling from the chamber. On closer inspection within the yellow light of the glass pipe, a colour akin to the brightest summer sun, he believed he saw a large blackish hill from which the smoke was emitting. This could not be, and yet, time and time again, he witnessed the same strange occurrence in the early hours before the sun was risen. The pipe, in daylight, reverted to transparency.

His friend (a young scholar of science, by the name of Henry Bertrand), did admit to being able to see something slightly amiss on close inspection of the glass pipe, when light was scarce. The transparent bowl had a seemingly yellow hue and he thought perhaps he could see smoke. Mr Bertrand made the suggestion that the pipe was, in fact, part of something much larger, an object or apparatus such as he had witnessed in the scientific laboratory. Still, it appeared that Mr Bertrand could, to some degree, verify Mr Smyth's remarkable story.

Mr Smyth took to visiting Mr Bertrand of an evening after the shop had closed, when he knew his wife would be tending to her ablutions. Slowly, with more practice, the picture within the glass grew clearer. It wasn't until, by chance, Mr Smyth draped the velvet cloth used to protect the pipe over his head, that he saw the true nature of the world within.

The view, as Mr Smyth described it to his friend, was of a wooded area, a tall black hill-like structure and a sea of a most remarkable lush green hue, akin to a well-tended lawn.

Mr Bertrand's approach was methodical and lucid, rather than fanciful. He made copious notes during Mr Smyth's visits, recording every detail of Mr Smyth's vision: the colourful birds that roamed the sky and the strange black sand. He recorded the angle at which Mr Smyth held the pipe and noted the time Mr Smyth announced the vision appeared.

Some weeks later, Mr Smyth witnessed hitherto unknown creatures in the glass he could only describe as large fish with legs. Mr Smyth's full attention turned to the sea beasts. They had curious tails, flat at the end like spades and feet that splayed out as if hands. Their eyes were small, situated on the side of large leathery heads, triangular in shape. They were fast in the water but lumbering on the land, as if they didn't belong. Or, like a young child, were taking their first steps.

It appeared to both men that Mr Smyth did not possess the only pipe through which this strange land could be viewed. On occasions, Mr Smyth was certain he could see a reflection in the glass that wasn't his, as well as the strange world beyond. As if someone else were also viewing the scene.

Where was this world with its green sea, black sand and constant yellow sun? If we believe Mr Smyth's story, we must also believe that the world he saw was somewhere in unchartered waters.

After several months, confident that Mrs Smyth had forgotten about the existence of the pipe, Mr Smyth relieved Mr Bertrand of his obligations and apparently took to carrying the pipe, wrapped in the velvet cloth, in the pocket of his overcoat. Thus, we must assume that he was able to conduct his experiments at will. Perhaps the world within the glass pipe became more real to Mr Smyth than his own.

Several months later, Mr Bertrand visited the small shop in Clerkenwell Green, eager to learn how Mr Smyth's visions were progressing. On his arrival, he found the shutters down.

Mrs Smyth opened the door at his insistent knocking. She explained to Mr Bertrand that Mr Smyth was dead. She had found him, several weeks ago, lying prostrate on the shop floor, clutching the glass pipe, a smile on his waxen face. She said he had taken to nocturnal wanderings and been dead for some five hours or thereabouts.

Mr Bertrand was overcome with guilt. He should have noticed the old man's decline; it was there in front of him. He asked Mrs Smyth the whereabouts of the pipe, to which she replied that it had been sold to a dealer, along with the stock from the shop. She informed him she would be vacating the premises now her husband was in the ground, for it was no longer a respectable position to hold.

Mr Bertrand repeated his condolences and hurried to the address Mrs Smyth had furnished him with. The dealer informed him the pipe had been sold to a young woman, who had no doubt purchased it for her father or husband. He had no address for her, he apologised, as she had said she was journeying and he hadn't wanted to press her, sales being what they are. Mr Bertrand left with assurances that the dealer would contact him should the pipe be returned to market, or he should hear of it.

Some months later, with no news forthcoming, Mr Bertrand was forced to abandon his search. With the loss of the pipe, he had no way to verify Mr Smyth's account. Regretful that he did not do more for his friend whilst alive, despite the absence of scientific evidence, Mr Bertrand wrote up Mr Smyth's discoveries. His peers would no doubt suspect a hoax.

With Mr Bertrand's notes and my recollection of Mr Smyth's conduct when I tried to acquire the pipe, my ideas on the matter are that the pipe was some sort of looking glass into another world, one yet to be discovered. I might perhaps suggest that Mr Smyth was not the only one studying it.

MOLLY

Tattio wants to kill the beast, gut it and throw its innards into the sea as a warning to the others but Molly manages to stop her, arguing that they must learn its weakness if they are to overpower it.

They must behave like the men of science.

To appease Tattio, when the beast finally passes, she has been promised its skin. She wishes to try to soak it, stretch it and scrape it, to make stiff pouches for medicine.

Molly enters the cave cautiously, as she has for the last two days, letting her eyes adjust to the half-light, tossing the scraps of fish and turtle flesh into the shallow salt-pool, before fully stepping inside. She's sure the beast would prefer a living creature to rip apart, but she's not willing to make that sacrifice. Still, she's learnt to respect the beast's strength, how fast, at full health, it can move.

She keeps to the edge, her back against the cool damp walls where Newt used to draw lines to mark the passing days, until there seemed no point. The beast will not survive much longer. Its skin hangs from its frame like a baggy woollen suit and its eyes are opaque. The shallow water where they have imprisoned it is not enough to sustain it, nor the food, but the goal has never been to save it, merely to observe.

Molly understands now why the Alienist, Dr Johnston, was so fascinated by her every move: the span of her hunger, the quality of her menses, the colostrum that dribbled from her poulticed breasts those first few weeks in confinement, even though her baby was dead. Without it he could not begin to understand the fight against puerperal insanity. He was not a bad man and she had given herself willingly for the use of his library. Dr Johnston even believed that it was possible for a gentleman such as himself to covet someone damaged like Molly. He'd shown Molly a book in his glass fronted cabinet: *Pamela*. It had a thick leather cover, embossed with gold. It was not impossible, he had said, for a maiden to be admired for her mind as well as her body. He was nothing like Edward, who took his pleasure when he saw fit, demanding Molly attend to her wifely duty even when she was unwilling, torn and grieving.

She'd been so lonely before she arrived here.

The beast shifts in the water, tracking her movements. It does not seem to see well through the piggy eyes stuck on the sides of its head but instead relies on movement, scent, and sound. The first bloody rag caused it to thrash around in a bout of malady.

Perhaps it has also lost a child.

She watches the beast resting, pulling the salt water through the slits in its skin behind where ears might form on any land creature. It does this continually, like it requires it to live. She gives it days at the rate its spirit is fading.

Molly watches the beast for a few more minutes and, satisfied it is resting, having lost all will for attack, she traces the wall to the opening which leads to the sacred well. Picking up one of the lighted jars, she begins to fill the buckets with the cool ice water for the community.

NEWT

Newt waits for Molly to leave the cave. Newt don't like the idea of her poking around, her daddles in stuff that don't belong to her but neither did Newt want to be the one to feed the beast. Let someone else risk their life. Newt's done with helping—don't get no gratitude from no one.

Take Betty. She's done got the morbs and if they was back home, she'd be in bedlam. Instead of being grateful she ain't locked up, she spouts words out her saucebox like an Autem bawler in his cackle-tub.

Betty don't think before she speaks or listen proper. She should try shutting her trap.

Molly's leaving the cave now, carrying two pails brimful of water, which slosh onto the dry path. She ain't as balanced as Newt, who don't never spill a drop.

It's quiet inside, not even the slap of water from the beast like yesterday. Newt lets her goggles adjust to the dim light, so different from outside where the sun nearly blinds you. She feels the beast watch her but it don't move, sick enough not to care no more. Maybe that's Betty's problem. She ain't got no fight left.

Newt moves swiftly to the back of the cave, stepping in the spaces between the rocks where the ground is less slippery. She picks up one of the glass jars and shakes it before ducking under the small arch. It's enough light to turn everything to smog, like the sky in London when night falls.

Lifting the largest black stone at the very back of the cave, Newt checks her stash: knife, sacking, shards of dried fruit-nut, bag of Tattio's remedies, and the broken glass pipe she found floating on the surface of the sacred well. She picks the pipe up now, turning it over in her hand. It don't make no sense to fashion something like this when bone and wood is stronger. How did it come to be in the cave? Running her hand along the edge, Newt contents herself with the fact that whatever it once were, the jagged edge is sharp enough to stab a man. Newt ain't like Betty. She knows men. If they come here, they won't think nothing of ripping open the legs of the 'mune and taking what they want. She will do everything she can to stop it.

Newt shakes the jar again to release the light, fading now the curious contents have settled into darkness. She peers through the glass at the tiny blue dots, wondering if they is alive and what else they can do.

MOLLY

The beast takes two days to die. Molly finds it on its side, with what's left of its eye rolled back in its head, its body empty of spirit. She feels a moment of sympathy for the creature who died alone, far from its kin and the familiarity of the sea.

She coughs. The carcass is starting to smell, the heat from outside the cave hastening the rotting of its internal flesh, which will leak out as liquid if they do not butcher it soon. She is grateful to have learned what she has about the creature, how poor its eyesight is, how it is drawn to scent more than sound, how it takes a breath not only through its mouth but the cuts below its ears, and more importantly, what it needs to survive. This information will help keep the 'mune safe. She does not have the stomach for studying what is under the thick skin.

She turns to the entrance. She'll need help dragging the body out of the shallow pool, for even at half the weight it was, she will not manage alone. Perhaps she'll ask Lightning and Rainbow to help. They've grown tall and strong with all the fresh air and will make short work of it.

Thinking about the children, Molly wonders if there's some truth in what Dr Johnston said, that humans, like animals, grow stronger than their kin when they have to survive. Or perhaps it is not that the children have adapted to the island, but the island has changed them.

There is movement outside the cave. Tattio and Newt must be back from their vigil, ensuring the beasts don't venture too close to the shore. It is only when the tide is high that they need worry. Molly has proved that the creatures do not have the necessary equipment to survive on land.

There will be no need now to involve the children in the removal of the beast, and for that, Molly is saddened, for the children must learn how to protect themselves.

Molly makes her way to the mouth of the cave. Pushing her hair back from her face—she doesn't want the stink of the beast on her—she combs it with her fingers, twists it into a rope and secures it with a whittled stick. Withdrawing her hand, full of shed hairs, she is surprised to see a grey strand amongst them.

NEWT

It seem Molly don't have the stomach for gutting. Once she's told them the beast has carked it, she moves outside the cave.

Newt lets Tattio get to work, holding the beast whilst Tattio makes short shrift of the carcass, scoring down both sides of the creature with a sharp flint and then peeling the skin back in one thick strip, as if it were fruit.

It certainly stinks like the fruit that rotted in the streets after market. Still, there were always something there Newt could pick through before the rain washed it into the gutters. She don't fancy eating the beast though, the colour don't look proper, its flesh greyed like it's been dead for days.

'Should we bury it?' Molly asks, still turned away, her hand covering her beak, like some gentlewoman with a hanky that don't want to witness the truth of it.

'Sand will ketch what we dun got need for,' Tattio says, holding up the spoils.

The skin she's removed is as thick and leathery as the seat coverings in the big-wig's carriages that gutter-crawled looking for fresh meat.

Anger bubbles in Newt's gut. She rips heartily at the remains of the beast as if it were a punter—separating the chunks of flesh from around the liver, slippery with oil. Heaving what's left of the beast onto a woollen cloth, laid flat on the cave floor, Newt steps back. The cloth don't do nothing to contain the liquid that seeps out.

Newt pauses and picks up a small metal disc from the cave floor, which must have been in the beast's stomach. Holding it up to the light, she finds it's a coin with two holes punched through.

'Damn creetuh eat everything,' Tattio says.

Newt nods, it's likely from the ship and the beast found it floating in the water.

When the shallow pool is clear of debris, and the parts of the beast dissected, Tattio places the skin back into the salt water and pisses on it, indicating for Newt to do the same.

'Softens it,' she says.

Newt looks at what's left of the beast, globs of flesh and bones, soft like torn nails. There ain't nothing to be scared of. The beast is flesh once dead, just like the rest of them.

BETTY

They need rescue now more than ever. They are women, not designed for battle in body or spirit. Betty is exhausted just adjusting her flags. Soon she will not be able to wear her best dress and all modesty will be lost.

She looks towards the ship, now a carcass of the past. She would board any ship today if she could, even if it was filled with ghosts like Master's stories, because it would take her somewhere, away from this godforsaken place. She could return to Master's house, pretend the incident did not occur. She would swap all of this world for one of Cook's pies and a scrub in the tub.

She shivers, despite the heat. The beasts is getting more confident, approaching the shallows more often. They care nowt of the sand when it sucks them down at low tide, rippling with their devilment. And they communicate, a high-pitched wail as they circle, and it's like nowt earthly: they are of hell's making.

Stretching one of the large glossy leaves from the rednut tree across two sticks to protect her skin from darkening further, Betty sits down on the path and looks past the beasts and onto the cloudless horizon, shimmering in the heat.

The community do nowt except set traps and patrol the shore, picking off the injured beasts whilst the numbers in the water increase and it is not for want of Betty trying. She has told them countless times. If there is a way onto the island, there must be a way off. Of course, she cannot swim, that is not summat a lady does, so it is not up to her to find the answers, merely to guide, as Master did for her.

As for the children, when they're not doing tasks in the camp, they run about like half-dressed savages.

In the silence, with only the swirl of water to break her concentration, Betty hears the tap, tap, tap of Clay's stick on the shell path.

Clamping her jaw tight, she tries to ignore it. The thought of Clay sickens her: that twisted limb and the long bleached blond hair, more suited to the fairer sex. It would be more tolerable here if she didn't have to witness it. Clay is a reminder of how wrong everything is, how unchristian.

She mutters a prayer:

Comfort me in my suffering, lend skill to the hands of my healers, and bless the means used for my cure.

Annoyed that she must move position from under the shade of her makeshift parasol, Betty scowls, picks up her skirts and walks further along the shell path, where the rednut trees grow thick and lush. She is not normally one for exploration, leaving that to the women whose skin can better tolerate the heat, who will never have the privilege of the pale beauty she is working so hard to regain.

Tap. Tap. Tap.

Gritting her teeth, she picks up speed, and heads into the forest behind where the ground is bumpy with low spiked shrubs which scrape the skin. The flies seem much more concentrated on this part of the island, and as Betty swats them away, she begins to see why the other women stay on the path. She needs to head further in, for she is not certain that the idiot child will avoid further injury. None of the children seem to possess the intellect to know their limitations.

Tiring, she sits down on a fallen tree to rest, and rubs the red ribbons on her legs that mark her journey. The forest is as silent as a resting place for departed souls, with not even the call of the rainbow birds, usually loud enough to deafen them until the sun sinks low and ends the day.

A rustle in the brush captures Betty's attention and she draws her legs up close to herself in case it's one of the scaly or squirrel creatures, which from the very beginning have seemed unconcerned by their presence, but nowt appears.

Sitting there, alone, with only her thoughts for company, Betty thinks that perhaps now is the time to take matters into her own hands.

It don't take much persuasion to get Clay to the cave. The child will do aught for a kind word.

'The sacred water will fix your leg,' Betty says, gritting her teeth. The child is uncomfortably close and has a musky smell. The sooner the cleansing happens, the better.

'Elder Molly say I is strong in other ways,' Clay says.

'Do you not want to run like the others?' Betty asks, stopping and folding her arms across her chest.

Clay's face reddens.

'Best you keep up then,' she says, turning.

She strides forward, her skirts brushing the shell path. She needs to be quick. There is never anyone in the cave at this time because they is waiting to sit down in the meeting place, but she will be missed when food is served.

Betty do not need to look back to know the child is following. She can hear Clay's stick, tap, tap, tap, mirroring her footsteps.

The cave is empty as expected.

'You must cover yourself with the sacred water to be baptised again,' she says.

'Baptised?' Clay asks.

'A new beginning. You will be reborn.'

'I dun understand,' Clay says. 'Will my leg be healed?'

'That's what I said,' Betty snaps.

Betty is frustrated by the child's constant questions. They should listen to their betters as she were taught to do.

She leads Clay to the back of the cave and through to the sacred water, shaking a jar to see better. The well is still and black.

'Get in,' Betty instructs.

'The Elders say flesh must not touch the sacred water,' Clay says, bottom lip quivering.

'Some of the Elder's have lost their faith in God and in miracles. I have not.'

Clay drops their stick on the cave floor and climbs over the lip of the well.

'It's cold,' Clay says, teeth chattering, clutching on to the rocky sides, 'and there is voices neath the water.'

'It is the devil in you,' Betty says, pushing Clay's head under. It is proof, if more were needed, that Clay's mind is sullied, and in need of purging.

Betty concentrates, trying to remember the scriptures, the right words to say.

'Let us cleanse ourselves from all filthiness of the flesh and spirit.'

Bubbles rise as Clay tries to resurface.

With all her might, Betty pushes down.

NEWT

Clay is missing from the meeting circle, their bowl untouched. Newt touches Molly's shoulder and points to the empty spot.

'Where is Clay?' Molly asks the children, already seated in the circle.

'Us is playing seek afore,' Star says. 'Maybe they is hiding?'

'Clay hides better than a stick-beast,' Thunder laughs.

Newt nudges Molly again.

'How long ago?' Molly asks.

When the children have no answer, Newt takes a spear and heads off.

When Newt finds Clay in the entrance to the cave, they is as sodden as a cloth left in water and their breath is scarce, barely pushing against their chest.

She presses her daddles against Clay's forehead and finds it clammy, cold as the leather on a wagon tyre. The child's staring straight ahead, back slumped against the damp wall. The stick, normally relied upon to walk, ain't nowhere to be found.

Newt looks about the cave for the circumstance that has knocked them into this state. The child has a gentle soul, don't mean no one harm—not like Lightning, quick to anger, or Star who will not take no for an answer.

Picking up a jar, Newt shakes it alight. There is some wetness on the rocks at the back of the cave, more than the damp that normally hang there. She traces it with her fingers, brings it to her nose and then tastes it. She has seen Clay do this. The wet is without salt.

She follows the damp, which leads her through the opening and to the sacred well. On the edge of the raised rocks that surround the water there is a sodden lump of bark. The tunic must have caught when Clay left the water.

Newt frowns, don't believe that Clay would enter the sacred well willingly. They is no rule breaker. Perhaps it were a dare? Or to hide? The cave is a good place to disappear. She pauses, that don't seem likely neither.

Letting the light drop, she looks at the floor and finds two sets of damp footprints: the child's larger feet, one turned slightly inwards and another, neater, smaller set.

There is only one person that still wears shoes on the island and Clay follows them about like a shadow.

Newt grits her ivories to stem the anger that don't have the opportunity to flow from her trap. But before she acts, she must hear the child's words, even though presently they ain't in a position to speak.

Clay do not speak when they reach camp, but their goggles give the game away. They look at Betty, who is seated in the meeting circle, like some mournful pup, but she will not meet their gaze. It is guilt. Newt saw it with the punters after they beat her, could not face the damage they'd done, though she never took her goggles from them, closed and bruised as they often were. Some threw a shilling onto her blood-splattered skirts, as if that was recompense for their actions, what with her left fighting for breath.

She must expose Betty's wrongdoing, for she cannot let Betty go unpunished like the gutter mongers who thought their fancy trappings made their lives more worthy than hers.

MOLLY

It's been two days, and no one can draw words from Clay, mute as Newt, their gaze downcast as if looking for truth in the soil. Molly knows that state, but for her it was the polished asylum tiles and the search for light in the blackness that descended after the death of her first child. Tattio has tried all the herbs in her possession, but this ailment is not physical, cannot be cured with a simple poultice. Clay's mind is sickening with something.

But why? What causes it? Clay's thin body has no marks of attack from a beast, though it was as sodden as if soaked by the sea. Has someone said an unkind word to Clay, to give pain and cause hunger to go? They are a sensitive child and barely ate anything before. Now they pick at roots like a baby bird. They have no weight to bargain with.

Molly looks over at Clay, sitting in the meeting place, a position they have assumed unless Newt is in the camp. It is an unlikely pairing, with Newt usually preferring their own company or that of a few select Elders, but perhaps Newt, without the words to elaborate, can understand Clay better than anyone. Molly has watched the children Clay is close to—Star, Rainbow and Lightning—try to encourage play, but it has yet to work. She wishes she knew what had happened. It is terrible to see one suffer so.

She turns her attention back to the hut, which only needs the roof edges woven before it is complete. Then she must take her turn patrolling the shore, when the sun is lower in the sky. She has good colour on her skin now, kept supple with the beast's fat, but it is still not hardy enough for midday. The naturally dark-skinned women are the only ones strong enough to withstand the heat of the sun. Molly does not know how the community would survive without them.

Newt will be back soon with the rednuts, and for once without Tattio, who is already in the food hut, concocting a new herbal refreshment for Clay. Something she hopes will lessen the tension that sets their jaw so tight.

Molly takes two of the raw strands of bark which stick out from under the hut roof and starts to plait them. Maybe she could ask Clay to help? A distraction might work as well as any medicine, it did for her and so many of the others when they first arrived on the island.

She walks over to the dusty circle.

'I need help to weave the bark for the roof and the others are busy on the shore. You are good with your hands,' she says. 'Will you work with me?'

Clay nods but does not look at her directly.

It is a start and maybe it will break through the silence.

BETTY

Betty stiffens, her body as hard as the weave of her salt-logged dress. Newt is approaching her, and she's alone, her stride purposeful. Has Clay said summat?

She adjusts her shade, trying to mask herself from view. Once picked, the large oily leaves of the rednut tree quickly dry out, the edges browning like the worn pages of a book. What Betty would do for one of Master's stories now, for there might be some answers to her predicament—some further steps she might take.

She scowls and focuses on the horizon, hopeful that Newt's appearance is simply her normal patrol of the shore and the firm set of her jaw is related to the beasts, which frolic like children at a fair near the sunken ship.

Betty shifts her position as Newt reaches her. Should she acknowledge Newt? She certainly don't want her company.

Newt sits down on the shell path, familiarly close, and Betty feels the heat from her glossy skin. The women have been rubbing all sorts of disgusting things onto their bodies to protect it from the sun. If they wish to keep their youthful glow, they should follow her example and stay in the shade.

There's summat glinting in Newt's hand; her small dark fingers do not quite mask the object. Whatever is it? The inside of a shell perhaps? The oysters back home used to glint when prised open, ready for Master's platter.

Betty starts to feel uncomfortable with Newt's unblinking gaze on her. She will surely go soon. But Newt do not move, and the silence eats at Betty like the pox, small blisters of discomfort forming into angry red eruptions.

'Clay did not wish to be a burden,' she says suddenly, unable to hold the truth inside her any longer, safe in the knowledge that the other women speak their minds when they see fit. 'I offered my help. That is all. You of all people should understand that.'

Regardless of whether the child has said aught, it's their word against Betty's—the stupid twisted child. Betty's been thinking about what to say ever since she pushed them down into the sacred well. She's frustrated that the words must exist at all. The child should not be here, it is everything that is wrong with this place.

Newt's expression do not change as Betty explains herself, but her grip tightens on whatever it is in her hand.

'Clay wanted it,' she adds. 'Nature's selection.'

Betty's surprised when Newt seems to relax. Even more so when she takes Betty's arm and runs her dark fingers down it. Her touch makes Betty shiver, it is both unwelcome and welcome—a connection of some sort—proof she is not alone in her thinking. The tears come then, leaking out of Betty's eyes and tracing her pale cheeks. All the worry that she will be discovered and punished evaporates. Newt is on her side.

NEWT

The girl do not see it coming and cries out as the blood spurts from her wrist, like blow from a pisser. Newt blocks Betty's escape, forcing her to stay on the path, her only option to step on the sand, which ripples with her cries, or to the sea near the rock pools, where the beasts is circling waiting for offerings.

Betty's goggles are wide, pleading but it don't cut it with Newt. Betty's the type that takes what ain't theirs: a life, a turn, honour for a shilling.

Now the beasts is coming, frenzied and thrashing towards them, splitting the dark sea with their fins.

The girl's chest heaves, like she's lifting something heavy, yet she ain't done a day's work since she got here—wouldn't know what real work was, sitting on her jacksy day after day, fanning herself like some corseted lady. If she had, she'd know the beasts can't reach them, with the tide so low, but it suits Newt for her to think she's dead in the water.

Newt wipes her blade on the cloth bag she carries, which contains the crushed false-mint leaves. She hadn't needed many to get the few drops of liquid needed.

The girl will know terror, like that she inflicted on the child. Newt don't need Clay to tell her they don't feel safe no more. She knows what it is to be in such fright that nothing spills from yer trap 'cept breath, and Betty just done admitted she did it.

Snot runs down from Betty's nose as she sobs and pleads, snivelling like a meater.

'I were only doing what were right. What the others don't have the guts for.'

Newt crosses her arms. Betty is not helping her cause, she should be repenting. Should Newt let the beasts have their sacrifice? It would be a just end for one who insisted on it. Newt don't doubt it's different now it's her.

The beasts is close, splashing in the shallows, their gib faces pointed at the path, their beady eyes fixed on the source—the stench of Betty's blood as it leaks from the cut. It would only take a small shove and Betty would be gone.

Newt's never killed no one, though she's had a mind to, and she's cut plenty. A knife in flesh don't turn her stomach no more than any butchery.

An image of her ma flicks into her head: her last shallow breath, her daddles cold, clasped in Newt's own. She'd bled out and it weren't from any wound. She done nothing wrong in her life but try hard to make circumstance better.

Newt steps aside, allows Betty to rise. It were only meant to be a warning, what could happen if she don't mend her ways. She grips tight to Betty's injured arm, stemming the flow of blood. Pulling her along, she leads her back to the camp, ignoring the sobs—that of a spoilt child, and the slap of her worn soles on the shells.

She hopes the girl has learned her lesson. Next time she will not be so merciful.

MOLLY

Newt must have found Betty on the shore, cut and bleeding. She probably injured herself on the rocks, but she won't speak. She should be more careful, what with the beasts so close, they don't need to excite them any more than necessary. Tattio's cleaned the wound with salt water and wrapped it tight with strips of sailcloth. Betty said no word of thanks for Tattio's ministrations. In fact, she said nothing about the incident, which is unusual. Normally, like all of them here, she does not hold back.

Should the Elders talk about Betty? She contributes little to the community except her words and though it does not matter what is said, often hers are not helpful. In fact, she creates problems: the fabric they so desperately need that lines the shore in the form of her flags. At least she's taken herself off to the far hut to lie down, she did look terribly pale but that might be the bleeding. She was lucky it wasn't worse, some of the rocks at the far end of the beach are like knives.

Placing more bark shavings on the fire and the bucket of water to boil, Molly makes ready for the herb tea and the root they will have for lunch. Now that the huts are nearly finished, she will be free to do other work. It is a pity the seeds Newt found came to nothing, withering within the first few hours. There must be something they can grow rather than relying on the fruits already here that dwindle in number with every meal.

Molly looks up as Thunder and Star run past, playing some type of game. She smiles at their speed, unhindered by clothing or rules. She thinks of the many times when she was scolded for her unbecoming behaviour—too many to count. Star looks like Dr Johnston, the aquiline nose, blonde hair and brown eyes, but that is where it ends. The children here have a freedom of spirit that would have been as alien to Dr Johnston as the feel of the chains he used to manacle his patients.

Thunder and Star clatter past again, kicking up dust in their wake.

'Be careful!' Molly shouts after them, holding back another smile.

Her warning is greeted by a flick of a hand. The children do not speak as much as Molly remembers doing at their age, even Star who is full to the brim with questions. Perhaps it is the sand, rippling at the slightest sound? Her father had called Molly a chatterbox, but not in a kindly way. Girls were to be seen and not heard, especially not to ask questions. Molly realises now it was training for womanhood. She has spent half her lifetime holding her tongue.

Well, no more.

BETTY

The hut is stifling, and Betty has no appetite, but Tattio says she must eat flesh to replace the blood she has lost. She has left strips of jump meat in one of the rednut bowls, just inside the hut doorway. Betty kicks the bowl, not caring that she eaten nowt for a day or that the meat is now ruined in the dust and will draw the beetles to it. It reminds her of Newt. She is the only one fast enough to catch the tree climbing creatures with her stupid pointed sticks.

Betty tosses and turns on the hard floor, sleep refusing to visit her. The hut is like an oven and her arm stings every time she moves, the bandage reddening with her injury.

The silent bitch, Newt, did this to her, and she do not trust her not to do it again.

'Move over.'

Betty's eyes prick open. Thunder's voice is hard to ignore in the hut beyond—she named them well. That means lunch must have finished, and the community are beginning to settle down for their afternoon sleep. Betty scowls. Soon she will be surrounded by the sweat of the other women, like animals in a barn. They will not leave her to herself for more than a day. Space is too scarce even though all eight huts have been mended.

'Stop playing. I'm trying to sleep.' It's Thunder again, their voice a boom amongst the soft chatter of the others.

Betty frowns, sits up, resting her back against the curved wall. What are they playing when they should be sleeping? What game is this?

She listens harder, catches a moan that escapes from another child and shivers in disgust. She knows that sound. It came from Master's lips when her skirts were pushed high and he pumped his seed into her—the moment of his weakness. She feels sick to the stomach. This is not a game the children should be playing.

She must let them know she has heard them.

'Go to sleep,' she shouts.

How has she missed the seeds of this immoral behaviour? It has clearly not been discouraged, for the children make no attempt to hide it. How can Rosie allow it? It must be Sarah that turn a blind eye, her own behaviour often unchristian.

There are giggles and a rustling sound, not what Betty expected. They seem unconcerned she is listening, that she *knows*.

Betty's face reddens at the horror of it.

Summat must be done and quickly before God strikes them down. She mumbles a prayer, an act of contrition:

Holy Mary, Mother of God, pray for the sinners and lead us not into temptation, but help us to stay on the path of righteousness.

MOLLY

It's after lunch, and the children are returned to their hut. It has become necessary to always rest when the sun is at its highest because it draws water from the skin like a flannel. The number of women has dwindled at the meeting place. Mostly they choose to sleep instead of talk and not just because of the heat. Nothing has needed to be decided for many months. But today, looking at Betty's pinched face as she approaches the small circle from the far hut, where she has been recovering, it's clear she has something she wants to get off her chest. She hopes Betty's put more thought into her words than the last time, when she spoke of sacrifice, and that her injury has not affected her mind. Her forehead does look wet with perspiration. She might still be fevered even after a whole day of rest.

Molly accepts the rednut cup of tea from Newt and takes a sip of the cloudy mix. Instantly her muscles relax. It's like taking a step back from the day.

'What is it?' Molly asks, eyeing Betty, hoping it's not another one of her mad ideas for rescue. They've wasted enough material making flags and fires when the tide's out. No one's coming, no one misses them; they were always surplus.

Betty takes a big breath in and what's left of the rags of her bodice stretch with it.

'It's time to separate the children,' Betty says, her face as stiff as the fabric which hangs off her in threads. She does not seem to see how ridiculous she looks.

Molly cannot help Betty if she will not listen. It is like an echo.

'What for?' Rosie asks. 'The bairns is grand as they is. Plenty of room in the hut.'

Betty flushes, her face even redder than before. She twists her hands, like she's wringing out a cloth. 'They're growing big, some is almost as tall as me, and boys have urges.'

'I ain't seen no difference in 'em,' Rosie shrugs.

''cept Lightning.' Sarah rubs herself between her legs and laughs, a coarse rumble. 'And they ain't got no tackle.'

Betty's face burns brighter as she crosses herself.

Molly watches Betty carefully. She was barely three-and-ten when they boarded the ship, practically a child herself and even though she is older now, almost a young woman, she is unable to adapt. Perhaps she's voicing her own fear from the past.

'Dey not got fathers to teach dem wrong. Won't be huffs and hawks like de men we knows,' Tattio says.

'Men cannot help themselves,' Betty frowns. 'It's in their brain. They's born like it.'

'Like us bin born slaves?' There's a growl this time in Tattio's answer.

'They ain't got the curse,' Rosie says. 'They's still young uns. Let 'em have their fun.'

Molly tries to gauge the other women's reactions in the small circle. They seem unconcerned by Betty's latest outburst, as if it is of no importance.

Tattio spits a leaf out onto the earth. Another is caught in her front tooth and she digs it out with her fingernail. 'It do no harm for dem to explore.'

'You would say that,' Betty snaps, her gaze accusing, her face now puce, sweating enough that it drips down her cheeks in angry tears.

Rosie draws lines in the dust before rubbing them out. 'I ain't seen no monsters in our bairns. Only in the sea,' she says. 'Our children is gentle.'

THE MUNE

The women are quiet for a moment. Perhaps, like Molly, they are thinking that the enemy is not within the community but thrashing in the waves.

'We cannot change man's nature,' Betty is firm. 'They is what they is. The girls need protecting.'

'This is bull-scutter. They can look after 'emselves,' Sarah says. 'Like what we done. They ain't stuck like we bin.'

'Men is stronger by nature.' Betty does not seem to be able to let the subject go.

Molly frowns, half expecting Flora to jump in and start agreeing with Betty, what with her always taking the opportunity to push God to the foreground, but she surprises her.

'They is no different from each other,' Flora says. 'This is nonsense—summat men do to hold our faces down in the dust.' Flora sweeps her arm around the camp. 'Look what we done without needing 'em.'

Betty's fists clench as she stands, turning away from the group before striding off in a hiss of fit, like a child that's been told no.

Molly waits until she's out of sight.

'I'm worried about Betty. We must do something to help. She is not sound of mind.'

Molly looks around the circle. Newt stares straight ahead, her back rod-straight, Tattio pokes at the fire with a stick and Rosie bites her lip so hard she draws blood. It will be a difficult subject for them to discuss, for they have surely all been accused of madness. It is the very thing that binds them.

BETTY

The women do not listen to sense, even Flora, and they have become savages, worshipping only themselves. They do nowt to pretend no more—Betty don't remember the last time anyone but her and Rosie said Grace, thanked the Lord for what they have been given. Instead, they thank the island! How can she fix them? What can she do about the evils that consume the children? It is a disease, summat which must be purged, but how can she purify them with nowt at her disposal: no holy water, good book or apparition?

She stamps onwards towards the beach, muttering and mumbling, trying to find a suitable solution. As she reaches the cave she wonders if the answer is in the sacred well where she first baptised the children, sprinkling their innocent foreheads with water. Was Clay's survival some kind of miracle to show her the way, guided by God's hand? Jesus did always favour the meek.

The more she thinks about the cool water, the firmer her resolve becomes. She will be baptised again, and it will be a blessed release to feel the ice water against her skin that burns like hellfire itself.

She stops to take in a breath outside the cave entrance. The journey has been harder than usual. Her limbs ache with the effort of simply walking and she feels faint. Perhaps she should have nibbled on the flesh or root before leaving the camp, but she cannot turn back—cannot fail in God's mission, as clear now as the water that will be her salvation. Her purpose has never been more transparent.

Betty has not been into the cave since the incident with Clay, but back then she had such a commitment of mind, she did not notice the stink left behind from the beast, like guts festering in a bucket. She wrinkles her nose in disgust, don't know how the others bear it. Probably got so used to it they no longer notice, like the men that bury the dead.

She thinks of Newt again. When Master's sister died of the fever, they hired a girl like Newt—a mute. Cook said it were supposed to bring good luck.

Well, she has brought nowt in the way of good luck to the 'mune. The very thought of Newt gives Betty the strength of purpose she needs to continue her mission. She will show them all. She will be the miracle the community needs, and God will reward her dedication with rescue.

Feeling her way to the back of the cave, her hands slapping on the damp walls, she retraces the path she took with Clay over the smoother rocks between the salt pools. Clay had been easy to entice, always wanting answers to questions that could only come from a sullied mind, and them voices Clay said came from under the water proved it.

She picks up one of the jars and agitates it, before ducking through the entrance to the well, surrounded by black rock. There is nowt to be scared of. She cannot be reborn unless she is free from fear and worldly goods. Carefully, she discards her dress and petticoats, which are stuck to her in some places where urine has dried against her skin. She is glad the light is not strong enough for her to witness her own nakedness, for that would repulse her.

Crossing herself, she climbs onto the cold rocky ledge and thrusts herself downward. Maybe she must be buried before she can live again.

As the ice-cold water envelops her, she feels a sense of release, as deep as the pain of her final contraction.

MOLLY

When Betty does not return for supper Molly is concerned, not by the state she was in when she left after lunch, fevered and angry, but because she hasn't eaten. It took several hours to rid the hut of biting insects, strange black spider-like creatures with tiny wings, which swarmed over the discarded jump flesh like a plague.

It had been one of the things the Elders had discussed when she'd stormed off—how little she valued their endeavours.

Molly is not the only one who has noticed her absence.

'Us must wait for Betty,' Star says.

Molly stirs the pail of fish stew with a stick and glances at Tattio. Tattio has already checked the shore and confirmed that Betty was not at her normal vigil.

'Betty do not do well in the sun,' Star continues, 'and must look proper nice when the boat come.'

Thunder nudges Star hard enough to produce an Ow.

'What boat be that?' Rosie asks, eyebrows raised. 'What tommyrot Betty be saying?'

'It's nowt,' Star mumbles, cupping the hot broth that is passed.

Molly puts a bowl of stew aside for Newt, who often misses meals when her hunt is going well. She wonders, as she scoops out the salty chunks, flavoured with rockweed, how much time Star has spent with Betty to know these facts. It is not healthy to dwell on what might be, when the land affords them survival. Perhaps she'll speak to Rosie later.

Molly leaves the children to rinse the bowls in salt-water under Rosie's guiding hand and follows Tattio to the food hut. Tattio ducks through the doorway and grabs her cloth bag of tricks, as commonplace now as if she were a doctor. Molly's fears remain unspoken as she waits.

'Us will find Newt,' Tattio says. 'E knows de island better den anyone.'

Molly bites her lip. Newt left the meeting when Molly had tried to discuss what could be done to help Betty, taking her spear and the empty pail, a sign she was going to collect water and patrol the shore.

Newt is angry at Betty, and she didn't need words to convey that. Perhaps it is because she always ends up cleaning the mess that Betty leaves in her wake.

'Newt is busy with the beasts,' she says.

Tattio narrows her eyes and Molly feels great discomfort. She should be used to voicing her concerns and not worry about what words are said, but this feels different.

'I worry she might have walked on to the sand,' Molly says. 'She has a fever and is not in her right mind.'

'Come.' Tattio hooks the cloth bag higher on her back and grabs the wooden spear she keeps stabbed in the earth. 'Us will find e and cure Betty's ills.'

Molly fears Betty's ailments will not be simple to cure.

NEWT

Newt is finished at the shore, two jumps speared. They is easy to catch now, using the sharp, stripped sticks she throws at them as they dart between the tall trees. It is best to aim high, for the creatures leg-it upwards when they sense her below. They is only injured when they fall but the false-mint oil on the tips of the arrows, helps slow their meanderings, allowing Newt to slash their necks; a swift end to their misery.

The children need meat. Tattio say it is good for their growing and Newt had needed to hunt, so consumed was she by the bile that poured from Betty's trap before. The children should be free from the shackles the Elders left behind. Free to love as they choose.

Newt stops outside the cave and leaves the spoils and her spear against the outer wall. There is only the bucket to fill and then she will head back to the camp, eat the stew Molly will have put aside for her. They is used to her tardiness, knowing she is hunting: the benefit theirs.

She pauses by the sacred well. There is clothes and undergarments, shredded and stained but folded neatly as if they's about to be packed in a fancy trunk. It don't take a high forehead to work out their owner. The only one of them that still wears the clothes they arrived in. Newt frowns, shaking the jar left beside them, even though she don't need light no more because she knows this place as well as any underpass.

Peering over the edge of the well, Newt agitates the water, careful to use the pail and not her flesh, which might corrupt it.

She can't see nor hear nothing beneath the surface, but then the water is as dense as the smog which chokes London.

Newt sits back on her heels. There ain't nothing she can do for the girl if she has taken it upon herself to enter the water, but it is better she makes her own sacrifice, than one of an innocent child.

Newt turns at the sound of others approaching. Footsteps pause outside the cave entrance.

'We should ask Newt about Betty.'

It is Molly outside, always mothering. Newt gathers the clothes up quickly. They is too big to secrete under the stone with her other finds, so she presses the bundle down behind a far rock. She will come back for them later—clap her hands, let the sand swallow them. It is better the camp think Betty is missing, than sacrificed herself. She has caused enough grief.

Emerging into the light with the full pail of water, she nods to Molly and Tattio.

'Have you seen Betty?' Molly asks.

Newt shakes her head.

'Us should check de shore again,' Tattio says. 'Where de rocks is sharp. Betty could be cut again and need tending.'

Picking up the spoils of her hunt, Newt turns away, heads back to camp. She knows how it feel when fear ain't able to be shed. With Betty gone, it might loosen Clay's tongue.

MOLLY

Their voices are hoarse from shouting.

'Us must leave,' Tattio says. 'De sea is rising.'

They have been searching for hours but there has been no sign of Betty, no evidence of her passing this way. The sea is rushing towards the island like it has no time to wait, eclipsing the black sand with a single stroke. It will not be long until it is high enough to draw the beasts in.

The night falls rapidly here and with no forewarning. In seconds the sky will turn black, as if someone has blown out a candle. At least the moon will be up tonight, low and swollen with light, and they can follow the shell path, which stretches like chalk on a board, marking their route.

'I will come to de forest early,' Tattio says.

Even early may be too late for Betty, but at least Tattio's journey won't be a wasted one. When the tide retreats, there will be spoils to be had: silver fish that flap, gasping to find water, their shiny bodies too silent and light to be sucked beneath the sand, and crabs that have scuttled sideways over the path to find shelter.

Molly is fearful for Betty, the night is no time to be alone, especially with the moon as full as she is. Should they walk back through the forest, to check Betty is not lost, rather than the easier route along the shore? But the trees here are so dense, and the brush sharp, their feet will be shredded—it will be like walking on needles and with no guarantee of finding her.

'Should we stay a little longer?' Molly asks.

'Us not risk anudduh life,' Tattio says.

Molly follows Tattio, keeping close enough to feel the heat rise from her skin. Tattio has the balance Molly is still trying to find after all this time, keeping herself safe whilst also able to think of others. They make their way to the path, as quickly and quietly as they can whilst treading carefully.

They arrive too late at the shell path, which is already under a thin layer of seawater. Their only option is to weave through the rednut trees, where the boggy soil will make the journey slower as it sucks at their bare feet.

Every moon draws the water further onto the island before it recedes again. The salt water in the pools in the cave, where they housed the beast they captured, is evidence that sometimes the sea washes deep into the mouth. Molly worries that one day soon, the beasts might come dangerously close to the sacred well—their only drinking water.

They trudge ahead, making silent progress. Molly ignores the thorny pain of the brown-leaved bushes, which sting like nettles on her bare skin, and thinks about Betty, her obsession with rescue, and how it consumed her.

MASTER'S BOOK OF SCIENTIFIC STORIES

The Automaton Nose

The day was not distinct from any other, though I do recall the sun was particularly bright and flooded through my open window, along with the whisper of leaves, the rustle of dry grass and the trilling of the blackbirds, singing for all their worth.

I left my hot apartment for a place which was unconstrained by walls and ceiling, clutching my volume to my chest. I threw myself down beneath an aged tree with a canopy redolent of a gentleman's umbrella. I could hear the wings of insects flitting in the gentle breeze, the burble of bubbles in the small stream near my warmed feet, and a single cloud scraping across the bluest sky I have ever witnessed. I never grew weary of hearing the changeful nature of my surroundings.

So curious was I, on hearing the rustle of ants that appeared to be marching across a crisp fallen leaf, that I was barely conscious of my reading until I happened upon this paragraph:

> *'The nose, which is the perfumier of the brain, detects fragrances so minute as to never register. It is not the fault of the apparatus itself, the organ of our detection, but limited by our ability to magnify that which is in front of us.'*

This was nothing new. I had long believed that my own sense of smell was superior to that of my acquaintances. I could often pick out a hint of raspberry, or another earthy aroma in the liquor they consumed that they could not themselves discern. One who was blessed with a larger nasal cavity, such as myself, might be at an advantage. I considered the scents of which I might be ignorant: leaves with the aroma of the autumn sun; the suggestion of the fish who have journeyed through the stream and the sweet sap of blossom.

Over the following days, I took to wondering if, like the eyeglass, or the automaton ear which magnified the detail we encounter and which is often unspeakably lost to us, there might be a similar solution for the nose.

Over and over, in the sleepless hours of the night, I asked myself: why not? What if it could be done? I would surely be famous and wealthy.

The idea clung to me like the sweet smell of jam on the lid of a jar and caused me confusion in my work. Some said I was ailing, my face the grey hue of rain clouds, but if the truth be told, I was tormented with possibilities. Thankfully, as a Professor, I was shortly to be released from my responsibilities, what with the summer hiatus looming. I would use the time to construct an instrument which would catch the most delicate of scents and I would conduct my labours without pause, until it was perfected.

I travelled to London and took possession of 'The Book of Perfumes', in order to learn enfleurage, maceration and expression. I concurrently purchased a nosegay and a selection of glass vials containing aromatic herbs and floral oils to magnify my olfactory senses. For days and weeks, I shut myself in my small apartment, maturing plan after plan which was followed by failure after failure. I sank into a despondency so deep I might as well have been drowning until one day, by pure accident, on inhaling oil of rose, the vial shattered, and the glass lacerated my septum.

At first, all I could smell was the blood that poured from the orifice, seemingly without end, and of course, the scent of rose also overwhelmed me. But after a period of dizziness, on sitting down, I was certain I smelt lavender and a waxy scent beneath the more obvious odours. Was I smelling the bee that pollinated the flowers and the plants that rubbed against the rose before it was harvested?

I discarded the metal nosegay and began the immediate fashioning of a glass implement which I might insert deep into my nasal passage. All the maddening doubts that had blackened my days suddenly departed. There was no tremor in my hand now and my heart was steady in its beat.

It was several days after when I raised the completed instrument to my nose and lodged it high in my nasal passage. I decided on oil of violet root for my first endeavour. I could smell it! Not just the pungent woody aroma of violet rhizomes but something else. I could smell the cool air in the dry cupboard where it was stored; the grains of earth which clung to the shafts before it was crushed and the sharp bitter leaves that once graced it. It was as if it was communicating with me.

My labours had been rewarded!

All night I practised with the instrument. The scents glistened and hummed, and my senses were alive with the history of their production.

I was anxious to guard my discovery against strangers and keep it secret and the desire for fame left me. I no longer cared to share the pleasure of my invention and I grew utterly indifferent to society.

I had not noticed my failure to wash or groom my beard during this period of intense labour, so intent was I on witnessing the boundless pleasure of the hidden layered perfumes I was absorbing. I could hardly recognise myself in the glass. My hair was unkempt, and my beard knotted, still crusted with blood. My skin was grey and my cheeks concave with hunger: fearfully haggard. My nose was an odd shape, my nostrils flaccid and without form.

I turned away from the mirror with an uncomfortable feeling. When I looked out of my window, I saw the fresh dampness of snow on the ground outside.

Had a season passed whilst I was labouring? Perhaps those dreadful noises I had heard, and which had angered me so, a thief on my concentration, were my colleagues, wondering where was I?

I happened to witness a woman of youthful years, but quite crumbled in appearance, walking past my window. She was wearing a torn woollen dress with a laced bodice. I suspected she was a woman of disrepute and it suddenly occurred to me that I might get her to test my instrument for there was no fear of betrayal.

I called for the woman to enter the building and once inside the narrow hall, I beckoned her into my apartment offering her ale for her health, which was surely lacking. She was clearly entranced by the scents on my windowsill, picking them up and inhaling them in their vials. Whilst her back was turned to me, I took advantage of her fixation and hit her over the head with my measuring scales.

When she awoke, my instrument was lodged in her nasal passages and when she inhaled the oil of lavender,

I witnessed her eyes roll back and her mouth become slack, as if in ecstasy. She murmured some words which I later recalled when I dragged her limp body into the hall and across to an empty apartment, a dirty bare room of a scent that turned my stomach. She spoke of a waxy smell that I had also witnessed when I first used the instrument, but also of a sweetness and warmth. Her life was of no interest to me, other than as proof of my success, and I left her alone, unperturbed by her cries.

Once more I inserted my instrument into my own nasal passage but this time I was met with a hard and diseased scent, which sickened me, and I could not clear it from my mind. My instrument was worthless! I removed it forthwith, and witnessed it was blocked by a clump of nasal waste. On washing the instrument, once more I was able to smell nature's true perfume. Relieved my labour was not in vain, I slept like a child, without fear or doubt and felt utterly refreshed on waking.

Looking out of my window that next morning and inhaling the freshness of the new day, which seemed brighter and clearer than before, I saw the woman of the previous day walking past. Her face was without injury, barring those same scars from the pox which had pitted her skin before my experiment! Was she a ghost? Was I still sleeping?

I searched for my instrument but all I could find was a broken glass vial and the fatty oils of rose staining my table.

My brain seemed to open up. I realised that over the last few weeks I had ridden the black depths of insanity but passed through unharmed. The woman remained alive and well, it had all been an imagining and for this, I praised our Lord the great Creator.

BETTY

Betty coughs as she gasps for air. Water spews from her nose. She is no longer in the water, that much is clear, for she is not fighting it. It took all her strength and trust in God to allow it to drag her down to its icy depths.

She shivers as cool air presses against her skin like ghostly fingers. Reaching down to pull her dress around her, she remembers that she folded it neatly by the well and is as naked as the day she were born. She flushes with shame, glad that it is too dark to see her flesh on display like some kind of wanton women, or the Elders back at the camp.

She feels around and beneath her. She is on some sort of hard rock, slippery with water, like the cave she just left. There is nowt to hear 'cept her breath, stuttering from her tightening breast and hanging in the air.

Is this purgatory? Is she a phantom?

Betty sobs, her chest heaving with her tears, falling unrestrained. This is not the rebirth she pictured. She should be free of her body, and its scars, free from all earthly desires. The world should be changed, but instead she appears trapped. Wrapping her arms around her knees, she protects her modesty as she rocks, just like she did on the shore waiting for rescue.

A light catches her attention, flickering from somewhere behind. Her heart lifts. She has heard about the tunnel of life and the light which draws forth your spirit into God's blessed arms and with it, sweet release. Will her mother be waiting at the gates to welcome her? She has not seen her face for so long. And what about her babby, thrown from the ship into the rough sea? Will it also be there waiting for her loving embrace?

Betty rises, forcing her shoulders back, eager now to complete her journey but also anxious not to slip on the unruly surface beneath. It is brittle, cratered, and cuts into her soft feet with each step. She walks towards the light and the entrance to heaven.

She pulls up short. The light is not coming from the back of a tunnel, but from an opening on the side of the wall, and is brighter than aught Betty has witnessed previous, even the sun on the island. There are people there, but it is not her mother. She colours a deep, shameful red, conscious of her nakedness, and the cold, thin air that has begun to make it difficult to even gasp.

This is no heaven.

A hand clamps over her mouth as she collapses.

NEWT

The snores of the community, and the insects which scratch and buzz, are the music of the night. Normally they soothe Newt to sleep, so different from the clatter of hooves on cobbles, and the mafficking. But tonight Newt is wide awake, goggles fixed on the grey rock where it curves away like a shapely rump.

She should have gone with Molly and Tattio.

Slapping at the biting bugs that never seem to bore of the taste of her, Newt flicks their squashed bodies from her skin. She is worried. It is late, the night is hot and heavy, like a hand pressed over yer mug.

The snap of a twig and a low murmur catches Newt's attention. Molly and Tattio must be rounding the grey rock, for no sound leaks from that side of the island until the broken tree is reached. There ain't no reasoning for the silence that falls over half the island. Some things ain't meant to be known, like heaven, or where Betty's ended.

Newt lies back, smiling at the thought of the young 'uns and their games of hide and seeks made so much harder with the island seemingly playing along.

Pulling the bark mat over her, the hard ground as comfortable as a feather bed now she knows the two is safe, Newt settles for the night. She is glad she don't have to pick her way to the shore when the sun rises and find they've kicked the bucket—ripped apart by the beasts. Especially as she knows their searching were for nothing. Betty has done what Betty always do, with thoughts only of herself.

The community will accept that Betty is missing, even without the evidence, now buried under the sand, for she's been missing since they arrived: refusing to nurse Ada's babe, never turning her hand to any work and instead, sitting on her jacksy on the shore in her woollen dress, and waving at the horizon like some porcelain dolly.

Tattio is worth a dozen of Betty: a healer and a hunter, and Molly has her uses. Every one of the 'mune have their role to play: cooking, mending, stitching, collecting and building, and each would be missed. They is family.

Betty were not made for somewhere like here. She belongs in the past.

Eyelids heavy, Newt allows sleep to claim her.

BETTY

Betty tries to remove the object, which was clamped unceremoniously over her mouth.

'Don't fight it. It will help you breathe,' a voice says.

Breathe? How can summat tight against the face help breath? Has she been chloroformed? Kidnapped by men who live under the water?

Everything is swimming in front of Betty's eyes, which are watering like the devil, and it is very bright here, with snatches of silver.

'The air is not the same here.' A person glimmers above her.

An angel? Is she in heaven after all?

'Try to relax.'

Betty cannot relax, and her face heats up as she remembers being lifted—the shame of it. She pats down her body to find she is not naked but covered by summat that crinkles under her touch. The floor is smooth and cold beneath her.

'Where am I?' Betty asks, her voice breaking.

'We call it *No Place*,' a voice says.

Purgatory?

'Is my ma here?' Betty asks. 'My babby? Are they waiting to take me home?'

'We must help her. Like we helped the child. And sterilise the water again,' a voice says.

There is murmuring before the thing that covers Betty's mouth is removed and something is pressed down onto her tongue.

Betty tries to spit out the hard berry but cannot find the energy. Then the room starts to spin, as if she is laying on the dumbwaiter on Master's dining room table, surrounded by hungry guests.

When Betty wakes again, she finds herself on a trolley, the kind they lay out the dead on, or tie women like Lady Harrington to, who cannot control their madness. She panics, tries to sit up, to find she is not strapped down at all, but free to move.

'Welcome back,' a woman says. 'I'm Doctor Adebeyo.'

Back? Have they taken her someplace else?

Betty blinks to get focus. The stranger beside her has a short, manly hairstyle and is wearing a tight silvery garment, which is snug against the body in a most unbecoming manner. Doctor? Whoever heard of such a name for the fairer sex? As if a woman could ever be as intelligent as a man! Betty shudders.

'How are you feeling?' they ask, pointing something shiny at her, which chirps like an injured bird.

'Very well, thank you,' Betty mumbles, glancing away, not wanting to witness either their immodest dress or this trickery.

This is an ugly place, cold and full of shiny boxes, trailing rope and flashing colours that Betty do not understand in the least. As for the landscape outside the room, visible through a flat, shimmering window, it is rocky, pitted like the walls of the sacred cave, and empty.

MOLLY

It has been three long days, or thereabouts and Betty has not returned. The camp is permeated by whispers of what might have come to pass. The children believe Betty has been rescued by a boat, but the Elders understand it is more likely they will soon uncover her remains. Molly's stomach churns as she thinks about the beast and how they butchered it, how quickly life is reduced to meat.

Molly hopes Betty's passing were not of her making because she has witnessed self-murder before. Her friend, Ruth, passed her time in the Asylum chained to the wall with her lips clamped shut. The cold showers and leeches, pressed against her shaved head, did nothing to cure her of her unreasonableness and she'd faded like a flower plucked too early from the ground.

What other choice did Ruth have? How else could she release herself from the manacles and surgery designed to cure her ailments, knowing what they all did, that once they were deemed well enough, they would be returned to servitude, the very place that caused their sickness?

Unlike Ruth, at least Molly had privacy of sorts in the Asylum, paid for by donations from her wealthy family, who had not quite given up on her. Edward on the other hand, who Dr Johnston reported had taken a much younger mistress, consigned Molly forever to history and the four damp walls of her tiny room.

Despite her heavy heart, there is something to be said for Betty's absence. Clay, so bound by silence before, has begun to open up like a bud drenched in sunlight, which suggests Betty may have contributed to Clay's state. She doubts Clay's words will ever run from their mouth like the other children, but their spirit is much raised, and they no longer sit in quiet solitude at the meeting place.

Perhaps also, it is due to the new tea with the barely remembered sweet taste of honey, brewed from yellow berries. Discovered in the forest whilst they were searching for Betty, it certainly lightens the mood. It also assists with sleep, which is no bad thing since there is no evidence of the heat abating.

With that in mind, Molly picks up a pail and heads out to the cave. Newt is busy with Rosie and the children today, distracting them from gossip by teaching them the ways of the shore, of survival, lest Betty's disappearance was more sinister than a journey to the next place.

The ground is hard and brittle under Molly's feet. As she reaches the grey rock and the cave mouth, she is relieved to find that the sea has yet to wash in that far. Rainbow is close by, arms wrapped around the trunk of one of the spindly trees, seemingly talking to it. The trees, which provide bark, seem to recover after the stripping when Rainbow is involved in the task, the young layers of regrowth green and soft until they mature. No one is quite sure what the child does, but it is a relief to have a never-ending supply of fibre which can be used for clothing, strong twine for the netting and to patch the huts. Perhaps Rainbow is communicating with the island? Molly shakes her head at her fanciful thoughts.

Molly waves to Rainbow, so easy to spot in the dry landscape with the decorated tunic. Molly likes the way the children have begun to embellish their garments, painting the edges with sticks dipped in crushed berries and the mashed false-mint. Rainbow's has intricate leaves carefully painted along the hem. It helps to distinguish them. With no dress coats, top hats or crinoline, and all with tight muscles and their hair falling past their shoulders, it is easy to confuse the children with each other.

Molly enters the cave, stopping to look at the walls in the entrance where the light floods in. The crude paintings they saw that first night on the island are fading but still recognisable as beasts. The other wall is part filled with small strikes; days counted before there seemed no point in marking them anymore. They moved on. Had to. Except for Betty.

Molly thinks about Betty as she draws the water from the sacred well, how hard she fought against change. She'll never understand how Betty, no more than a child when she boarded the ship, had such a blind belief in her Master, the very man who sullied her. Why would she want to return to that life of servitude when she could be free?

BETTY

Betty brushes down the satin skirts, checking the fit of the bodice. She admires herself in the looking glass. Her breasts are pleasing, rounded and pert, filling the pale blue, laced garment in a way they did not before. She is older than she expected, but perhaps that is the hard living on the island. Yes, this is much more fitting apparel for her return home to Master, which the strangers have promised to assist her with.

One last glance at her reflection and Betty begins to understand why Sarah called her 'a bit of jam'. She has a graceful line of neck and a delicate frame, curved with exactly the right proportions.

She smiles, trying not to think about the other clothes the strangers have said she will need to wear to travel, as they do. She will feel nowt but discomfort whilst wearing them; a suffocating second skin. Betty cannot imagine why anyone would fashion such a monstrous ensemble.

All Betty knows is the sooner she is back at the Manor and away from here, the sooner she can forget it all: the heat, the unpalatable food, and the unmentionable things the Elders did to each other on the island. Neither will she dwell on this place, the berries they use for nourishment, or where the persons found these garments. It is not her place to question, and she must remember that.

Betty unlaces the corsetry slowly, unwillingly, then watches as one of the persons seals the beautiful garment into a strange clear packet, which crackles when Betty touches it. She do not believe it will keep her new dress dry but what choice do she have?

'Ready?' one of them asks her.

Pressing her shoulders back, she takes one last look at her face, at her skin which seemed so much paler than the others in the 'mune, but here appears tanned. It is annoying to think her effort was in vain, still there are powders she might use to mask it. She smiles at the thought that, once properly dressed and toileted, Master might mistake her for a gentlewoman.

She allows the persons to fasten the strange silver travelling garment on her with its peculiar metal circles that appear to bite each other closed. Then comes the heavy foot coverings, which the persons have said she needs, in case of emergency, so she doesn't lift off like a rocket.

Betty has no idea what this rocket is the strangers refer to and she is beginning to worry that they are suffering from an ailment of the mind. People don't lift off. It is a ridiculous imagining, summat Master might read in his scientific stories.

'Are you sure you wish to return to Lord Harrington?' they ask her.

They have told her that even wearing this dreadful travelling outfit, hers will not be an easy journey. It will be different in her time than before—she has aged whilst her old world has turned slowly. Once more, this makes no sense.

'It is my home,' Betty says, wondering if the new girl the Master took in when she left has been sleeping on her mattress in the attic.

'Ready?' they ask again.

She nods, allowing one of the persons to guide her to a different opening in the wall from the one she entered through. There are three of these such openings, all seemingly identical, the door no thicker than the blade of a shovel and of a similar hue.

Clutching her dress in its special wrapping tight to her chest, she steps forward in her heavy boots, which is exceptionally hard going, like walking in your mother's Sunday-best shoes when your feet are too small.

Betty steps over the threshold. The small pool directly in front of her looks very similar to the one she emerged from, surrounded by the same black, pitted rock. They have told her she must hurry for the air in here is thin, even with the face covering. Crossing herself, Betty steps in, sinking down into the water, the boots making her journey faster than before. Her descent is followed by a clunk, as the door is closed behind her.

Gasping, her heart thudding and her breath hot in the strange mask, Betty opens her eyes to find herself below a small brick ledge. She is in a well, which has green moss growing on the sides and a ladder rising upwards.

Removing the mask, which steams up like the windows in the Manor when the weather is inclement, she heaves herself onto the ledge and sucks in a cold damp breath of air. It is a joyous moment to feel cold swell deep in her chest after the many months of stifling heat.

Is she home?

She dresses with some difficulty, for there is not much room on the ledge to turn and her fingers are too cold for lacing. She is astonished to find the persons were correct and the beautiful satin garment has remained unblemished in its packet.

Wrapping the travelling clothing in the transparent sack, she abandons it on the ledge with the mask and boots, and starts to climb the ladder, the metal rungs surprisingly clear of debris.

Anyway, it is of no consequence. There is nowt that Cook can't remove with soap and a bit of elbow grease.

NEWT

The children is full of chatter, their goggles on the sea instead of the spear clasped in Newt's daddles. They won't never learn to feed themselves if their minds is awandering all the time. They is plenty big enough for hard work now.

'Betty said the beasts eat folk,' Star says, gaze fixed on the horizon.

Star, as always, is full to the brim with imaginings but Newt knows that thinking don't feed you. Anyway, Newt has heard enough talk of Betty these past few days. Meater don't deserve no more of their attention. Nothing as cowardly as giving up yer life. Worse still to put yer family in danger. They is lucky the well-water ain't made them all sick.

Stabbing her spear into the shell path, Newt claps her hands together to get the children's attention back. The sand responds before the children do. Grabbing Star by the arm, Newt pushes the child forward, holding tight when Star loses balance on the sharp black rocks, because they is too busy looking at the ship. Newt points to the sparks of silver in the pools in front of them. Crouching down, she grabs one end of the finely woven net she laid there last night and pulls it gently towards them. Once the net is drawn from the water, several small silver fish flap about on the rocks. Newt holds one still and stabs it above the eye with the tip of her spear. She passes the spear to Star, indicating they must do the same.

The children need to know how to kill if they is to survive.

Star steps back, refusing the spear as if it is diseased. Instead, crouching down, picks up the dead fish, running a finger over its sunken eye. Newt don't have time to waste so points to Clay, the spear raised. Clay's still not up to dick after the incident with Betty, and it might help them with their confidence.

'Dun it hurt em?' Clay asks, frowning, voice almost a whisper.

'We has to eat,' Rosie says, from the back of the small group. 'It ain't nothin' but nature. God's bounty.'

Lightning steps past Clay and offering up a grin, takes the spear, dispatching the fishes one by one, and quickly.

'There, there,' Rosie says, patting Clay on the shoulder. 'We must do what we is best at.'

When Rosie leads Clay and the others back to the camp, Lightning stays behind with Newt. It ain't the child Newt would have chosen to learn hunting skills, but Lightning is at least quick and plenty bricky despite the constant jabbering that spills out of their saucebox. Newt shows Lightning how to tie and reset the net, for a few fishes will not feed the 'mune and the jumps is harder to catch.

At least, Newt decides, watching the sand ripple in response to Lightning's voice, it is a reminder of the danger, ever present on the island. They will learn that sometimes silence is safer.

North Yorkshire

BETTY

Betty has no idea where she is when she climbs out of the well. She has never walked further than her village or the gates of the Manor, and this don't look like one of them places. There is nowt here but rocky hills, clumps of dark green trees and brown grass.

She must find shelter, for the cold draws pimples on her skin and the fringed shawl do nowt to warm her. The gold coins the persons afforded Betty will do nowt to help her neither if there is no carriage to be had.

Her breath smokes the air as she searches the horizon for signs of life. There is a small stone wall in the distance, perhaps a track beyond or a farmer who might assist her. She starts forward, determined not to be undone, but there is no protecting her embroidered slippers as she sinks into the mud.

It feels like many hours have passed and Betty is stiff with cold, shivering with the intensity of it. For a second, she feels loss—the warmth of the island, the sun beating down, never having to worry about affording a coat, or paying for a meal. It is short-lived. She is determined to get back what is rightfully hers—the life she lost. She cannot stop now.

She reaches a road. In the distance there is some type of stone building—an inn perhaps, and beyond it the shape of trees. They might have food, a fire, and the means for her to continue her journey home to Master's. She cannot arrive at the Manor all muddy and out of sorts.

It is dark by the time she reaches the brown-stone building, the Saltersgate Inn. She is cautious when opening the heavy wooden door for she has never been in an inn before, though she has sat outside the alehouse in her village many times, waiting for her pa to sup up and be done.

There is a fire in the grate below a shelf of dark wooden barrels and Betty is drawn towards it, her arms and face numb and of a bluish hue.

'Dear lord,' a woman says, wiping her hands on her apron and emerging from behind a bar, fussing towards Betty. 'Are you lost, my lady?'

Betty glances around to see who the woman might be speaking to. She has never been called a lady before.

'I suspect I am,' Betty says, for it is not a lie she is telling.

'Come sit by the fire, me dear, I'll fetch you some ale. You'll be looking to stay? Nowt much will 'appen here afore the morning if it's a coach be needed.'

'That would be most accommodating,' Betty says, thinking how Molly would answer, using a long word when none is needed.

She sits down in the wooden chair, as close to the fire as she can get without fear of her skirts catching alight. The stone floor is warm and the heat soaks into her wet, mud-caked shoes. She'd like to take them off, but that's not what a lady do.

There is a gentleman traveller at the back of the room, seated on a high-backed bench like them in church, his top hat on the table in front of him. A cat washes itself on the windowsill pressed up against the diamond leaded window. This appears to be a good class of tavern.

'Awful quiet tonight,' the serving woman says. 'Weather changing end t'week by all account. I'll show you up to your room presently.'

'Much obliged,' Betty says, wondering if she's got the words quite right when the woman frowns. She passes her one of the gold coins from her beaded bag.

The woman's eyes shoot up into her heavy brows.

'Full board for a day and a coach to town, for I require some necessities. I'll also need a coach to Lord Harrington's at The Manor presently. Will that suffice? You may keep what's left.'

'Of course my lady. Bless you.'

When the woman curtsies, Betty has to hold in a snort.

MOLLY

Molly wakes early to the sound of scraping. Lately she's been having dreams of intruders, voices she doesn't recognise, though there has never been any evidence: no unknown footprints in the dust or new faces in the meeting place. Perhaps she has been thinking about the children's strange ways: Clay talking to every insect and bird as if it can understand, Star constantly seeking who-knows-what, and Rainbow, tending to the trees as if they are children.

Molly squeezes through the doorway, after stepping over Sarah, whose arm is draped over Tattio's breast. The nights have been getting steadily hotter, and the community has taken to propping open the woven frames they use rather than sealing up the huts. Molly's skin is pocked by insect bites this morning, itchy, and not helped that she's already slick with sweat.

Once outside the Elder's sleeping hut, she picks up one of the spears they stab into the ground, and treads carefully, tracing the strange sound, which makes the hair on her arms bristle and is not dissimilar to chalk scraped upon a slate.

Pulling up short behind the food hut, Molly hears a voice, deliberately low but recognisable as Star. Are they in trouble?

The children are gathered in the meeting area, seated in the same circle the Elders use to make their decisions. Molly hangs back, not wanting to interrupt them, curious as to their purpose. Do they do this often? Meet without the Elders?

'It's good, looks like Betty,' Thunder says, as the scraping noise ceases.

Molly has never heard Thunder speak quietly like this before. She moves carefully, crouching down in the dust at the side of the hut to afford herself a better view. Star has a stick in one hand and is painting on the smooth slab of grey rock that shades the camp. The scraping noise was the makeshift brush transferring plant dyes to the surface.

The picture Star has painted shows the outline of a woman, recognisable as Betty by the triangular dress touching the ground, drawn as two straight lines. The hair is neat, and Molly touches hers, knotted and curling past her shoulders. She's barely given a thought to her appearance since they arrived here.

It's strange the children should want to talk about Betty when the Elders have barely spoken of it, too frightened what it might mean for them in the future, for it is hard to believe, after being told for so many years that they do not all carry the seeds of madness.

'Do you think Betty will come back?' Star asks.

It's as if the children know something. Or perhaps it is because they are free with their feelings, not ever having had to be cautious or care about the consequences of their words. For all Betty's faults, she was an important part of the community, and the children recognise none of the burdens from the past that she carried around like a heavy sack.

Molly watches as Star sits back in the circle and Clay rises, taking the stick and dipping it in indigo dye. When Clay steps back, Molly sees a beast drawn on the rock.

'They dun come to hurt us,' Clay says. 'They look for summat.'

It worries Molly that the children see the beasts as anything other than a threat. The evidence is there: the attack on Tattio, and the way they writhe at the scent of a bloody rag. Should she step forward and say something? The beasts are animals with limited intelligence, working only on instinct. She cannot rid her mind of the image of the beast thrashing in the net, looking to maim, and the pungent smell of its rage. And yet, when it was dying, it had seemed to accept its fate, like it understood there was nothing it could do.

'Us must try to understand em,' Clay finishes, passing the stick to Rainbow.

Rainbow draws a simple tree, with but a few strokes of the stick. Instead of branches it has arms, which wrap around the trunk.

'The trees heal emself when us is kind and only take what they can give,' Rainbow explains. 'I smell their suffering.'

Though it is true that the trees Rainbow harvests bark from do not die, like so many stripped before, it is evidence that the children are not yet mature in their thinking, using their imaginations rather than evidence.

Is Molly worrying too much about them? Does it matter that they seem to have an understanding entirely different to that of the Elders? Isn't that what the community wanted? Perhaps the children think like they do because they have no past to fight against and no future to fear.

The island is their home, part of them.

The children are silent when Thunder stands and throws water at the rock, scrubbing away the evidence of their art. It is time for Molly to go. She does not want them to know she has witnessed their endeavours, but she must mention it to the Elders, for the children do not seem to see the dangers that lurk here. Molly will never forget the outstretched arms of Ada, or the look on her face as she sunk down in the sand, forever lost. If it had not been for Newt's bravery, Rainbow would not be here at all.

Molly's head starts to hurt, a thumping in her forehead that has nothing to do with the sun. What if the children, when told the truth about the past, change? They are free here—they suffer no shame, embarrassment, or limitation. They do not need beating with the strap to make them stronger.

Maybe the past is better left buried with Ada.

Leicestershire

BETTY

Betty stays seated when Master enters the drawing room that's had years of her hard work as a scullery maid polished into the wood. She does not flinch when he takes her hand and kisses it.

'What is a fine lady like you doing in these parts?' Master asks, his gaze firmly on her laced bodice. 'If it is the weather that has brought you here, then I suspect God may have had a hand in it. For you are most certainly an angel.'

Betty manages to hide her surprise in a blush, as his wet lips leave a damp trace on her new cotton gloves. The years she has been away have been kind to Master.

'I'm here about Betty,' she says.

Why does Master not recognise her? She may be dressed up in finery, but she is the same as she ever were.

'Are you an older distant cousin perhaps?' he asks, head cocked, preening like one of the birds in the coup. 'The family resemblance is quite remarkable.'

Betty blinks, confused, and withdraws the hand he has yet to release. One of her curls escapes from her hat, corkscrewing against her flushed cheek. Older? What does he mean?

'I'm afraid poor Betty was lost to the sea not two years ago. I'm surprised you did not hear tell of it. Perhaps you have travelled far?' he asks. 'The news may not have reached foreign parts.'

Has only two years passed since she was sent away on the ship? Surely it must be more? Two years is not time enough to blossom from a serving girl into the woman she is now, or for the children on the island to grow as they have.

She nods again, trying to hide her bewilderment. How can it only be the year of Our Lord eighteen hundred and sixty-five?

'It were a very long journey,' she says, truthfully. 'Two days by road, but not without its comfort.' She'd had a carriage fit for a lady, and the best rooms at the Inns when the horses were changed.

Betty is not ready to tell Master the extent of her travels, the journey through the well, or the persons in the silver suits, for it might well get her locked away like Master's wife. It is one thing reading imaginings in a book, quite another living them.

Betty feels for the gold coins in her beaded purse, thankful to the strange persons in *No Place* who gave her a small fortune, certainly more than she needed to pay for the carriage here and the new wardrobe, which is only fitting for a lady such as her, but they will not last forever.

'I have the newspaper still,' Master says, calling for John, his manservant who, as he ever was, is hovering nearby, 'which might answer your questions.'

Betty has yet to ask aught and wonders if it were always like this. Perhaps, she thinks, she should set her sights higher, now she has summat to barter with and leave the serving to someone less travelled. She presses her shoulders back, which exposes a little more flesh.

'You have a scullery maid?' Betty asks.

'Of course. A young wench from the village.'

'May I see her?' Betty asks.

'She will not know your cousin,' Master says, seemingly fixed on that untruth. 'But I will fetch her if it pleases you.'

John escorts a young girl into the room. She wears a patched woollen dress, and her eyes are downcast.

'Here she is,' Master says. 'What is it you wanted of her?'

'Nothing of import,' Betty says, swallowing down her dismay and feeling rather faint.

The girl that replaced her is but a child still, with freckles spread across her cheeks like abacus beads, yet in the same years that have passed, whilst on the island, Betty has aged many years more than is usual. Not only has she lost her position here in the Manor, but also her youth.

'I was sorry to hear of the loss of your uncle these few weeks past. He was a reliable labourer,' Master says, dismissing the maid with a flick of his hand.

Her father has died whilst she has been away.

Betty looks down, focuses on her skirts, smoothing the pleats in the silk, trying to hide her shaking hands. Biting her lip, willing back tears, she tastes the bitter tang of rouge.

Master must not witness her distress.

Part 2

1866

Leicestershire

BETTY

Betty checks her appearance in the full-length gilded glass, and dismisses the maid from her bedchamber with a nod of her head. She has not yet managed to regain the curves she lost wasting away in bed with the fever, but her pale countenance, stolen by the island, is returned. She will not need her powders.

Today Master is expecting a visit from the Earl of Cavendish and, as always, she will be on display.

'Mistress Bessie,' Master calls up from the bottom of the grand staircase.

This is the name by which he has addressed her since her arrival all those months ago. She has not corrected him.

Betty begins her descent in her full skirted gown, held plump by the hooped wires of the cage beneath. There is an art to sweeping down the stairs without falling and that is to step sideways and clutch tightly to the balustrade. Thankfully, Betty's fingers, which have turned white from gripping, are masked by soft, calf-skin gloves.

As Betty reaches the bottom stair, Lord Cavendish removes his top hat and holds it in front of his thick felted coat. He has not taken off his outside garments—a sign he is not staying long.

Betty half-curtsies and her silk skirts brush the polished floor. Cavendish is more important than Master. She does not hold out her hand though, because that would not be acceptable. Betty's learned much from *The Handbook of Etiquette*, unearthed in Master's library, poring over the pages by candlelight, teaching herself those things Master believes she already knows, relying on pictures when the words did not come easy.

Master teases her for daydreaming sometimes when she fails to answer him, but the fact is, since her illness—no doubt caused by the bad airs on the journey home—some days she simply do not recognise herself.

It's almost as if the newspaper story Master showed her, of the ship vanishing in the Pacific Ocean, is the truth and Betty's not Betty at all, but Bessie, a stranger who's had a bout of terrible malady, which has brought with it the imagining of another land.

Master has introduced Betty to many people since her recovery these last few months, calling himself her 'guardian', which he has seemingly decided is a respectable solution to their current situation. Betty is certain that the gentlemen who visit, whose eyes linger on her corseted bodice and tiny waist, know only too well what that means. Betty has no choice but to be agreeable, for she must offer some payment to Master for her board and medicine. Now she is down to the last coin the strange persons afforded her—the rest spent on gowns and perfumes—she has only her body to barter with.

As Master conjectures, much as he may wish to, it is not his fault he cannot marry her presently. Not only must he organise a divorce but, as befits tradition, he must ask her father for her hand. Betty has convinced Master that her father is in the Far East, on a trading expedition, and cannot be reached.

Betty does not allow herself to dwell on her circumstance and instead fills her head with daily details she must attend to, for when one is a lady there are rules for everything: dining, visiting, even walking the grounds, and all events must have a costume to match.

'Charming,' Lord Cavendish says, eyeing her bodice.

'I wish to visit my uncle's house,' Betty says, knowing she is remiss to even speak in front of such a distinguished guest, never mind asking a favour of Master in this manner. But perhaps Master might indulge her, distracted as he is with his important botanical illustrations.

Master fiddles with his red satin neckerchief, as if it is a fraction too tight. 'Very well. Fresh air will suit your complexion, I daresay. I will task John to make ready the pony trap and to accompany you on your journey.'

Betty hides her relief. Since her sickness, it often seems as if Master is fearful to let her out of his sight, lest she fly away.

It is bitterly cold, and the horse's breath mists the air, but it is no matter, for Betty will be well sheltered from any inclemency and she has been given vapours for her chills.

She has changed into her walking costume: a modest silk dress and a thick, embroidered cape, which is far less cumbersome for travel. She clutches her dark velvet headdress as she ducks inside the small wooden doorway, for it would be most unladylike to lose the sprigs of lily-of-the-valley the maid wove in so carefully.

The journey is bumpy along the muddied track until they reach the road to the village, flattened by many hooves. Betty allows herself the luxury of leaning back and looks out of the window at the passing countryside: at the horses ploughing the cold, hard earth into furrows and the children in their dirty woollen trousers scaring crows and collecting turnips in sacks.

They reach her father's cottage, a simple stone affair, on the edge of Stamford. With John's assistance, she alights from the carriage, careful not to soil her shoes in the ruts, full of muddied rainwater.

Betty watches two chickens peck at the soil around the tidy vegetable patch as John peers through the tiny window shaded beneath the overhanging thatch. He knocks on the heavy wooden door.

A woman answers, her arms full of a red-faced, screaming child. Her cotton bonnet is greyed with age and her woollen bodice frayed and stained.

'Help thees?' she asks, coughing, as wood smoke billows out from behind her.

Perhaps it is the child, or the simplicity of the woman's words that makes Betty feel faint, but it is as if she has suddenly lost her breath.

'Mistress Bessie is of the understanding her uncle resided here,' John says, doffing his cap.

'Nowt here but me and my Henry some years,' the woman says, jiggling the baby.

John turns to Betty. 'Happen it's another cottage, Mistress?' he asks.

The woman with the child is lying. Betty devil well knows the house she were born in, and where her mother breathed her last, but she cannot very well admit that. She is supposed to be a distant relative of Betty and one who might very well make an error such as this.

Betty had hoped to find a keepsake: a scrap of fabric from her mother's nightdress that her father kept so carefully, or his treasured pipe, but it is as if her family has been brushed away with the stiff broom propped up against the stone wall.

'No matter,' Betty says, with a flick of her gloved hand as she turns away, her jaw tight with emotion.

Still, it is some comfort, once back inside the carriage, to dab her eyes with a lace-edged handkerchief rather than the sleeve of a drab woollen dress. She will certainly not miss the vermin, or the damp that fingered the walls of the cottage, which were ever-present guests.

She must make plans, find herself some permanency: for this is proof, if needed, that her old life is lost.

Lord Cavendish has left the Manor by the time the carriage draws up outside the pillared entrance. Betty is quite exhausted from her journeying, chilled and clearly not yet back to full health.

John informs her, as she alights from the carriage, that Cook has kept a plate for her: pigeon pie with crisp pastry and a glass of ale, which will be restorative.

On her way to the dining room, despite having little appetite after the day's events, Betty spies a new collection of plant specimens on the bureau in Master's study and pauses to consider them.

She bites her lip. It will not be long before Master tires of her and she will need something to barter with, of more value to him than her body.

The Island

CLAY

Elder Molly's cough is worse and it rattles around their chest like the turtle shells in the chillun's hut. Clay pushes the sticky strands of grey hair from the Elder's hot face, and holds the cup to their mouth, the thin, hard edge pressed against their lips. They have a look of the sky bout em.

The spiked-bush tea they use for the Sharing ceremony seems to have some effect as it trickles into Elder Molly's mouth. Clay feels em relax, but it is short-lived as another coughing fit takes hold. Grimacing, Clay wipes the blood from the Elder's chin with a strip of rag. Elder Molly can barely swallow, even with Clay's attempts to make em feel comfortable. It dun seem long ago that Elder Molly clasped Clay's body close, while Elder Tattio strapped their twisted leg to heal it. Both Elders have shown nowt but kindness to Clay.

'I'm ready,' Elder Molly says, with a voice as thin as a piece of hammered bark.

Clay helps the Elder to sit up and shuffle back against the hut wall.

'Soon I'll not have the strength to do what's needed.'

Each word Elder Molly speaks is accompanied by a hack in the throat, as if summat is lodged there that dun belong. Clay dun want to leave the hut, but the Elder is adamant.

'There is other peoples,' Clay offers. 'I has seen em. They could help?'

Elder Molly's eyes flicker open, pupils unfocussed, and breath as shallow as the salt pools in the sacred cave.

'What people?' The frown that follows digs deep lines into the Elder's sun-wrinkled skin.

'Beneath the sacred well. They might have summat to help you. You should travel now, afore the passing.'

'People cannot breathe under water,' Elder Molly says. 'You must forget the stories you have heard. Betty did not have clarity of mind.'

Clay looks away, should not be burdening Elder Molly with suggestions.

'I have had a good life,' Elder Molly says. 'A free life, and longer than perhaps I would have had, certainly longer than many of the 'mune. Fetch Elder Newt, I wish to relay my plans.' Another cough interrupts.

Clay helps to arrange Elder Molly more comfortably against the wall, pulling the matting over to keep em warm. The Elder seems small—to have shrunk, is no weight at all. Perhaps that is why they is shivering despite the heat.

There is much Clay still wants to know bout life afore, some answers to the questions that fill the head, the things the Elders dun speak of. Is there nowt any of em can do to help Elder Molly: summat to prevent the passing? A new tonic or tea to rid em of the hurt that has taken hold? Elder Sarah, at least, had faded quickly when the sickness came.

'I must pass as we all must, as I have lived and given,' Molly says, dismissing Clay, eyes closing once more.

There is nowt Clay can do. Elder Molly's final days will be of their choosing, like everything here.

MOLLY

The tide is in, and the moon is rising. It's time. Molly can see the beasts, swarming below the cliff edge, some as big as the skiffs on the Thames. It's as if they know there's to be a passing. She will likely be dead soon after she hits the water but her body, even depleted as it is, will appease the beasts and give the community the breathing space they need.

She wishes she'd had the strength to get to the cliff without help, could manage this last part of her journey alone, but she can barely stand, the sickness having eaten into her.

At least the goodbyes are said. As Molly was too frail to leave the hut, the community came in one by one. Clay took her choosing harder than Star, her own child. In another life, perhaps it would have been different, but in that same life Molly would not have been able to watch Star grow or had the freedoms all the elders have enjoyed: being outside without a chaperone, deciding for herself how she wanted to spend her days, her body always her own.

She turns to Newt and Tattio, silent at her side. They are holding her up, having helped her here.

'I am worried about Star,' Molly says. It is hard to breathe let alone speak without coughing but the words need to be said. 'There is something of Betty in Star's moods.'

Newt nods, places her free hand flat on her chest. It seems they have all witnessed Star struggling with the morbs.

'Us will care for e like us always have,' Tattio says.

At least the children don't seem to be inclined to self-murder, but then they are not shackled, or their moods forcibly purged from them with ice baths and leeches. It is still a worry that, even though Star has been free to wander, they have yet to find a place they fit.

Molly turns her head, hearing others approach, their footsteps crunching on the rocky earth. Some of the children have come to bear witness to her passing. They stand silent in a knot behind her, their eyes wide and their expressions strained.

They are not really children anymore, as tall as the elders and almost all old enough now to bear their own.

Molly nods her assent and Tattio and Newt lift her to the edge of the cliff. She looks down at the deep green sea, cut through with rocks and fins. She has made the right choice to pass here, without the danger that the sand will claim her body, leaving the beasts unsatisfied. Breathing in the warm air one final time, another cough erupts from her chest, rattling through her bones. Every movement is packed with pain. She will not miss this struggle, but she will miss the 'mune, who have been her family for so long.

Tattio and Newt release their grip and step back. Molly allows herself to fall. As the sea rises up to greet her, she thinks of her journey to this place, and the bonds that were broken.

She would change nothing.

LIGHTNING

Lightning thinks bout grabbing the brown cup and licking out the last of the spike-bush tea. It's the best bit bout the Sharing ceremony, the way the tea makes you feel like yer head has opened up, the heat of the Mune in yer body, and that nowt matters but that moment.

It's the first Sharing since Molly passed. The Elders said the Mune needed a distraction from the empty place in the meeting circle—Molly was bigger than the space left in the dust—and new life must replace old.

Lightning's already done that.

Lightning looks down at their belly: full like they's swallowed the moon. They say it hurts bad when the cave splits opens and the childs is released onto the island, like a fish do when its guts get dug out. The Elders dun let the carriers have tea once the childs is inside, not even when the childs is ready to leave. Lightning hope it dun crack open like the rednuts when it's time, thinks maybe they should have paid more trouble to the six others when the child emerged from their cave, but it bin too interesting setting traps with Newt, to goggle much at the new life.

Not that traps did nowt. Lightning's seen the two ugly gib faces of the beasts that made it to the cave last night. It's like the beasts learned to tell where they's dug in the ropes, even though their piggy eyes dun see nowt.

Lightning leans against Star, shifting the weight of the childs inside. Star's behind the arc of white shells again, choosing not to take part in the Sharing ceremony.

'Sorry,' Lightning says, as Star shifts away. 'Legs hurt like beasts.'

Star dun like being touched but Lightning's not always got control of their body these days.

Star's the only one in the Mune who ain't ever done the Sharing, but they dun let the Elders press em, and Lightning likes that. Can't all carry chillun any ways, or there'd be no one left to bleed for the beasts. Elder Rosie says the beasts need the bloody rags, as much as the chillun need fingers to suck.

Lightning shifts again, rubbing the area where the childs presses hard against their back. It would be good to walk, ease the heaviness but no one can leave yet. Still, it dun take long, just until the ones who want to, feel the heat pass between em.

Lightning thinks of Thunder, Sun and Rainbow and the sharing that placed a childs inside the cave two moons ago. It dun matter who put the childs there—the childs belongs to the Mune.

Shifting again, Lightning sees Rainbow come out of the sharing hut, put on one of the tunics that bin discarded by the entrance and head towards the chillun's hut, where Lightning has no doubt they bin missed. Rainbow's sheened in sweat, like they all is after Sharing. Rainbow can't carry but can share and is good with the chillun. It's what's bin chosen.

Lightning won't choose to carry again. Dun want to end up like Sky, taking a last breath after the childs arrives, and later swallowed by the sand.

CLAY

Limping along the shell path with Lightning, guided by the full moon, Clay's too tired for this tonight, the pain in their leg like fire, scorching a trail along their bones. But what choice does they have? It ain't just the act of Sharing with Rainbow and Sun that's left Clay exhausted, but Molly's passing. Clay feels raw now Elder Molly's journeyed through the waters, like it was their own body pulled down to the depths. Sometimes, knowing what must be done for the good of the Mune, dun make it easy to swallow.

Clay presses a finger to their lips as they approach the cave entrance, gesturing that Lightning should stay back. Clay dun want the beasts excited by Lightning and it's their nature to attack when cornered.

'Us need to kill em,' Lightning hisses, refusing to let go of the bucket carried this far for Clay. 'Stab em in the mug.'

Lightning sees things as light or dark, but Clay dun. Clay ain't got a taut body, honed by yards walked, or Lightning's spearing skills, but strength ain't only carried in the limbs. Elder Molly understood that.

'Wait here,' Clay whispers, finally releasing the bucket from Lightning's tight grip.

Clay senses one of the beasts ain't well and the other is likely frightened, trapped as they is in the shallow pool. Their legs, which brought em here, is only forming on their scaly bellies and is weak, not big enough to carry their weight alone. They need the sea to lift em. They is like the new chillun in the Mune, tottering uncertain, not yet fully finding their feet.

Pausing at the entrance, not cause of the beasts, who ain't no threat despite what the Elders warn, but cause of memories, still fresh after all these years: Betty's words, which Clay once thought was meant to heal.

'*Let us cleanse ourselves from all filthiness of the flesh and spirit.*'

Sometimes the ceremonial tea gives clarity Clay dun wish for.

Clay shudders, remembering Betty's instructions, which was believed meant kindly. Clay needed to be covered by the water for their leg to mend properly, and to wash away sin. Clay had trusted Betty, until suddenly, Betty's grip on their wrists had loosened, pressure transferring to the top of the head. Betty's smiling face had blurred as Clay had plummeted down deep in the cold, sacred water, swallowed by the well.

Sometimes Clay thinks bout telling Rainbow bout the bottom of the sacred well, how instead of passing, two persons was waiting there. They'd known Clay's name, asked if they was hurt, then said hard words to each other bout not interfering. They'd wrapped a cloth around Clay's body, summat ain't felt afore, soft yet drying, and made Clay eat a small red berry, which had made breathing easier and pain recede.

It was not an imagining but the Mune will think it is. Clay fears, like Betty, they will say the devil have taken hold.

Clay sucks in a breath and steps into the cave. The beasts dun turn when Clay enters—as if they is a shadow, or a splash of water barely felt.

The beast near the entrance lies on its side, its tail slapping in the shallow pool. Crouching down, Clay cautiously places a hand on its belly, between the two front lumps of leg, which have pushed out of its scaly hide. The skin there is light and cracking where the water dun reach. The beast is too big to move alone, so Clay uses the bucket to pour salt water over the area, washing the skin dark grey again, avoiding the tail which could cause injury.

After several pails, the beast seems to relax, its tail now resting half in the water. Perhaps it will have the strength it needs to turn itself, now it ain't thrashing with hurt.

Clay moves to the back of the cave, sensing the other beast watching. The ground is slippery and wet where the movements of the beasts have splashed the rocks, but keeping close to the wall, near the faded drawings and out of reach, Clay uses the balance-stick to give distance. Even though the beasts dun see well, with their eyes too small and milky, they is quick to react. The one at the back dun seem to trust Clay and draws its lips back over its pointed teeth, as if grimacing. Clay sees it clearly cause the beast agitates the lightberries in the water with its tail.

Moving slowly, eyes kept fixed on the second beast, Clay makes it without incident to the sacred well. It is as if the beast is mirroring what they is feeling, so it's best to tread softly, and wear a smooth face.

There's a sudden scream, so piercing it makes Clay clamp hands over ears with the pain of it. Dropping the bucket on the floor, they limps over to the arch that separates the two sections of the cave, but there is nowt clear to see, no light from the pool that holds the second beast.

The air is thick with the smell of blood.

'You bin too long,' Lightning says from the entrance, hand on their bleeding ankle, a spear deep in the beast's side. 'Thought they done you in.'

STAR

The Mune—
steady beat.
Dull ache.

Star has walked all night and found nowt, no treasure washed up on the shore and no new herb for Elder Tattio. Finding is the only thing that makes Star feel alive. If the Elders would talk bout afore, what is beyond the everlasting sea, maybe Star would have a belly full of fire like Lightning, or a listening like Rainbow, summat more than words to offer.

The moon is waning, red light hitting the ocean. The Mune will rise for food soon, sit in a circle at the meeting place and chant their thanks to the island. Thanks for what? Star do not understand. Is it the strips of dry meat that feel like bark on the tongue, or the tea, which makes the heart beat slower when there is barely a pulse of life as it is?

Worse still, the Elders have started to check members of the Mune ain't alone and get angry if a place in the circle is empty, or if someone do not answer their name. They fear loss as badly as being ripped apart by the beasts. They is wrong.

Star decides to take the route back to the huts through the boneyard, the stony patch where they leave carcasses too rotten to use. Sometimes there is objects there to be found, things that do not fit: bits of broken bucket, and smooth stones, no bigger than a fingernail, scored with patterns.

The boneyard is along a narrow path on the island edge, across sharp rocks barely marked by footprints. Star is at the highest part of the island here, as far from the Mune as possible and where the sea swirls like stew below.

There is a sudden thrashing movement below the cliff. Lying flat down on the rocks near the edge, close enough to hang over, Star wonders briefly how it would feel to fall.

The thrashing gets worse. Is blood coming? The beasts can sense it long afore the first drop is collected. But no, there is summat down there, floating in the water: Elder Molly's tunic.

Staring at the clumps of tunic in the water, and the beasts who appear to be fighting over it, Star thinks bout Elder Molly, how much Clay feels the loss. Star feels nowt, but perhaps that is cause Elder Molly had no understanding of em, even though they looked a bit the same. Not their mouth though, Elder Molly had a turtle mouth, always snapping. It was like Star did summat wrong in always asking why the Elders never tried to leave the island.

'If only you knew how lucky you are.'

Star ain't never felt lucky. How is they supposed to believe the island is better than what bin afore when they's nowt to judge it by? It's like saying the silver fish taste better than the blue ones cause of the colour. What if outside holds the meaning Star is searching for? Summat other.

Rolling away from the edge, Star looks up at the black sky, and the moon which touches the water. Star fancies there's a light that ain't part of its true nature glancing off one side. If only it could be reached.

Standing up, Star takes one last look over the edge, beyond the beasts, at the spikes of wood in the distance just visible above the sea. It's hard to imagine they was once a ship now they is broken bits of branch and rusted nails. Could the Mune build summat to take em somewhere else?

The Elders would never allow it.

Leicestershire

BETTY

Master does not believe her, says Betty's tale is fit for one of his scientific story books.

'An island, you say, in another place?'

'It's called *No Place*.' Betty has explained numerous times, in many different ways, as many as she could find words for.

Master laughs at her, his head thrown back, exposing his rotted back teeth, as if she is nowt but an imbecile.

'And you say *you* are Betty?' Now he shakes his head, before raising his voice, and bringing his fist down on the polished walnut table. The wood judders with his displeasure. 'It is a manipulation of the highest order!'

Betty flinches. She has no choice now but to play her last card, which she has been trying to save. She swallows, feels it grate her throat. 'I were carrying your child when I boarded the ship that you believe sunk without notice. How would I know that if I were not Betty?'

Master colours, his face so purple she thinks he might expire, which would not do at all, because where would she be then?

He leans towards her, barely concealing his rage. 'It is obvious you are here to prey on a lonely man. Blackmail, no doubt!'

Betty clasps her hands in her lap to hide the tremble. She has not seen Master angered in this way before. It is different from his bouts of fevered passion, which sometimes bruise her.

'I did not know where else to go,' she says, squeezing her eyes shut.

She does not want Master to see her upset, for it is well known a woman's tears are often used for barter.

Master pushes back his chair, with such force it scrapes a mark onto the polished surface. The servants will have heard their exchange; John rarely strays from outside the doorway of whichever of the many rooms is of Master's choosing. They will think she is mad, like Master's wife, fit only for the Asylum. What was she thinking?

'Ready my carriage,' Master bellows, leaving the room, his footsteps heavy with contempt.

Alone in the draughty room, Betty sobs. She has paid a price in telling her truth and now her purse is empty.

It is not long before she feels a warm hand on her shoulder and the aroma of Cook's steeped milk drink.

'There, there, young Bessie,' Cook says, placing the steaming mug down in front of her. 'Most likely the sickness has muddled yer head. Master will calm down. He is a proud man but have a fondness for you. Best make yerself scarce until he do.'

Betty raises her head. 'But it's all true, Cook. I am sound of mind. I am Betty!'

Cook frowns, her gaze thoughtful. 'There is summat of young Betty in them eyes.'

Taking something from her starched apron pocket, Cook places it on the table in front of Betty. A small tarnished coin.

'If you really is Betty, 'appen you'll tell me what this be then?' she says.

Betty snatches it up. 'My sixpence! From the pudding—the year Master thought it were lost. You said to keep it neath my pillow for luck.'

Cook's face softens and Betty feels her study her, as closely as when she checks the kitchen girl's nails for dirt.

'Appen there might be summit in what you say then, lass, though I can't for the life of me understand none of it.'

Betty's spirits lift. Perhaps all Master needs is proof—scientific evidence—the type he spends his hours gathering.

LIGHTNING

The childs is coming, forcing its way into the world without Lightning's say so. The pain is like nowt felt afore, searing hot down the spine in vicious waves. Lightning can't be quiet no more. It ain't for want of trying these last few hours since it started, hoping it would drain away while they bit down hard on the rag Elder Tattio gave em.

Lightning grabs for Clay, who's lying next to em on the hut floor, and squeezes their arm hard. It ain't fair that the others sleep sound like chillun when they feels this pain.

Lightning screams as another wave crashes through.

Clay wakes and tries to shake off Lightning's grip, which is purpling Clay's skin in a pleasing way. Now Clay and Rainbow is trying to help Lightning to rise. Lightning punches at em, wanting em far away. Lightning's fist soon finds a fleshy target.

Then they is half-lifting and dragging Lightning across the dirt to the chillun's hut with Rainbow clutching their nose, which drips with blood.

Lightning's glad someone else is sharing.

The Mune starts waking as they pass the other huts. They shake jars, stoke the fire to burning, chatter too loud for Lightning's liking.

'Hurts,' Lightning screams through gritted teeth. It's worse than any cut or bite and they's had plenty of em.

Lightning remembers little of the last few steps of the journey to the chillun's hut, which passes in agonies. Outside the chillun's hut the sacred water breaks, gushing from Lightning's cave and turning the earth dark underfoot.

With Elder Molly passing, it is Elder Rosie that awaits Lightning, face flushed with feverous joy. Lightning would like to strike it out of em, but can barely walk, never mind raise a fist again, the hurt is so intense.

'Make it arrive,' Lightning shrieks as they is pushed through the hut entrance.

Elder Rosie holds one of Lightning's arms and Rainbow the other. Lightning can hear Elder Tattio and Clay outside, discussing the herbs that might be needed.

Elder Rosie lifts Lightning's white smock, which is smeared with mucus and bright red blood. Squatting down, Elder Rosie says: 'The child is ready to see the island.'

STAR

*Deeds
ripple back.
Bury you.*

Star has no choice but to join the Mune, seated in a circle at the meeting place to wait for the arrival of the childs. The third day of bloodtime is always the heaviest, and the most uncomfortable, but it is good that the beasts will have a thick offering to distract em from coming ashore. Star is worried that Lightning slaughtering the two beasts in the cave will have consequences. It ain't the first time the beasts have sought sacrifice for the loss of their own kind.

Star thinks bout Elder Tattio tending to Lightning in the chillun's hut, and how hard it must be after Sky's passing. Did em harvesting the beast's oil for birthing, trapping and killing it like they did, lead to Sky's death? If the beast had not bin killed the day afore the arrival, would Sky have lived to see the childs grow?

Star looks across at Ocean, the childs Sky chose to pass for. They is already on two legs, rather than crawling around like a bug.

Another ragged pain pushes down through the cave and Star thinks bout what it means to carry such an important thing inside you, and of the body changing as the childs readies itself for arrival at the mouth of the cave.

Star whispers to Thunder.

'My offerings is ready. The beasts must be tended to.'

Star leaves the circle with Thunder and heads to the bloodtime hut to change the rags, which are pungent and soaked. They must not waste a bloody drop. It is the only thing that can be done for Lightning and hopefully, it will be enough to satisfy the beasts.

North Yorkshire

BETTY

Despite the thick blankets that cover the bed, in the best room at the Saltersgate Inn, Betty has barely slept. Master is snoring, as he always does when prone on his back. It was a long day in the stuffy carriage travelling here, leaving even Master too tired for his ablutions. The evidence of their late meal of game pie is caught in the corners of his greying beard.

But it is not just a late dinner that causes Betty discomfort. The pain Master inflicted on his return to the Manor the day after she told her truth, that she was Betty and had borne his child, dead though it were, still smarts on her buttocks and thighs. The weals caused by his riding whip for her insolence: *a lesson she must learn for her own good*, have barely healed. At least the sexual relations that followed had been swift. It was as if Master enjoyed dishing out her punishment, despite seeming later to regret it.

There is a knock on the bedroom door. It must be the breakfast Master requested be brought to their room at first light.

Betty lights the lamp by the bed and hastens to dress, though it is difficult with her legs stiff from the beating and with no maid to assist her lace her garments. She fumbles, trying hard to cover herself before Master wakes, for he do not like to see the evidence of his fury.

The tray outside the door contains chops, fried potato, cold bread and a flask of ale. They will need sustenance if she is to retrace her steps and find the well today. It had taken every womanly charm to convince Master to accompany her on this journey to North Yorkshire to garner the scientific evidence he required. Without it, Master made no secret of the fact he would cast Betty out, penniless and past her prime.

The weather is temperate when they leave the Inn, unlike the cold, dark day when Betty returned from the island. The landscape has changed, now beset with purple and blue heather and dotted with sheep. If she were not under pressure to find the well, perhaps she might enjoy the excursion.

She looks out of the carriage window for the low stone wall that she followed, and will now, she hopes, lead her back. The landlady at the Inn had said there were abandoned wells on old farmland near Devil's Punchbowl.

The carriage rumbles and slows, struggling to navigate the increasingly narrow roads—little more than farm tracks.

'I fear I must walk if I am to re-trace my path,' Betty tells Master. 'For I had not the luxury of transportation that day.'

Master withdraws his gold pocket watch from his waistcoat. His pinched expression, as he checks it, indicates that Betty has already taken too long.

'I will give you one half of an hour,' Master says, knocking on the front of the carriage to indicate his wishes for the driver to stop, before settling back in the padded velvet seat and picking up his book.

He does not help Betty to climb down, which proves difficult what with her petticoats, corsetry, and silk skirts. At least the earth is dry beneath her feet.

MASTER'S BOOK
OF SCIENTIFIC STORIES

The New Cambry

The first event I can chronicle, after drawing water from my well, was opening my eyes on a scene at once so beautiful and strange that I leapt to my feet in amaze. I had only taken a brief respite in my cottage garden, to curb my indescribable rage after reading Mrs Humphrey Ward's open letter, but now found myself on a glass-like platform in a strange landscape, grey but with gay-hued markings set upon tall buildings, and walls embellished with brass keys, ribbons and trinkets.

My focus was fixed on the looking-glass windows that towered above me and the sea appearing to swirl beneath my slippered feet, when the voice interrupted my musings.

'By Jove! I say do you live here, or have you taken Opium too?'

I looked up to witness a young man perched atop one of the high decorated walls, like some apparition of Humpty Dumpty.

'I don't know how the deuce I came to be in this extraordinary place,' the fellow continued.

I advised him, unless gummed by the seat of his pants, that he should jolly well come down.

I observed that he was not of any great height, perhaps an inch shorter than my five foot one, but his proportions were acceptable, clad in a quite startlingly patterned suit of tweed. His moustache was certainly something to behold, rusty and elegant, and it appeared he had a penchant for stroking it like some favoured pet.

I was about to answer that I had not partaken of any drugs, when a specimen of a race, the like never seen before, appeared to glide before us.

'A goddess,' the fellow declared.

I deduced she was close upon seven feet in height and of magnificent build. A giant Venus with a most poetic motion. She wore a very peculiar dress, a modification of the divided skirt, like hosiery and in a silvery hue, which served to heighten her beautiful, symmetrical limbs. There was an accompaniment of a silvery bonnet, snug against her crown.

'What strange people!' she exclaimed, in a bewitchingly harmonious voice.

'I am the Honourable Horace Chichester. I daresay you are well acquainted with my name,' the fellow from the wall exclaimed.

The giant patted him playfully on the crown. 'Are you a child?'

'How dare you insult me so!' he cried. 'I am a man!'

The goddess called to her friends. 'Come sisters, I have found two curious creatures. One pretends to be a man!'

Three women of similar gigantic proportions glided before us. 'What funny little things they are,' said one and laughed.

'Where do you hail from?' another asked me.

'I am English,' I said quietly, afraid of being ridiculed.

They seemed astonished but intrigued by my answer. 'There is no such nation anymore,' they said.

I hardly knew whether to be amused or humiliated when we were led by the hand, as if we were the children they suggested and might stumble.

The building to which we were escorted was proportionate to the women who resided there, tall and covered with myriad mirrors that reflected the thick clouds. It was simply majestic to behold. In the dining room, I required a cushion on my chair to reach the high table. This was laden with a variety of dishes: a root of some type steeped in a creamy milk and garnished with small yellow berries, and other dishes I could not describe. All were sweet and luscious in the mouth.

'Micro hydroponics,' the nearest goddess told me, introducing herself as Flora. 'You must eat. Our dietists have discovered that this modified root offers absolute protection from disease.'

'The children do look healthsome,' I said, noticing swathes of them scamper in and out of large metal doorways that opened and closed by an unseen hand.

'Our children do not suffer the physical lassitude engendered by the sole focus on brain work, like the old world. They are instructed in physical activity from birth until they commence schooling at ten. They are splendidly robust. Of course, when children succumb to infantile disorders, they are sent to spend their probation in less material spheres.'

I did not have time to ascertain as to what exactly these spheres were, for the Honourable Horace Chichester, who was receiving attention from a bevy of other goddesses with an air of conceited nonchalance, was speaking very loudly across the table.

'I, of course, am the second son of the Duke of Chichester.'

Flora laughed. 'Your little male biped appears the same all the world over,' she said. 'What is he thought of in your country?'

I was interrupted again from answering by a commotion, the advent of a Lady Professor and two doctors who apparently wished to speak with me. When the Lady Professor enquired about my journey to their country, I told her of my awakening amid strange surroundings following the reading of an article that set itself against women's suffrage, and the desire for some water from my well to cleanse my palate. Perhaps I had fallen into it, though I had no recollection.

'Do you mean men are the only voters in your country?' she asked.

I explained only a few women dare show their real opinions and are reproached by less enlightened females. It was only then it occurred to me to ask which country I was presently inhabiting.

'New Cambry,' the Professor said. 'Though it is best known in history as Kent. A country of perpetual war and suffering before the floods.' She explained how, after the great floods swept the British Empire, Kent was completely cut off from the mainland and languished in a state of neglect. The effects of the destruction, in addition to space travel and war, reduced the male population, and women now vastly outnumbered men. It did not take many years before the surplus women proved they were capable of all manly undertakings.

'What year is it?' I enquired, for although Kent was not unknown to me, I was not party to news of any war or incidence of water.

'2289,' the Lady Professor said, before taking her leave.

'But it is surely 1889?' I positively averred to Flora, seated beside me.

'I think you have been asleep for many years,' Flora said. 'You must have taken Cryoberries.'

'What the devil are they?' I asked.

She explained it was an essence which puts people to sleep for a very long time and is used when painful disease visits and no cure is forthcoming, or when long journeys are needed to be undertaken, such as those to other worlds.

Her talk was awfully confusing, and I was relieved to be escorted to my room, up many more grey stairs. Flora afforded me new clothing, suggesting I might prefer to appear less of a spectacle the following day. When I donned the national costume, it fitted perfectly, designed, I concluded, to bring absolute freedom from bodily constraint as well as being surprisingly warm. To my chagrin, my tresses were too abundant for the cap, reaching near to my waist. Flora assisted me to remove what I had previously thought of as a woman's glory, but I found, once cut, had been both debilitating and inconvenient.

When Flora departed, I discovered a copy of the 'History of New Cambry' in my room. According to the strange, flat, symmetrical scribe set within, health of body, purity of morals and the highest technical and intellectual skill were ever the goal for this country. There were many religions listed but, from what I could ascertain from the pages, it was a simple moral existence, involving only worship to 'the Life Giver' and a firm belief that the route to the next life required the abandonment of all ignorance and imperfection in this one.

I slept wondrously in the luxurious, quilted bed, which appeared to move under me like a raft on the open sea, and the following morning, after breakfasting, we shared a water car, skimming through the quiet, grey streets of New Cambry. Flora explained that the State had control of all transport, business and utilities of the island. The water was always fresh and plentiful, owing to mechanical arrangements which existed to transform the sea water. I used my eyes diligently, but it was difficult to see anyone in New Cambry who was not the perfect example of dignity and refinement. There appeared no dirt, squalor, poverty or drunkenness in this unlikely landscape.

'How is it that I have seen no people of any great age?' I asked.

'There are many among us,' Flora said. 'I for one, am one hundred and fourteen.'

'But you possess no wrinkles,' I exclaimed.

'We use nerve generation and when our bodies are no longer a robust tenement, we liberate our spirit.'

'Self-murder?' I asked.

She laughed. 'We would never willingly shackle our spirit to a decaying body. Instead, we seek heavenly fulfilment with the Life-Giver.'

I was still trying to make sense of Flora's utterings when we met with the Honourable Horace Chichester, who appeared as entranced as I with this new land, having also exchanged his tweed for clothing more artistic and comfortable. He confided that he proposed to record everything about this place and insisted nothing would escape his notice. When I confided that I too, was considering publishing my impressions of New Cambry, he snorted.

'I daresay there is no harm in you trying but it is unlikely you will produce anything of merit.'

On our return from our tour of the strange watery streets we were asked to speak on the great platform by The Grand Mother, who appeared to be their ruler but was unadorned by trinkets, as one might expect. She asked that we speak of the adventures that brought us to New Cambry, particularly, how we had managed to avoid detention on the coast. I was not confident in Horace's ability to achieve this without arrogance, fearing he might get carried away by the sound of his own voice, leaving us open to ridicule. Far from acknowledging these natives' superiority, he seemed bent on maintaining existing prejudice.

'Ladies and Gentlemen,' he pronounced.

There was a distinct titter amongst the large audience, as if he had said something quite unfamiliar. The Grand Mother, who shared the stage with us, leant over to speak with him, suggesting 'people of New Cambry' was a more appropriate introduction and that might he consider I should speak first, given my natural superiority.

The Honourable Horace Chichester paid no heed.

'Perhaps I should call you children, as you did me on our first acquaintance,' he continued but his jest was met with silence and disgust. This appeared not to dissuade him.

'One day, I cannot recall when exactly, my companion and I frequented an establishment in Whitechapel to partake in some Opium. My dreamy state brought me here, and I found myself seated on a wall when one of you goddesses took quite a violent fancy to me. I have been treated well since my arrival, but it is a confounded nuisance not to be able to get hold of any champagne or to raise a smoke. In fact, the very thought of my deprivation has left me thoroughly distraught.'

Poor Horace sat down on his seat with a look of sour discontentment.

I was anxious to undo the unpleasant impression my countryman had made and though I talked fluently enough, I do not recall exactly what I said but it was something about lady luck playing a part in our arrival. I was greeted to a rapturous applause. Horace looked daggers at me.

I thoroughly enjoyed the next few days and was treated as a very distinguished person. It appeared that the women here coveted intellectual ability far more than any garment or possession, and the men appeared modest and thoroughly contented with their lot. One man, whose acquaintance I had the pleasure of, explained that nowhere else was there such health and prosperity as New Cambry and that, since the great flood, history showed how man's political influence proved corrupt and retrogressive. He informed me he had no ambition for political office, and described New Cambry as a cooperative, where profit was enjoyed by everyone not just the individual.

After some days, The Grand Mother asked if I was to make New Cambry my permanent abode and whether I might consider writing a book descriptive of my former life for their history archives, as much was lost in the flood. When I asked about Honourable Horace Chichester I was met with a look of disdain.

'I am afraid your companion will never be converted into a sober member of New Cambry,' she said. 'He has refused to wear the national costume, suggesting it sacrifices his British individuality and has demanded the attire he arrived in be returned. He appears to have a sickness of the mind. It might be a charity to release his spirit.'

My blood positively ran cold. My countryman's life was destined to be a short one if he did not embrace change.

Horace was not in good spirits when we met. 'I have been asked to earn my own living. Me! Who has never even had to clothe himself without assistance! And not one goddess has accepted my proposal. This would never happen in England!'

I kept my opinions about his suitability for marriage to myself and instead explained about Cryoberries and the route he seemed destined to travel.

Poor Horace was frightened out of his wits. 'Oh Lord, deliver me from this land of inequity,' he said.

He proceeded to tell me more of his life and I discovered Horace was a blackguard, a cheat who was not a Lord at all but had swindled his hard-working mother, Mrs Jones, from her last few shillings to buy Opium.

When he had finished lamenting his debts and his dreadful prior behaviour, he produced a small glass bottle from his waistcoat pocket, asking if I thought it might help his predicament. The substance was uninviting, but I held it to my nose to be certain and drew in a most surprising perfume.

I awoke, collapsed by my well, a small cut on my head and shivering all over. How long I had been subjected to the elements, I do not know.

CLAY

Clay waits for some time outside the chillun's hut, but the childs fails to arrive even when the sun begins its climb behind the grey rock, scattering light in an arc.

'E will need sacred tea,' Elder Tattio says, touching Clay's arm. 'De childs refuse passage.'

Clay ain't sorry to get distance from the hut, especially since Lightning's screams have reduced to a hoarse panting sound, recognisable from another whose childs took too long to leave the cave and, in the end, refused to take a breath of the island air. That childs' passage to the sea was swift. The beasts, at least, bin content with the offering until the moon rose again. They took the childs to the depths, gently, as if one of their own was returned.

It was different with Elder Molly who they seemed to fight over.

Clay walks quickly to the meeting place to make the spiked-tea, which will ease the pain, and help Lightning to feel the island's magic. Clay thinks, like the beasts, if a person that carries the childs is well, that childs will absorb the feeling and leave its place of comfort to meet em all.

The Mune is seated around the fire, the light-jars dulled and discarded in their wait to meet the new member. Clay's footsteps feel heavy with foreboding.

'Has it travelled?' they ask, as Clay approaches.

'I'm to make tea,' Clay says, glancing away.

There is hush as Clay takes a stem of the spiked-bush plant from the food hut and slices it so thinly that the green flesh is almost transparent. Working quickly, and ignoring the pinpricks from the hard spines, and the Mune's eyes, which burn, Clay steeps the flesh in water that's bin bubbling over the fire, later adding some yellow berries. Clay is careful to pour only a small amount into a rednut cup, too much and they may never rouse Lightning from sleep.

'Dis will help e to rest.' Elder Tattio nods, taking the cup from Clay when they returns to the chillun's hut, afore ducking back into the hut.

There is nowt for Clay to do with two Elders there, so picking up the empty water bucket from the meeting place, Clay heads to the cave. The Mune will need the sacred water once the childs arrives and they is running low.

The cave feels empty with the beasts no longer dwelling there and it stinks of death, like the jumps do when their bellies is slit and the meat lain out to dry in the sun. Still, all Clay has to do is not breathe deep and at least the feet can be placed anywhere safely now.

As Clay begins to draw water from the sacred well, summat bubbles up. Laughter followed by a voice. It's as clear to Clay as the water.

'*My future is set.*'

Clay shudders as the words reach the surface. It is a voice recognised from dreams; one that Clay's struggled so long to forget. Betty? Betty's spirit is alive in the water? How can that be? Is it the devil Betty spoke of, sullying Clay's mind again? Betty said the devil take many forms.

Clay drops the bucket, limping as fast as possible back to the Mune.

STAR

*A scream
unheard
releases nowt.*

Star emerges from the bloodtime hut just as Clay rounds the corner of the grey rock. Clay has empty hands and a forehead lined with sweat.

Blocking Clay's path, Star demands: 'What is it? Is it the beasts? Is they returned to the cave so soon?'

'Is the childs arrived yet?' Clay asks, ignoring Star's questions and glancing this way and that.

'Not as yet. Is the beasts returned?' Star asks again.

'No. It is nowt.'

Clay is lying. What has changed that they no longer feels they can share thoughts with Star?

'Where is the bucket?' Star asks, pointedly.

Clay looks down, frowning.

'Let us return to the cave together. Elder Tattio bin asking for water.'

Clay seems reluctant, stiffening under Star's gaze, which intrigues Star even more.

'Come. Lightning needs us,' Star adds.

'Yes, us must do this for Lightning,' Clay says, voice as flat as the sea.

Clay walks slowly, even taking into consideration the limp, hesitating when they reach the shaded entrance of the cave.

'I left the bucket next to the well,' Clay says, making no move to enter the dark space.

Star ducks into the cave. There ain't no evidence of aught that might cause Clay's unusual temperament, though the cave still holds the oily scent of the beast's slaughter, which had caused upset. Perhaps it's that reminder?

'Come,' Star says.

When they reach the back of the cave and the well, Clay just stands there, shaking.

'Do you h…h…hear aught?' Clay stutters.

Star frowns, listening intently.

'Nowt but the drip of water and maybe Lightning's screams. Though they might be fixed in here.' Star taps the side of their head.

Clay looks at Star for a long time afore speaking, shoulders hunched, seemingly carrying a great weight upon em.

'You can tell me,' Star says, keeping their tone light.

'I heard Betty,' Clay blurts out, loud enough to cause an echo.

Betty, Betty, Betty.

Clay looks more uncomfortable with each repetition the cave throws back.

'Betty?' Star frowns.

'In the water. I ain't sick in the head!' Clay's cheeks turn red as Star's rags.

Star looks down at the sacred well. The water is still and dark as always, and anyway sound do not carry through liquid. Star has used this truth many times to scream out hurt.

'You dun believe me,' Clay's voice is small, like it's bin squashed.

Star thinks for less than a moment afore pressing their face down, barely hearing Clay's warning to stop. They bin told many times that the body must not touch the water.

There is summat there, a moon of light deep down, beyond where it's possible to reach.

'It is forbidden!' Clay says, with a look of horror, yanking Star out.

Even cold and wet, Star's stomach fills up with warmth not felt for a long time.

'I think it ain't as it seem. The moon in the water waits for discovery.'

'Us must not,' Clay's voice is tight. 'The Elders….'

'Us ain't the Elders,' Star says firmly. 'And it is my choice, as it always is.'

'What will you tell the Mune?' Clay asks, 'bout the voice?'

'Nowt,' Star says, 'they will not want to hear it anyways with Lightning as they is.'

North Yorkshire

BETTY

Betty shivers. She is chilled through, the sun not yet warm enough to dry all the layers of fabric that were dampened on the climb down into the well.

'I must know more,' Master says, putting in his eyeglass and taking a closer look at the fine metallic weave of the suit Betty has brought from the well and back to the carriage.

It is the suit the strange persons afforded her for her journey back here.

Betty notes that the book of scientific stories has been tossed aside on the plush velvet upholstery, as if Master sets no store in the words anymore.

'But they are savages on the island,' Betty says. 'What is there to know?'

'Then they are not only ripe for instruction but for study.' Master looks at Betty, a smile spreading over his face. He shakes the fabric. 'This is like nothing I have witnessed before. Remarkable.'

There seems little Betty can say to bring Master to his senses. Betty's stories and this clothing appear not enough to satisfy Master's curious nature.

'There will be new flora and fauna to catalogue. There is much to learn from undiscovered lands. We must journey together to this place. There might be a book in the offing.'

'But I am not welcome there,' Betty says.

'That is an irrelevance,' Master announces, removing his eyeglass. 'I am your protector.'

Betty bites her lip, trying to stem the tears which threaten to wash down her face, as the carriage bumps back towards the Inn. She had hoped for an end to the past and to secure Master's patronage.

'I have kept my word. I have proved my worth,' Betty says. 'It is my wish not to return there.'

Master takes Betty's hand and pumps it. 'Perhaps then, I may persuade you to accompany me to this *No Place* you describe, as my betrothed?'

Betty colours.

'Betrothed?' she asks.

Master releases Betty's hand. 'I have put up with Lady Harrington's impossible nature for far too long. The divorce has been granted. My suffering is over.' He squeezes Betty's damp knee. 'A wife who cannot perform her duties has no place at a man's side.'

Betty's heart beats hard. It is all she has ever wanted—to belong. Does this mean she will be the new Mistress of the Manor, even without her father's consent, have all the clothes she will ever need and more besides?

'And my future?' Betty asks.

'Secure,' Master says, leaning forward. 'I had to be sure you were of impeccable health, Bessie, for I do not wish to be saddled with another woman fit only for the Asylum. Our betrothal will be announced forthwith. We will wed on our return.'

STAR

Life
circles round.
Rim of a bucket.

Star draws circles in the dust with a stick to pass the time. It has stretched on for so long it feels like summat soon might snap. The Mune have eaten: a stew of jumps, snails and nips. Star only picked at it, passing it to Thunder to finish. Thunder has a stomach like a leaking bucket.

There bin no sound from the chillun's hut since Star arrived back from the cave, and now with the sun sinking behind the grey rock, the birds is also falling silent, as if they too have nowt helpful to say. The Elders is chanting, but their empty words is an annoying itch behind the eye which Star would like to reach in and scratch out.

Thanks be to the island. Let the childs arrive safely.

Discarding the stick, Star signals to Clay to go to the bloodtime hut, aught to escape, even for a moment, from the endless repetition and the smiles that do not reach no one's eyes. They all know the danger Lightning faces. Sky's passing is proof enough.

Star can do more for Lightning than offer bloody rags to the beasts.

'I must talk to the moon in the well,' Star whispers, as they reach the hut.

'Us cannot.' Clay's bottom lip quivers.

'I ain't asking you to do it.' Star checks the rednut cup, snug between the legs, secured by ropes around the belly, and changes the rags to be sure. 'I need you to witness where I is gone. It is my choosing. Anyway, you must take the offerings to the pool.'

'Of course,' Clay says, flatly. 'Us must honour the beasts.'

It's odd that Clay says honour, when the others say satisfy. Star ain't noticed it afore. Perhaps Clay always hides truth behind helpfulness.

They leave the hut by the back entrance, the Mune still unwavering in their song. Only when Star rounds the corner of the grey rock, and the light is better, does the fear etched in lines on Clay's forehead seem obvious.

Star pauses, placing a hand on Clay's arm, not the way normally chosen to communicate. It feels uncomfortable. 'I has looked at the sea and thought bout self-sacrifice. I ain't frightened.'

Clay do not seem to relax, even with touch, but nods.

'I will do what you want…deliver the offerings to the net and stop on my way back to see…' Clay leaves the sentence unfinished.

'I will be fine, as you was when you entered the well,' Star says.

'What if my passage made Elder Molly and Elder Sarah sick?' Clay asks. 'The water must not be touched by flesh.'

'Then us would all be passed.' Star indicates the sky, which will soon switch from blue to black. 'Ain't us all still here, breathing the island air?'

It is only now that Star sees the worry Clay's bin carrying, enough to fill several buckets. Maybe this journey will help empty it out.

As they near the sacred cave, they take leave of each other. Star watches Clay go, limping along the shell path towards the sea and the rocks where the beasts will be thrashing, waiting for offerings.

Heading inside the cave and to the very back, to the sacred well, Star thinks only of Lightning and what must be done to help. There might be herbs, or words to learn where the moon waits.

There ain't no time to waste and after making sure the red-nut cup is still strapped tight, Star climbs over the lip of rocks that circle the well, takes a deep breath and drops down into the icy water.

North Yorkshire

BETTY

Master's grip is tight on Betty's long, white glove as he helps her down into the well. She is wearing her walking attire, designed, she hopes, to remain intact when sodden, something she will not be able to avoid. Betty does not wish to arrive back on the island in shreds, being almost the lady of the Manor now. She should have insisted on wearing the silver fabric the persons afforded her, because she knows with certainty that it will survive the journey through the water, but Master dispatched it in the coach earlier, to be held under lock and key. He says it is vital evidence that must be protected. From what, Betty is unsure. It will be useless if they cannot return and explain its provenance.

There is barely enough room for one of them on the ledge, let alone two, so Betty sidles into the corner, gripping onto protruding bricks to stop herself from falling into the water. She is not sure why, but she mentions nothing of the mask she left hidden on the ledge as she secretes it in her bodice. It is a flat shapeless object until placed on the face and she is certain Master will not discover it. She leaves the heavy boots where they are.

'You must go first,' Master says, filling up more than his share of the space, a habit he also has in the bed. He gives her a little shove. 'Send a signal that you are safe. I will follow forthwith.'

He pulls his heavy coat around him, which no longer meets over his stomach. He has grown round with contentment.

Betty says nothing about the coat and the weight it will bear once he descends into the water—he will not appreciate her warning. He knows best and Betty does not wish to release the passion he keeps hidden under his embroidered waistcoat.

When Betty hesitates, still gripping on, Master adds softly: 'There is nothing to be afraid of, if what you say is the truth, Bessie.'

It is not a truth Betty is yet ready to face but she has no choice but to comply, and taking a deep breath in, she steps forward from the ledge and drops down into the water.

STAR

Body—
a vessel
built to roam.

As Star pulls emself from the pool, their body shakes and their teeth chatter. Breath sits heavy in the chest, not wanting to escape. The floor is the same black pitted rock as the sacred cave, but the walls is different even in the darkness, smooth and with the shimmer of the silvery fish from the island. Painful to touch, skin sticks to it, turning a blueish hue like Elder Molly's lips afore they passed. Star looks frantically bout for any light, sees a faint glow further in. Light means someone has shaken a jar and might offer help.

Ignoring the pain of every step and the tunic, weighed heavy with water, Star shuffles away from the pool. They's always known there is more than tunic trees, jumps and rednut milk and here is the evidence. A place other than the island. A place that might hold answers.

The glow forms a square on the wall, an opening of some sort, and there's a silvery lump that sticks out on one side. The lump is as painful to touch as the walls but at least seems to want to move. Pressing against it do not shift it, so Star thinks the lump must do summat, like the handle on a bucket, which make it possible to carry. Star twists it, pushing and pulling until eventually the square swings inwards, releasing a wall of heat. It stays attached somehow—do not need to be lifted aside like the woven panels that keep insects out.

Star steps through. The room is made of a similar material to the cave, which echoes when Star clenches their fist and knocks against it. Blinking several times, Star tries to get their eyes used to the green glow that spots this strange new place. It is warmer in here, and each breath can be drawn deeper. It is also silent: there ain't no birds chattering, no suck of sand and no scurry of insect feet, nowt but a faint hum. Star pauses for a moment mesmerised by the quiet, summat never experienced afore, even in the boneyard, what with so many of the Mune always so close.

Searching the room for summat dry to put on, Star finds a pile of cloth: a long tattered brown tunic of the coarse fabric they use for sacks. What's left of the bark tunic is removed easily, coming away in wet clumps. The new cloth, though ripped and stiff, at least provides some warmth. It has ropes across the chest, but Star leaves em undone.

Star looks for evidence of the peoples Clay spoke bout but can only see shapes in the dust on the floor: footprints without toes. Is these peoples more like the beasts than the Mune?

Suddenly there is a splashing noise, which seeps through the wall where there is another opening with the same silver lump attached.

Star glances around, the sound seem to come from beyond. There ain't nowhere to hide—nowt in the room cept ends of coloured rope curled in the corners and shards of transparent rock littering the floor, as sharp as Elder Newt's flints.

Star cannot return to the island with empty hands, so follows the marks on the floor, which lead to a third opening in the wall. Perhaps the peoples that was kind to Clay is through there? Panicking, Star struggles again with the lump handle. Finally, it opens, and Star steps through expecting to enter another room, but there is nowt solid underfoot and within seconds, is plummeting through water again.

BETTY

The journey is worse than Betty remembers, despite only taking moments. It's cold, suffocating and there is nothing on arrival, when she clambers out of the pool using the hard raised edge, but an expanse of black rock in an empty metal room. There really is nothing here. It's as if someone dug a hole in pitted rock and then built a shelter around it.

Betty draws in several breaths, but the air feels sticky and thick in her throat, like Cook's treacle. She pulls the mask from her bosom and places it over her face. As before, it moulds to her face, claustrophobic in its tightness, but it gives a little respite, somehow seeming to thin the air and make it easier to breathe. She must signal to Master and leave this room as soon as possible, for he will not have the benefit of the facial covering.

'I am safe,' she shouts, through the strange mask and into the pool, unsure whether the sound will reach him. To be certain Master receives a signal, she agitates the water.

Turning to the door, which she recalls leads to the other room where the persons gave her the coins, she opens it a fraction. Warm air trickles out.

It is quiet inside, with none of the ticking and chirping of before.

There is a bubbling and then a slapping sound as Master's face erupts from the water. He is without his coat, which he must have discarded, but Betty knows better than to mention it. She removes the mask and secretes it again.

'There is nothing here to dry oneself with and the air is thick. We must move inside,' she says, struggling to speak, her breath stuttered now the mask is back in its hiding place, between her breasts.

'Inside where?' Master asks, glancing around, his face reddening as he also struggles to draw breath.

'I do not know what it is called,' Betty says.

'Why can you not remember? Try harder woman! Or are you an imbecile after all?'

She must not get upset. It is discomfort not anger that makes Master speak to her so.

'Wait,' Betty says, face pressed in the gap between the door and frame. 'I think I can hear a door slamming.'

'Out of my way.' Master's face is now puce, and he has one hand on his handkerchief pocket, where the heart beats beneath.

He shoves Betty aside, collapsing on the tiled floor inside.

Betty follows him, closing the door, any attempt at return now thwarted.

'There is no one here,' Master says, between obviously painful breaths. 'It is one of your imaginings.'

Betty frowns. The room is not as she remembers, and it is not the absence of sound, but the lack of shimmering pictures. But at least in here the air does not stick in the throat.

'Is this *No Place*?' Master asks, sitting up, his breath now even. 'Remarkable.'

Betty nods and drops of water rain down from her unravelling hair. The style is ruined, knotted and escaping from the pins. She is glad there is no longer a looking glass, for if she is aught like Master, she must look an unholy fright.

'There is another well which will take us to the island but it is very hot there. We will not need the layers we are wearing.'

Master will undoubtedly expire from the heat if he does not ready himself.

'Perhaps we should return when we are better prepared?' Betty continues.

'Nonsense, woman. We are here now. The adventure must continue.' Master smiles, seemingly delighted.

Betty hopes he will not be disappointed. She is barely healed from the last of his painful lessons.

'It is through there.' Betty indicates the door opposite, identical to the one they entered moments ago.

'That must be where the persons that afforded you the silver garment are hiding,' Master says. 'I will need to speak with them, tell them of my plans.'

'I cannot answer for I do not know. It is much changed here,' Betty says, picking a shard of black glass from the bottom of her satin shoe. 'They called themselves doctors,' she adds, her voice low, lest Master does not approve.

Master laughs so loudly that it echoes, banging around the room in punches.

'Whoever heard of such a thing!' he exclaims. 'It is no matter. There is much to learn.'

STAR

New words—
not beasts
to fear.

Summat grabs Star tight and pulls em forcibly from the narrow channel of water. The same thing removes the ragged bit of cloth and rednut cup from Star's body, pinching with fingers not made of flesh. Star is lifted onto a soft surface full of bubbles that do not pop even when there is weight on em.

With barely enough time to look around, summat like water but thicker and hot, starts to attack. Eyes closed, Star hugs their knees for protection, but cannot escape the burning or the bitterness. Everything is washed away, even the blood which trickled onto the bubbled floor. The rednut cup is lost. It is this wastage, not the bright lights or the strange smells that frightens Star the most.

A blast of cold, thick, grey air follows the liquid.

'3, 2, 1.'

Someone is speaking, but there ain't no body attached to the flat voice in the tiny round space.

'Decontamination complete.'

A chirping noise is followed by summat circular that lifts out of the floor around Star, trapping em like lights in a jar. A slight judder and the whole thing rises, travelling upward, washing bile into Star's mouth. Water leaks from Star's ears—painful, popping like purple sea plants. Raw and frightened, arms clutching their body and eyes closed, Star feels sicker with every shift of the floor.

The movement suddenly stops and the jar that traps Star slides down. Hands reach out and this time they is not from a tin beast but warm and welcoming, wrapped in skin. Star is helped from the circular floor and cocooned in a thick, soft cloth and within seconds, is dry and warm.

'Do not be alarmed,' a voice says. 'It is part of our protocol. We were not expecting a visitor.'

Star looks at the person who speaks. They is dressed in a silvery fabric, which covers all their limbs. Their hair is so short it is barely visible: a shadow on the scalp. Their skin is smooth and dark like Elder Tattio's, yet the words they uses ain't familiar.

There is only two persons in this room, and one is rushing to an opening to close it.

'Where am I?' Star asks, eyes flicking around but there is nowt which make sense here: lights which make you blink and walls darting with colours as bright as the bowbirds.

'We must take you to a safe room,' the person says. 'There is a lot to explain.'

Star cannot rest: there is too much to see, to understand, and there is stories that must be remembered, but the person says Star must wait. No one else must know they is arrived, it is against protocol, whatever that mean. When Star lies down on the soft thing the person calls a bed, which bears no resemblance to the sleeping mats at home, they cannot stop their eyes closing.

LIGHTNING

Lightning ain't awake nor asleep but somewhere in between: too exhausted to speak, body as heavy as black rock. Trying to grab the edge of the mat is hopeless. The twine burns, flakes and disintegrates with each attempt.

'E must drink more, or de pain will be too much to bear.' Elder Tattio's voice is as firm as the hands pressed against Lightning's cave bones, as they tries to turn the childs inside.

Lightning gazes up at the roof, where the bundles of grass twist in embrace. It bends down to whisper. Or is that Rainbow's voice? Lightning dun know, both is barely a breath.

'Try to drink.'

Fingers lace through Lightning's own, squeezing tight like the nets that trap fish. What is it like to be free in the water like the beasts?

A rough hand pushes wet strands of hair away and Lightning feels the edge of summat hard pressed against their lips. Coughing, Lightning tries to swallow the bitter liquid, but it is hard to breathe. Pain presses through their body but it twists further away than afore, as if it is summat to touch rather than feel.

Is the childs finally arrived? Is that this feeling of lightness?

There is a flash of silver, an insect, hovering for a moment above afore flitting away.

'It is hot and sharp?' Elder Tattio's voice again. 'De poultice is made? De water boiled?'

A murmur of assent. Elder Newt? It is the noise they makes when searching for their voice. Why is Elder Newt in the chillun's hut when they dun normally come inside?

The woven walls close in and faces drift out of reach. They is as hard to catch as the jumps. Lightning's body sinks further into the thin grass mat and down into the earth neath. Eyes heavy with stones cannot be kept open any longer.

'It is time. Make de cut.'

Another flash of silver and the scent of hot flesh—perhaps a ceremonial meal for the childs arrival drifting into the hut?

Shouldn't there be crying?

Rainbow's gentle voice, hot against ears: 'It ain't yer time to pass. Stay with the Mune.'

Lightning falls deeper, below the hard rock that shapes the island, and out of reach.

STAR

Moon
hangs heavy.
Even inside.

Star wakes disorientated, mostly cause of the silence, the lack of warmth from other bodies, and the cool air. It moves of its own accord and do not hang close. Struggling to sit up in the thing called a bed, which tries to draw em back down, Star fights it.

There is blood on the white fabric but it ain't lost. It can be folded and kept ready.

A knocking sounds.

'Can I come in?' The person's voice is so low, Star barely hears it.

Why is they asking Star this when places belong to all?

'Yes,' Star says, frowning.

It is the same person that told Star not to be alarmed when they arrived and to pretend they ain't here if someone else should come.

'I'm Doctor Adebeyo. It's good to finally talk to you, Star.'

'How do you know my name when I ain't told it you?'

'I will explain once you have eaten,' Doctor says. 'It is easier to show you than to talk. I hope the short time you have been able to rest is enough?'

Star nods and takes the flat bowl the person holds out, which has lots of sections, made out of summat that squeaks when rubbed. There is also two metal objects of a strange shape. They ain't heavy, but their purpose is unknown so Star places em back in the little dip they bin housed in. Star tests each thing on the plate first with fingers, then just a small bite. One is sticky, like the tree sap the snails' favour, and melts in the mouth.

'What is this?' Star asks, shoving the whole thing in.

'A sugar donut,' Doctor says. 'People your age like them. I couldn't get hold of much else without it being noticed.'

'You mean chillun?' Star asks. 'Though I ain't much of one no more, now I has bloodtime.'

'Indeed,' Doctor says.

'I need to collect it for the beasts.' Star looks up.

'I will get you something for that. In the meantime, I have found clothes for you. Things I hope you will feel comfortable in. I will close the door, wait outside while you change.'

'Outside?' Star asks, frowning.

'The room,' Doctor says, laying the pile of fabric down. 'To give you privacy.'

Once Doctor's gone, Star places the tray on the bed, but not afore running a finger around the place that held the sticky food and sucking it off. Picking up the fabric the person left, it feels softer than Lightning's carrying tunic but thicker, with fur on one side. It is a strange red creature they slaughtered to make this.

Another gentle knock and Doctor returns to the room holding a square thing.

'They call these Moon cups,' Doctor says. 'It was in the archives. I hope it will suffice.'

Star is surprised to find the object inside the box is not round like the moon, but floppy and a very strange shape for a cup.

'You put it inside you,' Doctor says.

'Into the cave?' Star asks.

'Yes, like this.' Doctor pinches the object between two fingers, so it is narrow, and uses their hands to show Star. They turns to go.

'I do not want to be alone,' Star says. 'Please stay.'

The new tunic is soft, warm and easy to move in. Star walks with Doctor back to the room of arrival. There is so many questions to be asked, not least the type of animals needed to make this tunic with legs, but Star must not forget bout Lightning.

'My friend is waiting the arrival of the childs and needs help,' Star says. 'It is why I came. Why ain't you in the other place?'

'*No Place*? Politics,' Doctor says, quietly.

'I do not understand.'

'That is a blessing,' Doctor laughs. 'It is simple really, we ran out of…' they pause, 'resources.'

'Food and water?' Star asks, thinking bout the sacred well and Clay's warning bout contamination.

'Something of that nature.'

Doctor puts their eye close to a square panel on the wall, summat chirps and doors slide open in front of em. Star bristles as they pass the indented floor, remembering the burning water from afore.

'I'm sorry last night was frightening for you,' Doctor says, seeming to notice everything Star feels.

Star's face burns. 'I is not frightened.'

Doctor stops in front of a wall, which lights up as their hand sweeps over it. Bright colours dance around like lightberries inside jars. A picture emerges: the sacred cave, full of young peoples in long brown tunics holding chillun. Even though they is now Elders, Star recognises some of their faces: Newt ain't changed much, cept for the greying hair.

'It is a digital memory,' Doctor says, 'taken just hours after the event, when the ship sank, and your elders found themselves on the island.'

Star reaches out but there is nowt to touch, only air.

'Event?' Star asks.

'Something unexpected. Sometimes when you are researching new sources of energy, it has consequences you don't foresee.'

'But you did see,' Star says, pointing at the image. 'So why ain't you helped?'

'It is complicated,' Doctor says.

This seems to be the reason for much that these peoples do and do not do.

'The Elders do not speak of what was afore,' Star says.

'It was a dark place, but you will bring light.'

'Me?' Star asks. Since when has anyone listened to what they has to say?

'Not just you. All of the community.'

BETTY

The heat wraps around Betty in a claustrophobic breath as she emerges from the sacred well, and into the damp cave. The stench is dreadful, reminding her of Cook's rotten eggs. She picks up a jar next to the well, which emits a faint glow, enough to make out the black rocks. Someone has been here recently. Betty shakes it to full light.

'We must hurry,' she whispers, as Master surfaces, his beard stuck in swirls to his chin. 'The 'mune do not like the flesh to touch water. They will act!'

Betty thinks of the way Newt so callously cut her arm after the accident with Clay, which Betty has been trying to forget. It has not been easy with the faint scar underneath her glove.

'The wishes of the Mune are no matter,' Master says, easing himself from the water, 'I will instruct them on what is best.' He stops for a moment and sniffs the air. 'Good lord, one might make good use of a nosegay here. Sulphur, if I am not mistaken.' He do not seem concerned that he is wet to the bone.

Turning to Betty, he asks: 'What is this thing you hold?'

'It is a plant or some such, of no importance now.' Betty glances around as Master takes the jar from her.

'I will decide what is important,' Master says, turning the jar in his hand, peering at the contents. 'Fascinating. Perhaps some type of seaweed?'

They need to leave this cave as soon as possible for with only one exit, they are trapped like the lights in the jar Master holds, but he is entranced. Betty fans her hand in front of her nose to eliminate the appalling odour, but it do no good.

She shivers. Her last journey from *No Place* to Master's made her sick.

'We must get dry before we catch a chill,' she says.

'Goodness woman. A little water never killed a man.'

'The 'mune will put up a fight, not wishing to bend to you as I do,' she says, her voice rising higher in pitch, and shaky.

Master slaps her face. 'You are hysterical,' he says.

Betty shocked, nearly stumbles, barely catching herself in time on the slippery rocks. Her lip quivers in upset but she hides it, biting down. Master do not tolerate unchecked emotion and she will need his support here. She has no choice. The 'mune will not celebrate her return, or Master's arrival. They will see it as some sort of dark trickery.

Master moves forward, leading the way and Betty follows, holding onto her long skirts. They are already ruined by the water, the hem filthy with dust. At least she has retained her modesty.

'And these?' Master asks, pausing to hold the jar up to the wall as they enter the main section of the cave, where the pools of salt water are found. 'Are this Mune responsible for these crude drawings?'

Master traces the faded brown outline of the beasts with a finger. Betty has not noticed before how smooth his hands are—the skin plump despite the brown spots that track his fingers like bugs.

'They was already here when we arrived,' Betty says, discomfort gnawing inside her.

She turns to the entrance, swears she hears footsteps, or a dragging sound in the brush outside. She's forgotten how miserable this place is, and hot, like Master's greenhouse.

CLAY

Clay pauses outside the cave entrance. All that's needed now is the hush-hush leaves that grow under the tunic trees. The bucket is already full of the yellow root they press into cuts, purple weed from the sea and the spiked-plant used for the calming tea. There ain't much room for aught else, but it is all needed to help Lightning return.

Elder Newt cut the childs out as the sun rose this morning. Rainbow said it was blue at first, but then red with screaming. Those who have chosen to care, take turns to hold the childs close, for it is connection with others, the feel of another heartbeat, that sustains life.

The connection ain't worked for Lightning yet, who still draws breath but ain't found the path back to the Island from the deep sleep. Since Lightning's bin moved back to their sleeping hut, it has a scent to it that often accompanies passing and it worries Clay.

At least, with all that's happened, the Mune ain't noticed Star is missing.

Pressing a bunch of hush-hush leaves into the bucket, Clay picks it up, ready to return to the huts, when voices bubble out from inside the cave. It ain't anyone from the Mune for they is all caught up with the arrival of the childs, and anyway, would have passed Clay on the path.

'This could be a new exotic animal to be presented at the Great Exhibition.'

'The beasts is dangerous, Master, not to be trifled with.'

Clay swallows hard, saliva grating like black sand. The second voice belongs to Betty.

'Dangerous to savages perhaps, but not for one who is well read, such as myself.'

This other voice is deep, rumbling through from inside, followed by a low throaty laugh.

Clay picks up the bucket and hastens to the dust path. Betty is capable of great hurt and who is this other? Why is they here? What is a Master? If they arrived from someplace else, does that mean Star is safe?

With an uncomfortable mixture of dread and hope, Clay walks as quickly as possible back to the Mune, ignoring the pain that shoots down through their leg.

The others must be warned.

BETTY

There is no one outside the cave and for that Betty is eternally grateful. She mutters a prayer of thanks, for perhaps the Lord is here with them after all.

'Holy and Righteous Father, I thank you for Jesus, who is at your side and knows my heart, struggles, and world.'

Master frowns, drops of perspiration already collecting in the lines of his brow as he squeezes water from his waistcoat and looks around.

'Where are the savages?' he asks.

To distract him, Betty picks up a bunch of discarded hush-hush leaves from the dust path. Though she has never collected them herself, she recognises they are freshly picked, not yet dried by the hot sun. She wasn't mistaken. There was someone here.

'These are used to treat ailments,' she says, hoping another exotic discovery will appease Master.

Master takes the leaves and rubs them between his fingers, before drawing them to his prominent nose. 'Interesting. They have the texture of animal hide, but with a foreign scent. I will need to record all of my findings, Bessie.'

Betty says nothing. Master will not find quills or parchment in this godforsaken place.

'I will show you the ship that we arrived on,' Betty says, trying to buy some time for there is a grumble of discontent, low down in her stomach, a sensation she does not recognise—not fear but something other. It is uncomfortable and she wishes it gone.

'It is on the route to the settlement?' Master asks.

'It is something to behold,' Betty says, not wanting to tell an untruth, for she knows the price for that.

'Lead the way then, Mistress Bessie.' Master tucks one of the leaves into his damp handkerchief pocket.

The path to the shore is wider than Betty remembers, and the shells that line it a brighter white. There are so many things she should have thought to bring: a parasol, or a broad-brimmed straw hat. She must protect her skin, for Master will not want her swarthy for their nuptials.

'It is not far,' Betty says, recalling the daily vigil she kept by the boat. 'We might see some of the beasts for they reside in the waters, but we must keep to the path.'

'I will decide where to walk,' Master says, hand firmly gripping her shoulder, his lips forming a tight line.

Betty flinches, but Master does not raise his hand this time. She must not forget herself. She decides not to tell him about the sand for he will see for himself how it mirrors sound, rippling its anger. He will be pleased at this new sight, and of course, more so when she saves him from sinking. She must think more in this way and save information for barter. Information is Master's favourite currency.

CLAY

The dust path is quiet cept for the call of the bowbirds high in the tunic trees and Clay's laboured breath. Clay rounds the grey rock, and the sound of the Mune rises in greeting. They is all still seated at the meeting place, sharing tea and the arrival of the new childs, but the celebration is muted. They have stopped chanting and the absence of words is a painful reminder of Lightning's predicament.

Clay limps over to the food hut, where Elder Tattio and Newt is busy.

'You found yellow root?' Elder Tattio asks, emptying the contents of the bucket out onto the earth, and searching hurriedly through the herbs. 'De wound must be treated again. Us have bathed it with de sea but it is reddening fast and dun heal.'

Clay nods, sucks in a breath. 'There is peoples come.'

'Here, ketch some water.' Elder Tattio fans Clay away. 'And sit in de shade to recover. You dun well.'

'Betty is returned to the island,' Clay says.

Elder Newt looks up at Clay, eyes narrowed, afore reaching for a spear. Nodding to Elder Tattio, Elder Newt leaves em, footsteps soon just dust.

'Elder Newt will find notin. It is just de sun make ghosts of de air. Us must tend to Lightning.'

It ain't the sun. Betty is here, flesh and bone. Clay ain't imagining it.

Shaking, but trying to put all energy into the job at hand, Clay takes the yellow root, and helps Elder Tattio to strip the bark from it, pounding it on a black stone with hush-hush leaves, until the juice seeps out. The mixture will be pressed into the wound while fresh, and more spiked-tea will be made to keep Lightning safe, until healing is complete.

Carrying the mixture in the rednut cups, Clay enters their sleeping hut. Rainbow is next to Lightning, body touching, trying to draw em back to the island. The Mune believe that em closest to the carrier is best placed to help healing and that connection is everything for survival. You dun win nowt when you fight alone.

Rainbow mumbles in sleep as Clay removes the arm, thrown over Lightning.

Lightning's wound is weeping, as if crying in anger. Red and raw, it puffs up around the twine stitched in a line under Lightning's cave bones.

Clay presses the fresh poultice gently into the wound, brushing away any grains of salt left on the skin. Lifting Lightning's head, the spiked-tea is dribbled into Lightning's mouth until swallowed. Even when a person is elsewhere, the body responds as it must.

Clay covers the wound with sun-bleached cloth, to stop insects from burrowing into flesh. Once certain it is tight, that there ain't no gaps, Clay takes Lightning's hand and, clasping it, sits back against the hut wall.

Clay dun expect sleep to visit, even though they is exhausted, not with Betty so close.

STAR

Onwards.
Footprints
is meant to fade.

Star has seen more pictures than it's possible to remember: the past when Star was just a childs, and the possible future, though it's hard to imagine the beasts standing tall like that and the island shaking, burning with fire. There ain't no images of Lightning: of the now. Doctor says visuals can only be maintained from the lunar laboratory and they bin forced to abandon it.

'I'm sorry we were not better prepared for your arrival,' Doctor says. 'Or that you cannot stay to learn more.'

Another Doctor enters the room. This is the one from afore and has light skin and short red hair but wears the same silver suit, which Doctor Adebeyo has told Star is a uniform: clothes designed for the laboratory and exploration. They says hair ain't nowt but an irritation when travelling.

The new Doctor is carrying a small metal box, which they places on the floor. Reaching over to Star, they presses summat hard into Star's palm. It is a red berry of some sort.

'For your friend, Lightning,' the new Doctor says.

Doctor Adebeyo puts a hand on Star's arm. 'You must not let anyone see this capsule, do you understand?'

Star nods.

'And you must never tell your friend that you healed them.'

Doctor has told Star several times that they is not supposed to interfere, only observe the island, and that these actions they is engaging in with Star, carry much risk.

'The skeleton shift will arrive soon to replace us,' the new Doctor says, glancing towards the door, deep lines cutting into their forehead.

Doctor Adebeyo nods, and takes the case from the floor, snapping it open and removing a document coated in a shiny clear substance, which is like water but not liquid, hard and spread tight over summat white. It is covered in strange marks.

'We cannot seem to agree the best way forward,' Doctor says, 'to make up for what has happened.'

'We?' Star asks, looking at the thin stiff object, unsure if this is what books look like. 'Yer Mune?'

'Yes. The research team.'

Star frowns at the marks on the paper. 'What is this?'

'It is a map of future events and instructions for this...' Doctor Adebeyo removes a palm-sized object from the case.

'What do it do?' Star turns the cold object over. It has a grey handle and a black square embedded in the main section, deeper than the night sky.

'It's an ultrasound scanner—to see the child inside. To make carrying safe,' Doctor says. 'It will change everything for you when you return to the Elder's old world.'

'How?' Star asks.

Doctor Adebeyo pauses as if they is measuring their words. 'Carriers will no longer be put at risk in childbirth.'

'Birth?' Star asks.

'You call it arrival,' the new Doctor says.

Star thinks of Lightning again as Doctor Adebeyo presses the side of the object, where there is a small lump. The black square turns the grey of beasts and Doctor Adebeyo rolls it over Star's hand. The screen shows white sticks, knotted together by smaller lumps and lines.

'This is what your hands looks like under your skin. It is what the machine does.'

Star snatches their hand away. This is what the body is? A mess of bits held together by thin ropes? Ropes fray and break. Is the body so fragile? Star feels sick as they thinks bout Clay's leg. Perhaps there is truth in it.

'We have simplified the design to allow it to be copied with the minimal of elements,' the new Doctor says. 'It may be converted to whatever energy is available, although we have witnessed many advances during the last few years.'

Star frowns. What is energy and how do this thing work? Do it have a heart?

The new Doctor speaks rapidly. 'There are three names on the bottom of the document, people to seek out who may have the skills to help in this process.'

Star looks at the marks on the bottom of the page, but they make less sense than tracks in the sand. Will they also disappear?

'Hertha Ayrton, Jessie Boucherett, and Sophia Jex-Blake all live in the Elders' world.'

'The Elders ain't going to leave the island.'

'They may change their minds if what we predict comes to pass.'

'The fire and the beasts?' Star asks.

The new Doctor nods. 'We cannot be absolutely certain, we do not know enough about your universe, but the way the island works, the erosion and the advanced evolution, staying there will become untenable. It may not be a choice.'

'Your job is only to keep these things safe for others to utilise,' Doctor Adebeyo says.

'What bout the water?' Star asks, thinking bout the return back to the island and how the tunic bin nowt but a wet lump when they travelled afore.

'The case will survive the journey,' Doctor Adebeyo says, placing the two things back in the thin grey box and clamping it shut. 'Keep it hidden until you are safe in the Elders' old world.'

'There is more danger than what I seen in the future pictures?' Star asks, thinking bout the beasts standing like peoples and the dead fish broiled on the sand.

'There is always danger when one tries to introduce change.'

BETTY

The ship is now little more than a few sticks sunk in the sea, not even enough to start a fire. When Betty left the island, it was broken but robust—its hull a gaping mouth. What is she to do? It looks like nothing of importance and the water sits so close to the path, she cannot even show Master the evils of the sand.

Betty stiffens at a movement behind the trees a little further on. Not the sort made by small animals but a heavier, lumbering sound. Are the 'mune already aware of their presence here?

'The ship has rotted because of the salt water,' Master says, in his booming voice. He rubs his rotund stomach, which is starting to growl. 'But the sea is a most unusual hue. It is of great interest, Bessie, but we must hasten to the settlement. A man cannot survive on water alone.'

As they walk, Betty wonders if Master imagines the women wear aprons ready to serve. Whilst it is true the 'mune have lost their faith and their modesty, with their cloth coverings and dark skin, underneath perhaps they are not so different—trying, like her, to survive.

This new thought makes Betty uncomfortable but thankfully she is distracted by another sound, louder this time and closer: a thud as if something heavy has fallen. Perhaps it is a rednut, dropping on the hard earth under the large trees?

'We must rest, Bessie,' Master says, looking once again over the green sea and to the horizon. 'You are not accustomed to this heat.'

Master is a proud man and even though it is him, sweating like Cook over a hot pot, Betty must make allowances.

'I do feel rather faint,' Betty says, drawing her gloved hand across her forehead to emphasise it.

'We will seek shade under those trees.' Master points further up the path to the dense foliage that lines the shore. 'And allow you to regain your strength.'

Master do not wait for an answer but steps off the path and into the wood. Betty follows, careful to avoid the spikes from the low bushes and the bases of the trees which seem to have been damaged, shards of bark protruding like sharp teeth.

Master settles on a fallen log and, lifting his shirt coat, sits down, not waiting for Betty, who pauses to pluck a thorn from her shoe. She scowls, seeing the thorn has torn a small section of the beige satin.

From here, if Betty squints past the trees, she can see the rock pools where Newt used to spend days standing with her spear, stabbing fish. She supposes when one does not have breeding, one has to learn patience.

Betty hesitates before sitting down on the edge of the log with Master, worried she might add further stains to her ensemble, and there is that uncomfortable feeling she has, that won't go away—that they are being watched.

Betty allows her eyes to close for a second.

'Not one movement, Bessie,' Master says, quite suddenly, and not in his normal tone.

Betty turns, cannot help herself.

There are two beasts behind them, which must have come from the direction of the cave and the 'mune. Betty stares at their black, beady eyes and the stubby legs which protrude from four corners of their flat undersides. The fin, stiff and sharp-looking, erupts from their grey leathery backs. They have the look of monsters.

Have the women sent them? Have they befriended these large creatures, as Master has his wolf hound?

Betty bites her lip hard, stifling a scream, as Master shifts on the log beside her. Betty sees a flash of gold embroidery in her periphery.

'Master?' she whispers, but there is no response bar a crunch of undergrowth.

One of the beasts shuffles closer, sniffing the air as it raises itself up. It moves forward, crushing the prickly bush in its path. It does not seem to feel the thorns and wears them in its hide like jewellery. Opening its mouth, baring pointed, stained teeth, it launches itself at her.

STAR

Alone—
cold
if ain't chosen.

Breaking through the sacred water, Star removes the transparent mask and breathes in the hot island air once more. There is only the faint murmur of distant voices. Perhaps the Mune is hunting by the shore?

Pulling the metal case from the water, Star removes the white, shiny rope from the handle, letting it curl back to the bottom of the well. They open the metal case, strip off the silver suit, which is dry, despite the journey, and take out the bark tunic that the Doctors seemed to have a collection of. Changing into it and putting the silver suit and mask into the case, Star shuts it. Doctor told em bout a black rock in the cave, which moves when weight is pressed against it. Eventually, after pushing many of the black rocks, one finally shifts exposing a deep hollow neath it. In the dip is already many strange objects: a small glass tube, a bundle of dried rednut flesh, and a small silver blade with a wooden handle. Star picks up the glass tube and looks closer at it. Is there something moving inside, a thin grey smoke? There ain't no time to question what or whom these things belong to now; Star must take the red berry to Lightning to heal em afore it is too late.

Pushing the case into the hollow, Star heaves the rock back over, obscuring it. Wetting the tunic, and smearing dirt on it to make it look more worn, Star takes a deep breath and leaves the cave, heading straight towards the Mune, the red berry gripped tight in their hand.

BETTY

There is nothing Betty can do but raise her arm to protect her face as the beast bears down on her, teeth as stained as Cook's butcher's knife.

'I'll get the devil, young Bessie, don't you fear!' Master shouts from behind, flourishing a branch in one hand.

He launches himself at the beast, hitting repeatedly at its flank, but with no more impact than a feather brushed along its leathery hide.

Betty tries to scream as the beast connects with her flesh, sinking its teeth deep into her arm but no sound comes, her shock is too great. Blood soaks through her glove and the sleeve of her cream satin dress.

Master hits out at the beast again and Betty can smell the sweat of his effort spreading through the thick layers of his clothing. Finally, he manages to jab it in its eye and it rears back, ripping fabric and with it a strip of Betty's skin. It peels away like badly hung wallcovering.

The second beast, who up until this point was merely watchful, now raises itself up on stout back legs, and lumbers towards Master. Master jams the stick into its cavernous mouth as it reaches him, and it emits a high-pitched cry—a wounded sound that makes Betty's ears smart. Then there's a thump and a thud as Master is thrown backwards onto the ground by the weight of its lifeless body.

Master do not move, and now the beast that first attacked Betty is sniffing the air again. It reminds Betty of the time Newt pulled her away from the sea. It is blood this beast lusts after, and it flows from Betty's arm in a river.

The beast raises itself up, facing Betty, ready to attack again but then suddenly falls forward with a thud, knocking Betty from the log, and landing across her legs, pinning her down onto the spiked brush beneath.

Deep in its side is a spear.

There's a faint rustle as Newt walks out from behind the thicket of trees. Her face is expressionless as she stands over Betty, but it is not the first time Newt has witnessed Betty's arm bleeding. Then Newt turns and heads towards the shore, leaving Betty prostrate and alone.

There is still no sound coming from Master, who is almost hidden under the grey hulk of the monster and Betty cannot turn to witness his injuries anyway. Not able to contain her sobs, Betty lets them flow. Stuck here, she will surely bleed to death.

Why did she come back to this godforsaken island?

CLAY

The sun streams through the hut opening, yet it ain't the light or the ache from sleeping upright against the stiff grass walls that wakes Clay, but the commotion outside. Whatever is happening, Rainbow has left in a hurry, forgetting to replace the woven screen.

Clay drops Lightning's hand, which is clammy and white where it bin gripped too tight. Lightning's lips is a similar blue to Elder Molly's in the days afore passing, and the skin around the wound is hot to touch. It ain't a good sign.

'Clay?'

Rainbow is at the entrance, frowning, the new childs strapped close against their body.

'Elder Tattio needs yer help in the chillun's hut. It ain't safe for the new childs to be there. I will sit with Lightning.'

Safe? The word brings Clay round as if Rainbow had slapped their face. It can only mean one thing.

Clay feels sick to the stomach.

'There bin an attack,' Rainbow says, ducking through, the childs held close.

'Betty?' Clay asks, hopefully. Perhaps Elder Newt found em.

'I dun recognise the scent.'

Rainbow sits down next to Clay, adjusting the childs afore reaching for Clay's cheek. It feels rough and comforting. Clay knows every callus, every scar and every line of Rainbow's body. Their lips meet in the gentlest of touches.

'Go,' Rainbow says, placing their hand on Clay's heart. 'You will find me here. Always.'

The Mune is gathered around the fire, watchful. Water is boiling in the buckets and Clay recognises the bitter scent of spiked-tea. There ain't no sign of Elder Newt but the spears, normally lined up against the food hut, is missing.

STAR

Childs
push through.
Dun matter the harm.

Star traces the dust path to the Mune, enjoying the familiarity of the heat, the scratch of tiny stones under bare feet and the island smell: of knowing what and where everything is, cause if Doctor speaks the truth, soon it will change.

There ain't no chants of celebration as Star rounds the grey rock but instead, the sound of many footsteps slapping on dust. If Lightning bin of health and the childs arrived, it would not sound this way.

Star hastens forward, almost bumping into Thunder coming the other way. What if they is too late?

'Is the beasts stopped?' Thunder asks, shifting their spear into the other hand.

The tip of the spear is smeared with the false-mint oil that takes fight away.

Star lets out a breath. The Mune clearly do not know they's bin missing. Thankfully, Thunder, as always, do not pause for a response.

'Elder Newt cannot fight em alone.'

Star wants to ask what has happened but cannot, cause Thunder will wonder why they do not know.

'I must go to the bloodtime hut,' Star says, conscious of the Mooncup tight within, which must be emptied onto clean rags and replaced with a rednut cup, so questions ain't raised. Whatever has occurred, it seems the island is in need of blood.

Thunder nods and gripping the spear in the attack position, continues on.

Star arrives at the bloodtime hut without seeing no one else. The blood is thicker than expected when the Mooncup is emptied onto strips of cloth. With nowhere to hide the object given to em by Doctor, Star squashes it into the bottom of a rednut cup, covers it with fresh rags and straps it around the cave bones. Clutching the red berry tight, they heads off to find Clay.

CLAY

Elder Tattio is outside the chillun's hut with Elder Rosie, talking in whispers. They look up as Clay approaches, but not afore some of Rosie's words is caught: *protect the children.*

Clay frowns, unsure of the meaning.

'Us need herbs,' Elder Tattio says, 'but first us must wait for Elder Newt to return.'

'Is it Betty?' Clay tries to glance around em to see inside.

Elder Tattio nods but moves to block Clay's view. 'It was not de sun dat made you sense a presence.'

'Who is the one with the voice that rumbles?' Clay thinks bout the low laugh that caused a feeling of coldness through the body.

A look passes between Elder Rosie and Elder Tattio that Clay cannot quite define.

'Nothin' but a stranger,' Elder Rosie says bluntly. 'Don't make no difference to us.'

'But how...' Clay continues, wanting to know if they came through the sacred well. If that means Star is safe.

'Questions will be answered later,' Elder Tattio says, 'Dey is both badly hurt. It is best dey stay in de chillun hut for now.'

Best for who, Clay wonders, already knowing half the answer. If the past shows aught, the Elders may never give the answers needed. Clay is beginning to understand Star's desire to search outside for em.

'I will collect the yellow root and hush-hush leaves. I dun need to go to the shore for those,' Clay suggests.

''em beasts attacked in the wood,' Elder Rosie says. 'There ain't no place safe.'

Even so, Clay would rather be with the beasts than Betty, for although they might attack, it is expected—they dun hide their true feelings under a seemingly kind smile.

'Is Lightning returned to us?' Elder Tattio asks, brushing an insect from their tunic and standing firm.

'Rainbow sits guard, but I will return and tend to healing. There is tea made and the wound is clean.'

Elder Tattio nods. 'De 'mune is us priority.'

Clay walks quickly away from the chillun's hut, keen for distance, detouring to the food hut to check the amounts of herbs there. Lightning must have enough for recovery. The strangers can wait.

'Clay!'

Clay turns towards the sound, which comes from behind the food hut, from the thin strip of shadow.

'Star?'

'I is returned,' Star says, but dun step forward.

'You is safe!' Clay feels the black rock that bin weighing heavy, being lifted.

'Why is you hiding?'

'I has summat for Lightning, but you must help me. It ain't summat I can do alone and it must not be witnessed.'

STAR

Hope—
herbs
for the head.

Star ducks through the opening of the sleeping hut with Clay. For the first time in many days, the four friends is together again. Rainbow is sitting up, back propped against the hut wall, a childs held close against the chest, and Lightning is lying in the far corner, stomach bandaged as tight as the ropes under Star's cave bones. Lightning's face has a green tint to it and the hut smells of sickness, of turned meat, which ain't a good sign.

'You is back,' Rainbow says, stroking the childs' damp head as it sleeps, and smiling at Clay. 'The strangers is well?'

'Strangers?' Star asks.

In the rush to administer the red berry to Lightning, Star has failed to ask questions, summat unheard of. Clay digs an elbow into Star's side, but it is too late, Rainbow has noticed.

'Where you bin that you dun know?' Rainbow asks, scrutinising Star.

Star's skin prickles. Rainbow's gaze always reads em things hidden neath the surface.

'Bloodtime made me lose my way,' Star says, quickly. It ain't that unbelievable. Rainbow knows Star's mood often changes.

The childs wakes, distracting Rainbow as it snuffles for food.

'I must take the childs to the meeting place for milk,' Rainbow says, frowning at Star, the conversation clearly not forgotten.

Clay touches Rainbow's arm as they passes. 'Us'll talk later.'

Rainbow nods and ducks out.

'Rainbow do not believe me,' Star says, stomach knotted. 'I should not even be speaking to you.'

'This ain't the first time we have spoken of things that ain't usual. You listened to me and now it is my turn. What is it you must do for Lightning?' Clay asks.

Unfolding their palm, Star shows Clay the small red berry clasped within. Clay gasps.

'What is it?' Star asks.

'I has seen this afore,' Clay says. 'Us must hurry.'

Clay do not wait for Star but takes the half-empty rednut cup next to Lightning and cradling Lightning's head, presses the cup to their lips. As the spiked-tea trickles in, Clay motions to Star to put the berry into Lightning's mouth.

There is a gurgling sound and Lightning coughs, but when checking Lightning's mouth with a finger, the berry is gone.

'What now?' Star asks.

'Us wait,' Clay says.

BETTY

The children's hut has the pungent smell of unwashed bodies and excrement, which does not help Betty's indescribable agonies. She cannot raise her arm, strapped as it is in rough sacking and smeared with some type of repulsive muddy mixture—certainly not something she recognises from before. Her dress is ruined, soaked with blood and the oily flesh of the grey monster that fell atop her. To make matters worse, Betty had to endure the shame of being helped back to the 'mune by Newt, who dispatched the monsters, with Master's help of course.

Where is Master? Betty looks for him in the dark but can only make out his shoes, placed near the entrance, their polished leather visible in the strip of light that seeps under it. Her own feet are also without the proper coverings. In fact, it appears the 'mune have stripped her of all valuable belongings. At least she is still wearing her dress. Is she a prisoner here?

'Master,' she hisses, not wanting to draw attention to herself, or suffer further indignities at the hands of the Elders.

When there is no answer, she shuffles across the grass matting, which is difficult what with every movement causing a spike of pain down her injured arm and having to hold her skirts to maintain modesty. It does not matter that there is no one here to witness it. God has eyes everywhere.

Master is prostrate at the other end of the hut, behind a row of hanging beds. Why do the 'mune still keep them when the children must be far too big now? Perhaps, with the limited food and loose morals, the children have failed to grow properly. Or like that awful child, Clay, have caused themselves bodily damage with their savage ways.

Betty listens hard but hears nothing but the murmur of adult voices outside. There is no sign of the whimpers and squeals of young children.

Leaning across the beds, for there is not the room to manoeuvre around them, Betty sees Master's face looks grey, as if the beasts have left an imprint on him. The women have not stripped him of aught but his shoes, unlike her. His waistcoat, dress shirt and breeches appear intact, albeit muddied. He has no obvious wounds, but he is not breathing as he should, and the rise of his chest is stuttered.

Betty shuffles back at the sound of the door being pulled aside. She closes her eyes, pretends she is not yet awake. It is the only way she can think of to learn more about the 'mune's intentions. People speak more freely when they think no one is listening.

From under her lids, Betty sees Newt enter the hut. Damfino. She will not learn aught from the mute, but a few seconds after, Tattio also enters, dragging in a sack. The sun lights their progress as Newt checks Master, putting an ear to his mouth, before raising him up, while Tattio wedges the sack, which spills dried leaves, under him, until his upper body is higher than the rest of his length. Betty is surprised by how old Tattio looks.

It isn't long before Master's breathing eases. Can it be the women are trying to help? More likely they want information, and no doubt Molly will be the one to try to prise it out of them. But they underestimate Master. When Master wakes, he will teach them a thing or two. Betty shivers—Master's lessons are not always pleasant.

LIGHTNING

Lightning wakes with eyes so dry, it is as if they bin rubbed with sea. The pain in the cave, so debilitating afore, is gone, but there is summat that constricts movement. Reaching down, Lightning discovers a wrapping, gripping their body tight.

As they tries to loosen it, a scent is released: bitter and metallic.

The belly is flat under it. Ain't the childs no longer within?

Faces now come into focus: Star and Clay, leaning over, close enough that breath might be caught.

'The childs,' Lightning says, throat feeling like the dried husk of a rednut.

'It is arrived safe,' Clay says, grabbing the hand Lightning uses to tear at the wrapping.

Lightning tries to push Clay away but finds it hard to connect. It's like swatting a bug in the dark, nowt is seen sharp enough.

'Take it slowly, you is healing,' Star says, grasping Lightning's other hand.

Lightning stiffens. Must be summat wrong if Star is touching the body.

'I cannot move as I want,' Lightning says.

Star and Clay share a look Lightning dun understand, which makes anger bubble deep inside. 'Tell me!'

'You was in the other place for some days,' Clay says, voice wavering.

'I dun remember,' Lightning snaps, but it ain't wholly true. There is memories of heaviness, of sinking neath the sand, of voices too far away to hear and emptiness: summat lost.

'I will find Rainbow,' Clay says, clearly keen to leave the hut. 'And the childs. So you can witness it is safe. And Elder Tattio to check healing.'

Lightning dun wish to see the childs that caused this harm, but it is good that Clay is leaving. Lightning dun need protection, just truth and Clay dun speak it.

Ignoring the spinning in the head, round and round like a childs game, Lightning shifts to face Star, who is crouched beside. 'Why is these cloths tight around me?'

At least Star will not soften the words.

'Elder Newt cut the childs out,' Star says.

Lightning vomits, the bitter taste of spiked-tea washing the mouth. It trickles onto the mat in a thread. Star dun attempt to clean it up or explain further. Dun seem to want to.

'Why ain't I passed if flesh bin cut?' Lightning demands.

It dun make no sense.

Only now do Star look uncomfortable, biting their lip so hard there is indents.

'It is a miracle,' Star says.

Even feeling the sickness, Lightning sees Star's words dun fit the face they wears.

STAR

To heal—
truth
must be hidden.

Star cannot tell Lightning bout the berry, though it pains em not to. The way the herbs spread through Lightning's body, glowing under the skin, like lightberries. It is proof that there is truth in Doctor's words, for there ain't no other explanation for Lightning's swift recovery when, as Lightning said, once flesh bin so deeply cut, they should have passed.

Star must find a way to show the Mune the truth of the island, the rumbling beast that lies neath waiting to breathe fire, cause words ain't enough. Who cept Clay will believe Star passed through the sacred water to a different place, and learned this information?

Can other friends be trusted with the things Star has witnessed? They all seek answers: Rainbow from the trees, and now Lightning needs a reason for recovery. But the persons said Star must keep the metal box hidden until the Mune is safe in the Elders' old land.

'I will get you food,' Star says, desperate to leave the hut and Lightning's scrutiny. 'Elder Tattio is arrived.'

Star heads to the meeting place but Clay ain't in the circle with Rainbow as expected.

'Is it true that Lightning has returned to us?' Elder Rosie asks, shuffling towards Star, whilst rocking the new childs, who seems content sucking on a finger.

Star nods.

'Thank God and the island for summat good this day.'

'Has Clay gone for water?' Star asks, not wanting to admit they still do not know what else has occurred.

'Left recent,' Elder Rosie says, kissing the childs damp forehead, where thick, black, curly hair springs up like young plants.

Star glances around. Thunder is near the food hut with Elder Newt, busy gutting beasts and Rainbow is sitting with the other chillun in the circle. There ain't no one available for guardianship.

'I need a bloodtime guardian, but I will find Clay,' Star says quickly.

Elder Rosie sighs. 'No further than the cave, mind. Be watchful, 'appen the beasts is growing.'

BETTY

Master's breathing is easier since the women raised him up, and he has started to snore, which Betty thinks must be a good thing, as it is something he does when well and simply asleep, rather than crushed under a monster. A few moments ago, someone left bowls of food in the doorway. They didn't enter, just pushed them through a small gap in the screen. Betty shuffles over and picks one up to sniff it. She tosses it down, not willing to eat the stewed muck they have offered up. What if the 'mune have added poison to it? She wouldn't put it past them.

She leans back against the wall and groans. The pain in her arm is not abating and it's so hot in here that even her eyelids are perspiring.

'Bessie? Where the devil am I?'

Master is awake! She is no longer alone. If it weren't so dark, he'd see Betty's smile, stretching across her face.

'I am here, Master. By your side as always.'

'I cannot see you.'

'I will come to you, Master.'

Betty shuffles across the hut, this time pausing to move the line of beds out of the way. It is hard to do, what with only one useful arm and the beds so cumbersome. They are barely more than sticks and old woollen dresses, roped together. She wasn't part of the industry when they were being made, instead keeping a close vigil on the shore, hoping for rescue.

Who is going to rescue them now? Master's family thinks they are in Yorkshire, on a tour celebrating their engagement. Betty checks herself—now is not the time to dwell on their future.

'Are you well?' Master asks, as Betty sits down next to him, exhaustion soaking through to her petticoats.

'As can be expected,' Betty replies, hiding the grimace as she rests her injured arm in her skirts, out of Master's sight.

Master is quiet for some time.

'Perhaps,' he finally says, 'the women here are not so different from you, for they have tended to me, as is their wont.'

Betty doesn't respond, doesn't know what she thinks about the 'mune, for it is true they have tended to their injuries, but they will not have done it freely, for in her experience there is always a price to be paid.

'I feel nothing but sympathy for these women,' Master continues. 'They have had no firm hand to guide them, forced to do men's work. They are all but lost.'

Betty frowns, thinking about the absurd number of gatherings at the meeting place those first few weeks after they arrived on the island, the baskets of shells used to make decisions, and how eager some were to discard their dresses and take up spears.

'You are right, Master,' she says. 'They lack guidance.'

'Do not fear, Bessie,' Master says. 'I will help them.'

CLAY

There ain't no sign of the beasts near the cave, and no movement to witness amongst the trees, but there is a change in the air. It is heavier to breathe. The faint smell, which reminds Clay of the bowbird's broken eggs, with their half-formed chicks, is stronger, more pungent.

Clay feels no trepidation entering the damp cave, but instead there is a feeling of curiosity, of what might be heard from the bottom of the well. The fear, carried like a tunic weighed with rocks since Betty accused em of being possessed by the devil, is shed. The peoples neath the well saved Lightning with their herbs, and perhaps it is summat Clay might learn, to help others during a childs' arrival or to heal after hurt: more than the spiked-tea, yellow root and hush-hush leaves offer.

Putting the buckets down onto the slick black rocks, Clay looks over the lip of the well, concentrating hard to see the moon that Star described.

'Clay?'

Clay jumps at the sound, nearly losing balance and slipping backwards, afore realising it comes from behind, near the entrance of the cave and not from the water.

'Star?' Clay asks, turning.

'I bin looking for you,' Star says, walking forwards.

Clay frowns. There is a shadow behind Star, summat that ain't yet close enough to see.

As the shape draws closer, it is accompanied by a lumbering tread. A beast is outside, just moments away from Star. It stops and sniffs the air. It must be Star's bloodtime that has drawn it to the cave.

'Walk slowly to me,' Clay says, placing a finger to their lips.

They must find summat quickly to mask the bloodtime scent and distract the beast.

'The rags,' Clay says, drawing water from the well.

As Star hands Clay the bloodied cloth from the rednut cup, summat drops to the floor and bounces away, but there ain't time to see what it is.

Clay drenches Star's legs with water from the bucket, diluting any remaining scent, afore moving to the front of the cave with the rags.

'Wait here.'

'Be careful.' Star's whole body is shaking, more than it would from the chill of the water.

'It ain't going to hurt me,' Clay says, moving further away, rags clasped tightly.

'You do not know that!' Star voice sounds tight.

'I know it, like you know words,' Clay says, standing tall.

BETTY

Betty is hungry and the waiting is interminable, but as least Master has perked up and is able to raise himself to a seated position without assistance. There have been no more visitors to the nursery hut since he awoke.

'Tell me about these creatures,' Master says, taking a sip of water from the cup Betty holds close to his lips.

'Beasts,' Betty says, frowning.

She wonders if Master is imagining them stuffed and on display at the Manor. Many of his acquaintances have exotic pets in their stables and animal skins adorning their floors.

'There is something to be admired in them,' Master says, thoughtfully. 'They are creatures of purpose.'

'They are monsters,' Betty says sharply, spilling the water.

'Careful now, Mistress Bessie,' Master says, wiping droplets from his shirt. 'One must maintain one's decorum even in the most trying of situations.'

'They nearly killed you!'

'They were merely acting according to their true nature, as we all do when faced with danger.' Master pushes away the cup. 'I must speak with the Mune, as you call them, to discover more about these creatures' behaviour.'

Betty sits back and smooths down her skirts, as best she can. She must be careful with the delicate fabric, for she will not be seen in one of those ghastly coverings the women wear, with all flesh on display. Thankfully Master has not yet been forced to witness their nakedness and control his natural urges.

Betty does worry that Master's insatiable quest for knowledge will surely be the death of them. It is as if he is doing nothing more dangerous here than reading one of his scientific stories.

'Introductions must be made,' Master says. 'And soon.'

Betty would rather walk into the sea or take her chances on the sand, than say one more word to the women here.

'I wish to return home,' she mumbles, longing for a cup of Cook's warmed milk, a plate of food that she can recognise, a warm bath and a feather bed to ease her aching bones.

Master frowns. 'You said yourself that these women need my assistance. Who else is there to put them back on the right path? To protect them?'

'They do not listen to reason,' Betty says, thinking about the months spent amongst them.

'They will listen to me,' Master says, with authority.

He pats Betty's knee, but instead of the usual gratefulness, she feels agitated.

CLAY

Clay approaches the beast, each foot placed carefully on the damp cave floor, so as not to frighten it with sudden movement. Star has listened to Clay for once and moved out of sight behind the cave wall. If there is to be a connection with this creature, for they is all different in temperament, there must be no distraction. Clay, like the rest of the Mune, has witnessed their frenzy when blood flows.

Clay draws in a breath. The beast is now just an arms-length away, but it appears relaxed rather than tight, even though it is displaying its teeth, which protrude in two sharp points.

Is it a smile? Clay would like to imagine it is but is too guarded to risk being mistaken.

Stopping at the mouth of the cave, ignoring the pain deep in the leg, Clay squats down to the same height as the beast. There ain't no sense in towering over it—Clay remembers only too well that feeling of dread when in the shadow of Betty.

Reaching out, offering it Star's bloody rags, Clay is careful to fix a neutral expression on their face. There must be no fear shown.

The beast snorts as it catches the scent of the blood but remains as calm as Clay pretends to be. Reaching forward, Clay gently lays the rags on the floor between em and moves back. This close, with the sun on its back, Clay can see its hide is different from the others that needed tending to. Afore, in the cave, the skin was dry and cracked without water. It now appears thinner and smoother, as if it dun need the constant relief.

As the beast inches forward, Clay stays as still as possible, to show there is nowt hidden, no spear or net that might cause injury or pain. The beasts dun see well, and it might mistake

Clay's caution for hunting. After a few moments, which feel like many more, the beast drags the rags backwards, its tiny, black, protruding eyes never leaving Clay's face.

Then unexpectedly, it lies down, its body obscuring the rags, reminding Clay of the chillun when they attach emself to a scrap of cloth or one of the wooden toys Rainbow make, that seem to give comfort.

Clay reaches out and places a hand on the beast's side, careful to stay clear of its head. There is a gentle thud that ripples under the beast's skin, much slower than Clay's heartbeat.

Clay sits for some time with one hand on the beast's body. It feels right, summat they both need. There is more to these creatures than the Mune understands.

One thing is certain though, if Star was not at the back of the cave witnessing this moment, no one would believe it.

STAR

Fear
hunts prey.
Scent must be shed.

Clay's hand is pressed against the beast as if it is Rainbow's leg neath and not a dangerous, vicious creature. Star cannot stop shaking and it ain't the cold in the back of the cave that drills through skin but worry. Why do the beast curl up as if in sleep when bloody rags should send it mad? Is this beast different from others?

A loud voice comes from outside the cave, interrupting Star's thoughts. It sounds like Thunder. The beast rises in response. Star turns away from Clay, presses their hands to their ears. They do not want to hear their friend hurt, especially when they ain't got no help to offer.

'Star?'

Clay's voice, drawing closer, and the lumber of heavy tread.

Clay is safe?

Star wipes away tears, shed with imagining the worst, and peers around the cave wall into the main area. Clay is drawing the beast inside, rags clutched tightly, to where it is dark enough to be unseen whilst the lightberries lay undisturbed.

'The Mune dun understand,' Clay says. 'Please help me.'

Clay never asks Star for nowt, is always the one who tends to others, often ignoring their own discomfort.

Taking a deep breath in, Star steps out into the main section of the cave, conscious of bloodtime dripping sporadically onto skin. Each foot pressed against the cave floor feels as dangerous as treading on sand.

'Hurry,' Clay says.

Star cannot hurry, not knowing how to move faster, legs heavy with dread, remembering how Molly was pulled down in the water. But the beast do not move as Star passes close. Star must trust that Clay understands what ain't usual.

'Star? Is you alone?'

Thunder is at the entrance to the cave, brandishing a spear.

'Clay is collecting water from the sacred well,' Star says, trying to keep their voice steady. 'What is wrong?'

'You must return to the Mune, there is work to do.'

Thunder's eyes drift down to Star's feet.

'Us is nearly ready to return,' Star says, swallowing, imagining Thunder can see bloodtime dripping down skin like damp on the cave walls.

'Us is fine,' Clay calls out.

'Elder Newt is at the shore. There bin sightings.' Thunder clutches their spear tighter.

'Beasts?' Star asks, trying to hold Thunder's gaze and not blink. 'How is Lightning?' Star adds.

'Well enough to fight bout joining in the hunt.'

Thunder turns but then pauses.

'Us do not need a spear, us is safe here,' Star says, not wholly convinced yet the words is true.

BETTY

It is Tattio that is the first to visit the chillun's hut with Master awake. She ducks through the small doorway, carrying a cloth bag, and do not close the screen behind her.

Master's skin looks grey and drawn in the natural light that pours through, worse than Betty first thought.

'And you are?' Master says, voice booming, by way of introduction.

Betty winces but tries her best not to let it show. Clearly, Master has not attended to her words of warning about these women.

Tattio, hunched over due to the low ceiling, if that's what the rough, twisted grass can be called, says nothing but Betty notices her jaw tighten in response.

'Lord Henry Harrington.' Master nods in Tattio's direction. 'Much obliged by your ministrations in my hour of need.'

Tattio does not acknowledge him, which causes Master to frown, but not from continuing to speak. It is as if the mood in the hut fails to touch him.

'Lord Harrington,' he says again. 'Are you in charge here?' He speaks slowly, every syllable pronounced, as if Tattio cannot comprehend his words.

'They are all in charge,' Betty huffs, unable to hold back any longer. 'She can understand you perfectly.'

Why do he not listen? Betty feels every uncomfortable moment in the claustrophobic space, like a corset bound too tight.

Master ignores Betty's outburst and Betty feels her cheeks getting hot as he dismisses her with a wave of his still outstretched hand.

'You are one who heals so, to an educated mind, it would make sense that you are in charge,' he declares.

'Dat is yer way, not us,' Tattio says, finally breaking her silence.

'Well, it's a good job I'm here to help you sort out this muddle,' Master smiles.

'Us dun need no help,' Tattio says, firmly. 'It is we who rescued you.'

'I am better equipped now I have more information.'

'Dat will make my job easier,' Tattio says calmly, dropping the bag next to Master and turning to Betty. 'De powder will ease any pain,' she says, her focus on Betty's arm, 'and rags should you need dem.'

Betty feels her cheeks burn. These are private womanly matters, not to be discussed in front of Master.

'Where are the things that were stolen from me?' Betty snaps, feeling great discomfort under Tattio's glare.

'Us have no need for trinkets here, as well you know,' Tattio says.

'Where are they then?' Betty raises her voice. 'I demand they be returned.'

'De Mune mend dem.' Tattio's response brings another flush to Betty's cheek. 'Dey will be returned in good time.'

'I wish them to be returned immediately,' Betty says, concerned now that they will be used for barter.

Tattio does not respond or linger further, failing to have even the good grace to wish them good health or to close the screen behind her.

Master raises himself up.

'You will have to tend to my needs, now that you have angered that foreign woman,' he says.

Betty wants to assure Master that Tattio is not foreign but she don't. Instead, she forces herself back to Master's side and opens the cloth bag, though it is a struggle with her arm not easily moved. Inside is a rednut cup, ropes and rags, as well as a bundle of herbs and smaller stiff bags of powder of some sort, which Betty has no idea how to identify. She do not wish to poison them.

'She will return,' Betty says, confidently, tying the bag back up.

The 'mune will not leave them unattended, for surely, they have many questions.

'It is not in man's nature to wait upon a woman's whim,' Master says. 'As soon as I am able, I will find someone who can better understand the word of a gentleman.'

As Master closes his eyes, Betty shudders, thinking about the curse, which will visit her soon.

LIGHTNING

Lightning moves quick, away from the chillun's hut. Elder Tattio dun stay as long inside as expected. Still, it bin long enough to hear two voices—one of which spoke words as muddled as Star's. No one in the Mune is saying nowt bout these new peoples, but they must come from somewhere. Another island? Perhaps they arrived by boat?

The Elders said Lightning weren't ready to hunt on the shore, even though with the strangers here, and the beasts venturing further onto the island, they need all to help. Lightning scowls, feels perfectly well now their body ain't heavy with childs.

Heading round the back of the food hut, Lightning avoids the meeting place. The chillun will all be in the shade now, what with the sun so high. Lightning dun want to sit and make cluck-cluck noises like the others. They agreed to carry, not to care.

Taking one of the spears from the earth at the side of the food hut, Lightning heads to the path. There is answers needed from Star and Clay. Lightning ain't forgot Star's face and the lies spoken bout recovery.

Lightning hotfoots it down the dust path to discover Thunder at the entrance of the cave. Lightning hides in the wood, waiting for Thunder to leave. Thunder dun know Star well, like Lightning do, and misses the change in Star's voice on speaking and Star's clenched hands, which normally hang loose by the side when they is looking at the sky. Star is also without the rednut cup, Lightning can smell bloodtime, like it bin coming from within emself. It dun make no sense, what with the beasts needing the offerings.

'Lightning?'

It's Rainbow, coming up the dust path behind. Lightning puts a finger to their lips and motions Rainbow to stay back. Rainbow frowns but ain't one to argue, so is quiet as asked.

Lightning waits until Thunder's dull tread is lost to the shore and Star is back inside the cave, afore stepping forward.

'What is you doing here?' Lightning hisses.

'Clay is taking too long with the water. The Mune need it.'

Lightning nods, points to the cave. 'They is inside but quiet, which ain't normal with em two always questioning.'

'Wait here,' Rainbow says, glancing at the spear in Lightning's hand.

'Words dun protect no one.' Lightning grips the weapon tighter.

'Clay cannot hide the truth from me,' Rainbow says.

Lighting nods. That at least is true.

Lightning mutters to emself, as they watches Rainbow enter the cave, fed up with waiting like some bit of damp bark no one has use for. Staking the spear into the dry earth, for summat to do, Lightning leans against one of the thin trunks of the tunic trees. A voice comes from the tree, rising from the roots—from as deep a place as Lightning was sent after the childs was cut out.

The island is dying.

No. It ain't a voice but a smell, burrowing through the nose and into the head, like an insect breathed in by mistake. It holds the scent of fire and fear. Lightning shakes it away. It do no good to listen to the mind's imaginings, however real it seem.

Maybe the Elders is right and recovery ain't complete.

CLAY

The object which fell to the floor at the back of the cave, is made of a fabric like nowt Clay has seen afore or could begin to imagine. Star said the peoples in the other place gave it em.

Is Star able to approach the beast, resting in the salt pool, without incident cause they's using this object? Or is this beast unconcerned by Star's bloodtime now it has the rags? Clay's mind is spinning with thoughts, none of which is easy to separate into threads, but there might be answers, ways of living with, rather than against, the beasts.

Clay strokes the beast's thick hide. It likes being touched neath the small cut that looks like an ear, but less so on the chest. Clay rubs at the mark, raw on the wrist, the beast's way of saying it weren't happy. It is barely a scratch, already healing after being bathed in the salt pool. It dun mean to, ain't its fault it has teeth sharp as flint.

'Clay?'

Rainbow is at the cave entrance, backlit by the sun. Clay must be careful what is said, for Rainbow will sense what is neath words.

'Clay?' Rainbow calls again. 'The Mune need water. Why is you so delayed?'

'Us bin busy,' Star says, stepping forward in the darkness and standing next to Clay, shielding the beast from sight. 'Can you take the buckets back? They is filled and waiting.'

'Why dun you return with em yerself?' Rainbow asks.

The beast slaps its tail in the water and emits a high-pitched sound, like that blown upon a plucked leaf, held tight between fingers. The cave lights up as the berries is agitated in the pool, Clay cannot prevent it.

Rainbow sucks in a breath, clear as the water in the sacred well, and Clay waits for Rainbow's next reaction.

'Lightning is outside,' Rainbow says, drawing nearer, a frown on their face, 'with a spear.'

'I will not let this creature be injured.' Clay's jaw is tight. 'It ain't any more of a threat than a childs.'

'I will make Lightning understand,' Star says, rearranging their tunic.

The beast lies quietly, the rags now tucked under its bulk, as if it is hiding em. Clay trusts Rainbow with life itself—they never reacts without deep thought. Surely it is safe?

'I will know if this beast means harm,' Rainbow says, crouching down next to Clay, and placing a hand gently on the beast's damp back.

Rainbow concentrates, body as still as when they touches the trees. After some moments, Rainbow lays their face flat on the beast's skin.

Only then do Clay exhale.

STAR

Words
wound.
Deep as spears.

Star finds Lightning jabbing a spear in the ground, just off the dust path opposite the cave. Their skin looks red, which is odd—the sun do not normally touch em with its heat. There is also a deep frown between their eyes that do not disappear with blinking.

'What did you do to return me to the Mune?' Lightning asks. 'I dun feel proper.'

Star for once, is lost for words. Could the red berry have done more than mend Lightning's body? Clay said voices started to be heard more often, after travelling through the well. Has the berry changed the ears?

'What do you mean?' Star asks, keen to know but keeping their face neutral, though it's hard with Lightning squinting like that.

'It's nowt,' Lightning says, scowling, and more like emself again.

'Takes time to heal,' Star tries.

Lightning's gaze penetrates, making Star feel chilled. 'What you doing in there that take so long?'

'Us bin worried bout the water, what with the strangers arriving.'

'What's the sacred well got to do with em?'

Star decides to use this as a test. If Lightning can be persuaded, maybe the rest of the Mune might listen?

'I has seen the moon at the bottom of the well. So has Clay.'

'The moon is in the sky,' Lightning says, back to jabbing the earth. 'Where yer head is stuck.'

'There is another place,' Star continues, trying not to be hurt by Lightning's words. 'Different from here, reached through the water.'

Lightning laughs and it ain't a kind sound. 'Next yer be saying the persons in the chillun's hut came from there, swimming like beasts when the tide is full.'

Star says nowt more. Maybe silence will help Lightning understand, cause Star's words is bouncing off, like stones dropped on rock.

'I'm going in,' Lightning says. 'Done with waiting.'

Star grabs Lightning's spear and holds on tight. 'Not with this,' Star says, finding courage, which ain't normally there.

'I ain't nowt without the spear.' Lightning's eyes water as they lets go and the spear drops to the ground.

'You carried a childs,' Star says, 'that take more strength than killing.'

BETTY

Master is improving quicker than expected and is now able to move his limbs after a fashion. Perhaps it is the desire to toilet or to bathe. The pungent odour of her own perspiration is enough to turn Betty's stomach. How many days has it been? It is difficult to know when it is marked by bowls of slop and tea, which make the day drag.

'Assist me, Bessie,' Master says, shuffling towards the opening.

He do not seem to care that his breeches are soiled, the stain spreading with every movement.

'It is not easy to raise oneself up when one has been forced to be still,' he adds.

Betty crawls to the screen, which was pulled across last night when darkness fell. It is quiet in the camp, the sun yet to rise fully past the grey rock, but there is enough light to see the other huts.

Betty pulls back, stiffens. There is movement outside, the light pad of naked feet on dust. The 'mune never used to rise this early.

'What is it Bessie?' Master asks.

'Nowt to worry about,' Betty says.

'Nothing,' Master corrects. 'You are a lady now and must present yourself as such. None of this gutter talk.'

Betty nods, straightening her dress. Master is right. It is imperative she present herself with good grace and bearing, for one is always judged by appearance.

With the 'mune quiet again, Betty ducks through the doorway, turning back to assist Master. She is glad whoever was creeping around the camp is gone, because it is not a graceful scene. Master stumbles and clutches onto her for support but he is a heavy man, and she is unable to maintain an upright position, falling to the floor with the weight of him. She gasps as her injured arm takes the weight.

Stomach filled with dread, Betty is surprised when instead of anger and reproach, Master unexpectedly laughs, a bellow that cuts through the silence of the camp. If the 'mune were not aware of their movements, they most certainly are now.

Out of nowhere, two persons come to assist them. Likely they were spying on them. They are not much younger than Betty, two slender girls with long hair and smooth skin. Are they visitors to the island too? Has there been another shipwreck? They are wearing the dreadful stiff tunics, which the 'mune favour, leaving little to the imagination. The skin on the dark one glistens as if they have been bathing and are not yet dry. Betty shakes the pair off, feels quite nauseated at their touch. It is not proper.

'I am quite capable of standing,' she snaps, gritting her teeth and struggling to get purchase and rise.

As Betty bathes in the dust, they turn their attention to Master and assist him instead. They appear strong and he accepts their help, perhaps because his legs have yet to remember their purpose, being so useless these past few days. He wobbles but, before long, is upright. It is only then that Betty sees how tall one of the girls is. She feels a brief rush of sympathy for her, for they also appear to have been cursed with thick hair above the lip. There are things that can be done for women who look fit for the freak show.

Betty will advise them on how to disguise it. It will be good practice for when she is Lady of the Manor and must manage the servants.

It seems that her purpose on the island may not have changed. She must help Master lead the women back to the path of righteousness.

STAR

Elders—
rigid
as shell paths.

It has fallen to Star to tend to the beast until the sun lifts itself above the sea again, cause it ain't uncommon for em to wander, so they will not be missed. It ain't a hard task, the beast is content to lie in the pool, occasionally beating its tail and lighting up the cave, the rags tucked securely underneath it. The only sound is the bubbles when it chooses to breathe through the water. It seems it has that choice.

Star pats the beast on the side one last time, afore heading to the front of the cave. Lightning should have arrived by now with food, for the beast must need sustenance. What has kept em?

It is Clay that finally limps up the path, carrying a bucket.

'Where is the others?' Star whispers.

'They bin delayed by the strangers. Us is safe for now. The Mune's eyes is fixed on em.'

Star nods. The distraction is a good thing, for it gives em the day to decide what best to do. The beast cannot be kept hidden in the cave for much longer. It must be reunited with others like itself. It has its own Mune in the sea, where it is safest.

Clay passes the bucket to Star and moves straight towards the beast, tossing some dried fish into the pool. The beast sniffs the air and then falls on its side, exposing its belly and lighting up the cave with the movement. It is as if it trusts Clay with its pale underside, that part of it that is softer and more easily gutted.

Clay do not move to rub it, no doubt the last time, and the hurt, is still in the front of its mind. Perhaps it is a test?

'Look,' Clay says, frowning.

Star moves back across to where Clay is pointing. There is a small red lump buried in the beast's skin, near its back legs, which has caught the light.

'What is that?' Star asks, peering closer.

'It is like em stones that Betty arrived with that is worn on a string round the neck. The ones Elder Rosie is mending,' Clay says.

Star wants to touch it, to feel the surface, check it is not a trick of the lightberries or the shadows that dance on the cave walls, but dare not get too close.

'It is as if it has always bin there,' Star says, staring at the small round object sunk deep into the beast's hide, in its stomach, like the hole in a childs belly once the cord is cut.

BETTY

Betty is seated at the meeting place alone. The 'mune has still not yet risen. The two girls that helped Master to stand have taken him to the section in the woods they use to toilet. He is not quite ready to walk unaided.

Betty scowls.

They were not both girls and Master does not yet realise he has been tricked. The taller one is, in fact, a boy, with a deep voice that matches Master's. His appearance is clearly a disguise to fool them into thinking that they are not in danger of attack, as men are apt to do when faced with a superior of their sex. The boy had shrunk away when Betty, not able to disguise her horror, had shown it plainly on her face.

Master had not been close enough to witness the brief exchange, and Betty, in shock, had not had the courage to tell Master, lest his good mood change.

It is possible the children here do not have the mental faculties to understand their place in the world. She thinks of Clay, and Lightning, the interminable questions, and how they had not an ounce of regard for their own safety when she knew them. It would not surprise Betty for any child left under the guidance of Sarah, Rosie and Molly to be lacking in mental agility. Betty glances around. Where is Molly? She were always the first to rise, apart from the mute. She expected to see her as soon as they arrived at the 'mune, always with her nose in everything, pretending she cared.

Betty shivers with disgust, cannot push from her mind that she might be in some way responsible for this abomination. It were her suggestion they bring the children up as one, but not like this. The devil has clearly been at play.

Betty crosses herself, mutters a quick prayer.

The Lord is my strength and defence. May his words heal me.

She must tell Master about the boy at the first opportunity. It is evidence of the madness of the island and the 'mune. It might be enough to persuade him to leave.

They are returning. Betty recognises the shuffle of Master's shoes, which make a different sound when set down upon the ground. There is now only one of the 'mune helping him, the dark girl. Is she a girl? It is hard to tell with the tunic skimming the curves one should be proud of.

At least Master is gaining strength, not needing two arms for support.

Betty must content herself with the fact that Master will soon be back to his usual self. She holds in a breath as the dark one helps Master to sit down. There is much relief when they say, in a voice with female qualities, that they must leave them, they have tasks to attend to. Perhaps it is only the one boy here who does not know if they are Adam or Eve.

LIGHTNING

Lightning dun know what to make of the strangers. They dresses fancy, speaks funny and dun seem grateful for nowt, as if the Mune is there to please em. They dun seem comfortable neither. The one that needed an arm to walk, had tried to hide their nature, like they's summat Lightning ain't witnessed afore. Lightning had turned away once they was crouched, which seemed to make em content, but what kind of person fears the body and its waste? What goes in come out—it's nowt but nature. And calling em both lassies, whatever that mean, in the same tone Elder Sarah used when they done summat wrong as chillun. Lightning ain't here to please no one that dun please back, especially when what's meant is muddied like dirty water.

The taller one, Master, from the wood, is now settled by the fire but dun say thank you for help or offer up summat in return. They's both sitting there like sacks of sea, no help to no one, when they could be getting the Mune ready for breakfast.

Is that why Rainbow left so sudden? Fed up of em expecting? Or was it cause of Betty in the long tunic? Betty said summat to Rainbow with a face pinched like they bin smelling rotting fish. Lightning dun remember Betty from afore, but Clay said Betty was not kind and Lightning's beginning to think that there might be truth in that.

Anyways. The Elders can deal with it. Ain't Lightning's problem. Got enough to do and thinking dun put food on the table.

Lightning grabs a spear from the food hut and heads out to the cave. Can't be too careful whatever Clay think bout the beast and anyways, they need to feed it. There could be other beasts when out hunting that ain't the same, like these peoples that have come. Yesterday Star said the peoples came from the water and Lightning had laughed. Lightning knows what happens when you go under the sea—ain't no breath to be had without the sky.

Scowling, Lightning picks up their pace, fast enough to kick up dust on the dry path that winds around the grey rock. They's later than what bin planned.

Leaving the path, Lightning heads past the tunic trees and deeper into the wood where the rednut trees start to grow and the jumps like to play. Last night a trap bin set, full of the sweet yellow berries the jumps like to eat and covered with the thick green leaves. The jumps is lazy, wanting always to play. They take food where they can.

There is a jump, trapped in the woven bark, seemingly given up fighting to be free, and laying there like it's already passed. Has it bin there all night? Lightning takes a hush-hush leaf, rolls it in the hand and presses it into the jump's mouth. The kill will be quick but all creatures deserve a good thought afore death.

The life taken, Lightning wipes the blood on the ground, picks up the dead jump and traces their way to the shore, in case the beast dun like nowt to eat but fish.

Lightning stops short on the shell path, near what's left of the ship. There's a few silver fish washed up on the sand, which ain't usual and they is already dead. Maybe Elder Newt left em or the beasts bin playing a game.

When Lightning picks one up, it's warm and black on the belly, like it's bin cooked a bit.

No matter, it's only for the beast.

CLAY

The beast dun eat the dead jump Lightning arrives with, or the fish. It's still on its side like it dun have the will to move.

'I think it is sick,' Clay says to Star, worried.

'It ain't sick,' Rainbow says, hand on its side. 'I'd feel it.'

'Maybe it just dun eat like we do,' Lightning says, tossing the rotting jump carcass out of the cave.

Clay stands, a frown forming.

'Maybe it needs others like it? I felt summat similar while away from the Mune,' Star suggests.

'When you bin away?' Lightning demands, arms crossed.

'You was ill in the other place. Star dun keep it from you,' Clay says, hoping that might soothe Lightning's temper, which is back to being quick to spark.

'Through the well?' Lightning asks, eyebrows raised, and laughing.

Star sighs.

'Look for yerself,' Clay suggests.

Lightning will clearly need to experience it to form any belief.

'Jump in the well? Dun you care for me?' Lightning puts their hands on their hips.

'I will come too,' Rainbow says, leaving the beast's side.

Lightning pauses, maybe realising that Clay would stop Rainbow if they fears any hurt might come to pass.

'The peoples in the well helped me to make you well after the childs. They gave me berries,' Star says, biting their lip.

'I knew it weren't no miracle.'

Maybe Lightning is thinking of the risk Star took to help em as they speaks, cause their voice softens. 'When I left the Mune, the strangers was seated at the meeting place,' Lightning says.

'Us must go now then,' Rainbow decides.

'I brought summat else back with me that will help,' Star says.

'More herbs?' Lightning asks, raising their eyebrows.

Clay frowns as Star shakes a jar, and rushes to the back of the cave. Why has Star kept secrets when there ain't no need?

Clay checks the beast is still resting afore following Star through the partition and to the sacred well. With some difficulty, Star shifts one of the big, black pitted rocks aside. There is a metal box in the dip and other things Clay dun recognise. Star removes the box, clicks open the lid and takes out a clear piece of cloth.

'It will help you to breathe but there is only one.'

'Rainbow must have it. I can hold breath inside when needed,' Lightning says.

Clay watches as Star fixes it to Rainbow's face. It moulds itself against the chin and lips, like a cupped hand.

'You must travel as nature intended,' Star says.

As Rainbow and Lightning shed their tunics, Clay feels a moment of panic deep in the pit of their stomach. The beasts have changed. What if it's the same for the water?

'Us will be fine as you both was,' Rainbow says, lifting the face covering and kissing Clay afore stepping over the edge of the sacred well and plummeting down.

'You dun get rid of us that easy.' Lightning's spirit has returned, and they follows close behind.

As the ripples still, Star takes Clay's hand, which is unexpected.

'We need em to understand for change to happen. There is strength in many voices.'

Clay cannot argue with that.

THE MUNE 287

BETTY

The smell of the 'mune seated so close sickens Betty, it mixes with the putrid fish drying on lines close by and makes her stomach turn. In contrast, Master seems comfortable, as if he is at the head of a table rather than on his bottom in a dusty circle. Do the younger children not know it is rude to stare? Clearly not, as Betty is forced to push one of them away, trying to hook a grubby finger in the brocade on the hem of her dress. They are no better than street urchins. It is odd that she do not recognise any of the children though.

'Where is Molly?' Betty asks. Surely Molly cannot be at ease with this lack of discipline? As irritating as she is, her snout in everything, she has at least got reasonable manners.

'Elder Molly is passed,' a woman says.

'And who are you?' Betty snipes, irritated that she did not know—that Tattio did not have the good grace to inform her of Molly's death.

'Elder Rosie. Remember?'

Betty frowns. Rosie was no more than four and ten when they arrived here, a little older than Betty. How can her face be so lined and her fingers so knotted, when Betty is at full bloom? She hasn't been gone from the island that long. Perhaps it's the harsh outside life they lead, or the constant heat. The shapeless stiff tunics they wear do not help matters.

'I remember,' Betty mumbles, picking up the rednut bowl despite having no appetite for the mealy porridge.

'Almost as good as home,' Master says, with a bright smile. 'Is there a spoon I might acquire?' he asks.

Tattio snorts, ignoring the request, and tips her bowl to her mouth.

'Like the natives,' Master chuckles, copying. The pulpy, grey food sticks to his beard, where it dribbles down.

Betty grimaces.

'What is the ingredient of this?' Master asks, searching for a handkerchief. His brow is lined with perspiration, yet the sun has barely shown its face above the grey rock.

'Get up early enough and you can help make it,' Tattio says.

Betty bristles, expecting Master to lash out—how dare a woman seek to command him like that! But Master do not even appear to be controlling his rage, he is as interested in the food as he is his insect collection, pinned to boards in his study.

'Is it a root of some type?' Master asks. 'I would be most interested to see where it grows and its foliage.'

'Surely, we are not staying?' Betty asks, frowning.

They have achieved their aim. Master has seen the island and collected several mementos. They are both healed and should leave while they are still sound of mind, unaffected by the devilry here.

'I am not yet finished with my exploration,' Master says, passing his empty bowl to the child that moves around the outside of the circle to collect them. 'I have many questions.'

He nods as if pleased by what he has seen. How can that be? He said himself they were nothing but savages. How can a few plants be of more consequence than her?

'I must speak with you alone,' Betty places her hand on Master's arm to garner his attention, and lowers her voice. 'There are things you do not know that will surely change your mind.'

'Bessie,' Master says, patting her hand. 'A gentleman is never swayed by a woman's loose tongue.'

Betty removes her hand and tucks it amongst her satin skirts, out of reach.

LIGHTNING

It dun need a breath held in as long as it do to touch the bottom of the sunk ship, but it's cold in the well. What feels good in the throat dun feel good touching the body or pressing up the nose—it prickles like handfuls of thorns rubbed against skin. Lightning's relieved to pull emself out of the water and join Rainbow on the hard black ledge.

Star ain't telling fanciful tales, for they ain't bin claimed by the water in the well as feared, breath is still in the body, though it smokes from the mouth like damp fire.

'Us should move from here,' Rainbow says. 'I dun like the feel of it.'

Lightning inhales but smells nowt. Perhaps that is what Rainbow means? The cold that fills you, taking all else. It certainly ain't the same here as the island, and it ain't just the air neither. The walls is smooth and glint like fish in the darkest part of the sea.

Rainbow is right, they need to move, warm the body up cause it shakes of its own accord and is starting to make the teeth hurt. There ain't no other way to go but to the back of the cave.

'An opening,' Rainbow says, pausing by a square cut into the wall, marked by dull green light. 'There is warmth within.'

'Someone's in there?' Lightning checks, wishing for a spear held tight in their hand. Why did they not bring one?

'I think it is a trace left behind,' Rainbow says, twisting the handle. 'Like that on the skin when someone passes by.'

Lightning pushes through first, blinking, getting used to the light that seem to come from dots in the ceiling, as if someone has punched holes in it. There is nowt in the room cept a pile of face coverings in the corner, like Star gave

Rainbow, and a line of bright blue dots on the far wall next to another opening like they came through.

Lightning approaches the dots cautiously, shielding Rainbow, for light can blister skin and Rainbow's skin dun darken, is pale like rednut flesh. What is it? Is there a gap in the wall letting a blue sun creep in? Reaching out to check, summat flickers to life. Lightning pushes Rainbow further back.

A voice: *Welcome to No Place.*

Lightning checks around, clenches their fists. 'Who is speaking? Show yerself!'

No one steps into the room.

A picture has appeared on the wall above where the blue dots was. It is too fancy to bin dun with fingers or bark and it is flat, without the ridges that earth leaves.

'Look,' Rainbow says, voice echoing in the empty space. 'Home.'

It is their island, recognisable by the grey rock and the huts.

The picture starts to move, other parts of the island is shown. It is as if a big eye sees everything, all at once without needing legs to carry it.

'It is a trick!' Lightning scowls. 'The well cause sickness in the head. It is what is wrong with Clay and Star.'

'Wait,' Rainbow says, voice soft, as if there is nowt to fear. 'We cannot ignore what is in front of us, just cause we dun understand it.'

'It is meant to confuse us, as it has confused the others. I dun wish to be trapped in imaginings like em,' Lightning snaps, turning away from the picture.

As Lightning takes another step back from the picture, the door next to it opens.

BETTY

Betty has made her excuses and left the meeting place because Master is under a spell, and it is maddening to witness the 'mune's trickery. She has started to feel invisible, like a trinket worn on the arm: easily discarded. Perhaps it is the bare flesh on display, which all men are wont to admire. She draws her shoulders back, correcting her posture. She must attend to her toilette, clean her attire, set an example to remind Master of home. What else can she do in this disagreeable place?

She do not need assistance to find the dust path that begins by the smallest hut and leads to the sacred cave. It is as ingrained in her mind as the dirt under her fingernails, despite her gloves. She will not be asking for assistance anyway, now she has learned the two that helped Master are Rainbow and Lightning. They are older than she were when she first arrived on the island, which cannot be right. How have they have grown so quickly, with just two year or so passed in England? And how are there infants and babies that were not here before?

It is quiet walking on the path, what with the 'mune still breakfasting, and not yet starting their chores. Perhaps Betty should have offered to fill a bucket, but it did not occur to her, so keen was she to put distance between herself and the community. She will not let the island and its evils consume her, as it has Master.

She pauses. The 'mune will accuse her of being lazy if she does not show willing, like Sarah, who always prefers late mornings to rise. Betty has not yet seen or heard Sarah in the camp. Despite her brashness, Sarah at least kept the children in line. Is she dead too?

Betty sighs, but the air she inhales is not restorative but thick and like treacle in the throat.

A feather drops down like an arrow, coming to rest on the path in front of her. It is a myriad of colours, serving to remind Betty of a rainbow, and the name of the boy that pretends to be a girl, who bears the name she chose for them. She kicks the feather away and shudders, despite the full sun bearing down on her.

The cave is further away than Betty remembers but perhaps it is not distance but heat that slows her down. The temperature makes one sluggish, more inclined to seek respite. She finds a fallen tree and rests upon it, smoothing out her skirts, which are beginning to look old and worn already. There is hope her dress can be rescued, that the mark the beast left on the sleeve can be scrubbed out. Cook would know what to do to rid Betty of this constant reminder: the pain as teeth ripped through her flesh and the weight of the beast as it pressed her into the hard, thorny ground.

She tries to raise her arm, but it is stiff and unyielding under the wraps, and there is a scent of decay. It is a smell remembered from her mother's final days, of bloodstained rags held to her mouth and ruptured sores. Will the 'mune's medicine be enough to cure Betty of her ills, or will she expire here, forgotten? She no longer has a father left to remember her.

She decides to rest for a while longer—regain her strength, then she will find a way to persuade Master to leave the island, and if that fails, contemplate leaving by herself.

LIGHTNING

Lightning dun ever run from danger and ain't running from this creature covered in silver scales that has burst into the room. Even without a spear there is ways of protection.

'Stop!' Rainbow says, holding Lightning back by gripping the arm. 'It ain't a beast!'

As Lightning struggles to get free, the creature puts down a sack and peels the scales back from their head, revealing red-coloured hair and a pale face.

'It is a person,' Rainbow says softly, staring at em without pause.

Maybe it is the hair that has caused this reaction, so similar to Rainbow's, but cut close to the scalp in a second skin.

'It is a stranger,' Lightning snaps, thinking of the two new peoples in the Mune and the troubles they brought with em.

'Do not be frightened,' the person says, stepping forward, hands held at their side. 'I am not here to hurt you.'

'What do you want?' Lightning says, finally managing to shake off Rainbow's tight grip.

'My name is Doctor Stuart. I have brought medicine.' The doctor lifts a clear sack, full of red berries.

'Us dun need no help,' Lightning says.

'You must be Lightning. Star told us all about you.' The doctor smiles and it dun seem false to Lightning.

'You met Star?' Rainbow asks, looking at the sack, mouth hanging open like a fish caught in a net.

Lightning tenses, hands clenched into fists. Rainbow is too trusting.

The doctor nods, their gaze focused on Lightning. 'Are you well now? Did the child survive?'

Lightning feels hot, uncomfortable. How do this person know so much bout em that they dun know emself?

'What did the herbs do to me?' Lightning demands.

'They killed the bacteria and allowed your organs to regenerate…to heal. It is a common… herb…in my world.'

Lightning feels sick.

'What is *my world*?' Rainbow asks, frowning.

Doctor flicks their hand over the picture, and it changes to a green and blue round shape, a jagged grey shape, and the moon. That at least Lightning recognises hanging like it do in the black sky at home. There is ropes knotting the bits together.

'This is your island,' Doctor says, pointing to the jagged shape, 'and this is my world.'

'Yer world is blue and green?' Rainbow asks.

'It's how it looks from the moon,' Doctor says.

'The moon cannot be touched,' Lightning says, sharply. 'However much it might be wished for.'

'Touching it caused your island to appear, and your Elders to disappear,' Doctor says.

'Yer head is stuck in yer imagination, like Star,' Lightning scowls.

'What is all em paintings?' Rainbow asks, hands indicating the wall.

'Part of our research data.'

'What do that mean?' Lightning says.

'The things we have seen,' Doctor says, flicking their hand in front of the wall. Another picture appears.

'The Elders' ship?' Rainbow asks, with a worried frown. 'How is it whole when it is nowt but sticks in the sea?'

'It has been part of my job to record what happened after the…event.'

'Event? What is *event*?' Lightning scowls again.

'We were searching for…' Doctor pauses.

Lightning laughs. The stranger dun understand what they is saying emself!

Rainbow puts a hand on Lightning's arm, but this time it is gentle.

'I think the paintings is easier for us to witness than words,' Rainbow says.

Doctor nods, waves at the screen again. There is a picture of the sacred cave, with many Elders inside. Lightning leans forward. They is wearing long brown tunics and look young. It causes discomfort in the belly looking at those who is painted here, yet have passed.

'This was recorded the day your Elders arrived on the island,' Doctor says, with another flick of the hand. 'When you were just babies.'

'You mean chillun?' Rainbow asks, frowning.

'Yes,' Doctor says. 'And this is what will happen.'

There is now a painting of the grey rock, but it has fire and smoke pouring from the top.

'There ain't fire in the grey rock,' Lightning says. 'Only in the meeting place.'

The picture changes again: dead fish washed up on black sand.

Lightning swallows, stepping closer to the image. 'I seen fish washed up. I thought it was the beasts playing their chillun's games.'

'It is the volcanic nature of the island,' Doctor says. 'If the fish are already dying, you do not have much time. The passageways will become unstable.'

'The sacred well?' Rainbow asks, turning to Lightning. 'I felt heat when I spoke to the trees and summat deep neath, unsettled. What if the beasts is not trying to attack but escape? What if Clay is right?'

Lightning blanches, thinks of the feeling experienced earlier when touching the tunic tree.

The island is dying.

'We will try to help you for as long as we can,' Doctor says. 'It is the least we can do.'

STAR

Cups
hold life.
Water and lost childs.

Star ain't normally one to pace, for it leaves no room for thinking. To think properly is to hold yerself in the moment, not to run away from it, but Rainbow and Lightning bin gone for too long. What is they doing? Isn't it enough to rise from the well and know they is someplace else? That what was said in this cave, is true?

'Breakfast will be over soon, and questions asked,' Star says.

'We cannot leave the beast unattended,' Clay replies. 'What if…?'

There's a crack outside: a snapped branch. Star feels their stomach rise and is glad they ain't eaten yet. Moving across the cave to Clay, finger to lips, Star wills the beast to remain still.

No one calls out to em but that do not mean they ain't there.

In the darkness there is footsteps, barely heard, the lightest touch of skin on rock. Someone is heading towards the back of the cave to the sacred well, and do not want to be noticed. Who would do that?

A jar is shaken and shadows dance behind the partition, and then there is the sound of stone being scraped across rock.

Star has held the breath in so long, it feels like it might fill the cave if exhaled. How do the person know bout the stone?

The beast moves, emits a faint light, enough to see Elder Newt walking towards em, eyebrows raised, carrying Star's metal case.

'I can explain,' Star says, stepping forward.

Elder Newt puts the case down, knows exactly what to do to unlatch it, then takes each object out and studies em.

Has Elder Newt noticed the beast behind em? Clay is only partly shielding it.

Star must distract the Elder.

'Peoples from another place gave those to me to take back when we leave. The island is changing,' Star stutters, adding. 'They said it ain't safe to stay.'

Elder Newt raises a thick eyebrow and points to the sacred well.

Star nods. 'I travelled through.'

'Like me,' Clay says, standing. 'When you found me afore. And Betty.'

The beast shifts again as Clay speaks, nudging Clay with its tail, like a childs wanting more tickling. Elder Newt's attention switches. There ain't no hiding it now.

Elder Newt commands em to step aside with a flick of the hand.

'It ain't hurt us. It ain't going to hurt us,' Clay says, pleading, still yet to move aside, and instead placing a hand back on the beast.

Elder Newt packs up the case and clamps it shut afore slowly moving to the pool. There ain't no urgency in the movements, no anger. Is it curiosity? It is sometimes hard to tell—Elder Newt wears the face like a mask.

Bending down, Elder Newt runs a hand over the beast's side. It responds by rolling over.

Elder Newt frowns as the cave lights up with the movement, their focus on the lump exposed between the beast's legs, which Star now thinks of as the navel, like any childs.

When the Elder turns, there is tears in the corner of their eyes, as if summat sad bin remembered.

BETTY

Betty stifles a scream, the touch on her arm unexpected, so wrapped up is she, in thinking of what must come to pass as she continues her journey to the cave: that woman she saw in the family cottage in the village that denied her parent's existence, holding her red-faced brat of a child. Betty will not live a life unremembered, like her father and mother. She has worked too hard to find her place in the world, one which relies on Master.

How is any of it fair?

'What?' Betty snaps, skin prickling at the touch.

It is Newt, silent, her expression seemingly judging Betty, as always.

Newt is not alone. There are others with her that Betty do not recognise and one is cowering behind a tree, as if they wish not to be near her. She has done nowt to warrant this behaviour!

Newt beckons to her, and there is nowt Betty can do but follow. There might be a beast, or summat worse, one of the 'mune bathing in the pools in the cave, exposing their most private parts, without consideration of what might be witnessed.

Betty is outnumbered both by bodies and spears.

Newt do not enter the cave but continues to the shore. Betty's skirts are heavy, and she is forced to lift them to protect the delicate fabric from the thorny bushes that lie in clumps as they approach the sea. More used to a promenade on Master's arms, and her meals served in her chambers if so required, she has quite forgotten the exhausting nature of this place.

Betty is careful to keep her feet firmly on the shell path and away from the black sand, which glitters in places where the sun hits. Her steps are painful in her satin shoes. They have shrunk, and where the fabric has stiffened, pustules have appeared on her heels. Perhaps, if she leaves the shoes out in the sun they might bleach as light as the shells?

She fair bumps into Newt, who has stopped by the rock pools, where the small silver fish are caught by the tide. But it is not fish contained in the largest pool but a brute of a beast. Betty stiffens. Has Newt brought her here as a sacrifice? Why did she not tell Master of her intentions when leaving?

Newt does not grab Betty's arm or push her forward as expected, and Betty is surprised to find the beast does not notice or care they are there. It behaves as if the pool is a bathtub in the middle of the kitchen, and it is waiting to be scrubbed.

But she does draw in a sharp breath when Newt lays a hand on its side.

The beast rolls over, like a well-trained dog, exposing its stomach above the shallow water.

Newt beckons Betty forward, and points at something between its short legs.

Grimacing, Betty takes the smallest of steps, but it is not enough to witness what the mute points to. Another small step brings Betty close enough to see.

Betty gasps and staggers, and without thinking, grabs onto the arm of the nearest child, who has been standing quietly behind. Pain comes from deep within her, a raw place she has tried to soothe with Master's generosity.

Embedded deep in the beast's skin is the ruby stone given her by Cook when she left Master's service, part of a necklace Lady Harrington destroyed in a fit of pique. Was Molly lying when she told her she wrapped that same gem in the shroud with her babby, moments before it were tossed overboard, and buried at sea? Moments before the ship sunk?

Reaching out, Betty touches the stone and the beast's smooth hide. She gasps as it draws pain from her, a raw wound deep down which has failed to heal.

Tears streak her cheeks as she remembers her babby's blue-tinged skin, how it never uttered a single cry. How, after all the months of praying for its safe arrival, it were stripped from her. Without even a name. There weren't no memorial for her lost child and she must make it right.

'Let the little children come to me and do not hinder them, for they belong in the kingdom of heaven...'

The beast seems calmed by her words as they are spoken aloud, and there is a feeling of lightness inside her as she touches its skin, as if God is listening. She presses on:

'Oh Lord, we commend this little life, which has been such a joy and a blessing to us all, into Your strong and loving hands...'

'We must leave. Others will come.'

In her periphery, Betty sees Newt raise a warning hand, as if to quieten whoever speaks.

Betty continues, for these words must be said—should have already been said. Why were they not said on the ship? Why was her child not prepared for their journey to heaven? What if their soul has been lost for all these years?

Betty's voice falters. 'Lord, keep them safe until we meet.'

Someone tugs at her dress, but Betty ignores it. She is not stupid; she sees the ripples that are forming near the sunken ship, but she is not yet finished. She *must* finish her prayer. Not just for her own babby, but for all the children who passed on the voyage.

'I entrust them to your care.'

Her dress is tugged again but this time a section of the fabric tears, the sound ripping through the silence.

'Remove your hands from my person.' Betty snaps, turning to face the culprit, her cheeks reddening with fury.

It is the child who spoke before, warning about the beasts. Do they not know this is Betty's only dress?

The beast whines—a sound that causes Betty to remove her hand from its back and to cover her ears.

'You've upset it,' she accuses.

Her hand removed, the connection is broken, but there is now only a dull ache where a few moments ago, there was searing pain.

As Betty splashes her face with water from one of the smaller pools, for she cannot face Master so dishevelled, the beast seems to calm again. It is as if it does not like confrontation. Or perhaps it does not wish her to be upset. That is more likely.

Dress smoothed, and hair adjusted, Betty is ready to leave.

The child from before, who damaged her dress, looks at Betty with something other than understanding. Perhaps they are envious, wishing they also had silk against their skin rather than bits of tree. They have quite a delicate frame, which would suit the current fashion. Perhaps that is why they tried to ruin the dress?

'Has no one taught you it is rude to stare?' Betty says.

STAR

Water
trapped in body,
stagnates.

Star cannot understand Betty's words, which is plentiful, but seem not to follow any truth easily understood. Why is it rude to look at someone, when what is behind that look is an effort to understand what lays hidden? To witness the person under the skin rather than the paint on the tunic?

Star listens for movement as they pass the cave entrance, for some kind of proof that Lightning and Rainbow is safe, but there is nowt bar the dull drip of water that sheds from the walls. Star cannot even check to see if the discarded tunics is gone cause questions will be asked if they is found still to be there. There ain't no excuse for wasting cloth. Did Elder Newt notice the tunics when searching under the stone or when they returned the case? Nowt was indicated, but then Elder Newt has always bin quiet in purpose and there was moving the beast to hold the attention. But if Elder Newt knew bout the well afore now, that it led somewhere new, why ain't they investigated?

Star frowns, glances back, cannot comprehend it. Clay is trailing behind, trying to hide the limp by using small steps, and even further back is Betty, a scowl back on their face. Star thinks perhaps it is cause Betty is more used to hiding tears than letting em fall.

Star cannot see Elder Newt, such is the distance between em, but imagines em holding tight to the spear, prodding Betty on. Star remembers little of Betty afore the disappearance cept the stories they told and information shared at bedtime, which ain't bin spoken of since: of beds made of feathers and dark skies speared with light. Perhaps Betty might hold the answers to what is beyond *No Place*, where the doctors insist they must return? It would add to the pictures witnessed on the doctor's walls, of the babies sheltering in Elders' arms in the sacred cave. Star cannot quite believe they was ever that small, despite witnessing new childs arriving.

There is disconnection between what is felt and what is known. Perhaps the melding of things must happen—like herbs which need to be boiled in water to release their healing properties.

There is a sudden bang from the shore and a low rumble neath the earth. Star grabs onto a tunic tree, which bends but do not break.

CLAY

They have moved into the trees to avoid the rock tumbling from above. Clay clamps their hands over their ears and crouches low to the ground. But it ain't the sound that rumbles neath em that causes Clay to wince—the beasts is screaming, a painful sound, like blows to the head.

'Us must hurry to the Mune,' Star says, close by.

Clay cannot move, even with Star's encouragement. Is the beasts passing? Why else would they make such a terrible sound?

'Us must help em,' Clay says, struggling to stand. 'They is frightened.'

'Us must save the Mune,' Star urges. 'The island is angry. There ain't time to wait.'

'It is not angry,' Betty says, emerging from nearby, brushing dust from their fancy tunic. 'Master says it's the nature of it.'

Elder Newt steps past Betty and helps Clay to rise, a worried look upon their face, indicating they should indeed hurry.

The meeting place is deserted when they arrive, littered with dirty breakfast bowls. The Mune must be sheltering, worried bout the earth shaking. Clay would like to shelter from the noise, still ringing in the ears, or perhaps lie down, bury their head, try not to think bout the beast left alone in the rock pool and those in the sea.

Elder Tattio emerges from chillun's hut, looking annoyed. Master is close behind.

'I told you Betty's outburst was of no consequence.' Master's voice is loud. 'And the shaking is nothing that isn't expected on an island such as this. I have read much about it.'

'You brought bad luck,' Elder Tattio's voice is without its usual calm.

'It will pass. It is merely a tremor.' Master sounds confident.

Elder Tattio scowls and steps towards Clay. 'Thank de island yer safe. Where are de others? Where is Lightning?'

Clay steals a glance at Star, but Star has their teeth firmly sunk in their bottom lip. They ain't going to answer.

Thankfully other members of the Mune start to drift out of the chillun's hut.

'Where do the smoke come from?' Elder Rosie asks, consoling a crying child and looking up above the rock, where puffs of grey rise.

'It comes from the sea, of course,' Betty says, pushing past Clay.

Turning to Master, Betty continues, 'And I'll have you know, it were not an outburst, Master Harrington, but distance that were needed. There is much you do not know about this island.'

Clay frowns. Why does Master have two names when one is enough?

'Now is not the time, Bessie, I think you would agree. We must learn more about the volcanic nature of this unique place.'

Betty flushes red and stomps away, towards the food hut, kicking up dust.

Star's stomach rumbles loud enough that Clay is reminded of the ground afore. They must not ignore it, whatever the stranger says.

LIGHTNING

The covering makes it easier to push through the water, though Lightning dun like the feel of it stuck on the face, like some piece of wet sea-plant. They dun have a clue how it works, but it seem to turn water to air as the body travels upwards, with no need to hold in the breath.

It is a relief to break through the surface of the sacred well and feel warm air wash over the body. It will take a while for the cold to go, longer than it do after a swim in the sea. Stripping off the face-covering, Lightning tosses it into the corner of the cave, not wanting Clay or Star to think it was needed.

The cave is quiet.

Pulling emself out of the water, Lightning waits at the edge to give Rainbow a hand. It bin good to have Rainbow at their side afore, in the other place, stopping em from reacting so quick. What's needed for hunting ain't always the right thing for understanding. The body know what to do when faced with killing—you can't take no time to listen, else you might not do it, whereas thinking need the body to be still.

Rainbow breaks the surface of the water, seems at ease with the face covering and dun rush to rip it off like Lightning. Their voice sounds usual when they speaks.

'I dun notice the smell so strong afore,' Rainbow says, inhaling, and taking Lightning's offered hand.

Dun look like the nose is affected by the mask neither.

'Most likely we bin used to it,' Lighting says. 'Knowing nowt else.'

Rainbow frowns, shaking the water off. 'Or perhaps it's a sign that what the doctor said is true?'

'Us dun know nowt for sure,' Lightning says, passing Rainbow a tunic. 'Best stick to what us seen.'

Rainbow frowns. 'I dun know what that is.'

Lightning shrugs. 'Maybe it ain't for us to understand.'

Lightning shakes a jar of lightberries to life. It ain't just quiet when they enter the main part of the cave, it's empty. Even the beast is gone, though the scent of its oily body hangs in the air.

'Summat has happened,' Rainbow says. 'There bin others here. I can sense em.'

'Us must get back to the Mune.' Lightning puts down the jar and turns to head out of the cave, momentarily blinded by the sunlight, so different in colour to the room with the pictures. There is grey stones on the path and a thin cut in the ground that runs towards the trees as if a spear or summat has sliced the earth open.

'Us was not gone that long?' Rainbow asks.

'I ain't bin counting our steps when us bin busy talking,' Lightning snaps, worried by the changes.

Rainbow seems confused as they sniffs the air, as if there is summat not quite making sense. But it is not the how or why, but what they must do that matters, as it always has.

Picking up the spear, left propped up against the tunic tree but now flat on the ground outside the cave entrance, Lightning leads the way down the dust path to the Mune.

CLAY

Clay limps along the path towards the cave, sweat soaking the fabric of their tunic, dust clagging their skin.

Collecting water is not the reason for Clay leaving the meeting place, but an excuse. Star is right that it is easy to hide purpose when summat is needed.

The cries of the beasts is still heard in the head and it ain't in Clay's nature to ignore hurt, do nowt to help. The beasts is no different from anyone else in the Mune.

'Clay?'

Lightning is on the path ahead, skin clean of dust. Rainbow is behind, wearing the face covering from afore.

Clay puts the bucket down as Rainbow draws close. There is respite found in Rainbow's embrace, as soothing as hush-hush leaves pressed into a wound.

'What happened?' Rainbow asks.

'Thank the island yer safe,' Clay says, clutching Rainbow.

'What happened?' Rainbow asks again, voice tight.

'The island shook and there is heat.'

'The paintings Doctor showed us.' Rainbow glances across at Lightning.

Clay looks up and touches the strange fabric which cups Rainbow's square chin, summat they would never be able to do to Star.

'It helps breaths like Star said. I dun feel the heat in my throat from the air, or the cold from the well in my chest.'

'There is more of em in *No Place*,' Lightning says. 'Us saw fire burning in the grey rock.'

Clay frowns. 'Grey rock? But the heat is in the sea!'

'There is much to tell,' Rainbow says, stroking Clay's back afore stepping away. 'But us must be quick and warn the Mune.'

'I must go to the shore.' Clay's lip quivers. 'Us moved the beast.'

There is safety in releasing feelings after being held close by Rainbow.

Lightning steps forward. 'Rainbow will take water back to the Mune, and I will guard you.' Lightning bangs the spear against the ground.

'I ain't going there to fight,' Clay says.

'The beasts is all different. Like us. Us must be awake to it.' Lightning is firm.

'Go,' Rainbow says. 'I will use the walk to think of what to say.'

Afore leaving, Clay lifts up Rainbow's face covering, and presses their lips firmly on Rainbow's.

'Find Star,' Clay says. 'They holds the words you need.'

The smell hits Clay long afore the dead fish is witnessed, scattered on the black sand. The crack that started near the cave is bigger here, like a mouth gaping open and it cuts through the shell path near the pools. Beyond the crack, there is beasts, some laying down, others moving into the wood beyond.

'It ain't safe,' Lightning says, touching the water, and bringing the hand away quickly. 'It burns, like tea.'

Clay coughs, smoke clawing deep in the throat, and looks for the beast from earlier, but it ain't possible to recognise. If only it had a name.

Lightning grabs Clay's arm and tugs backwards.

'Us cannot let the beasts reach the Mune afore us,' Lightning says, starting to run.

BETTY

Betty watches the Elders push their dry grass brooms over the ground. It is a pointless exercise when the sky is starting to turn grey above the rock. The children, who would benefit from a lash to the rump, run about, as if it is snow falling. There is nothing to be built with ash that disintegrates in the fingers, certainly not a man.

Why does Master not see the seriousness of this new situation? Whilst it is true that he is busying himself, his focus appears not on their return to safety, but rather collection. His pile of artefacts is ever growing, threatening to take up more space in the hut than Betty herself.

How does he intend to transport them home? It is not as if a ship will pass, and he has barely spoken of any plans since her return from the shore.

'You!' she shouts, at the slim child from the shore before.

Perhaps they might be used to sway Master? The child would be pretty if they tied their hair up and used some decoration, rather than scraping it back from the head and twisting it round a stick in the harsh manner the' mune all seem to prefer.

The child frowns across at Betty, as if they have no comprehension. Or perhaps they do not see her in the doorway, looking out.

Master is approaching the hut, his arms full of samples again. Betty smooths down her skirts and tucks the knotted lock of hair behind her ear. It will be a devil for her lady's maid to comb out when she returns to the Manor.

'Surely we must make preparations to leave?' Betty says, trying to honey her tongue as she moves aside for him.

'The event has passed.' Master is assured, as if he has seen the future.

How does he know so much when there is not even proper tea leaves, or cups, here to be read?

'We still have plenty of time to learn about the island,' Master says, placing the items he has amassed onto the pile: the skeleton of a jump, a section of bark and a strip of dried fish. Betty doubts he has asked permission to take them, he has likely taken advantage of the 'mune, too caught up in cleaning to notice.

'The creatures they call beasts, bear the markings of an ancient species. I must catalogue their existence,' he continues, his eyes alight.

It is as if he is inebriated.

'The smoke gets thicker,' Betty says, wrinkling her nose against it.

The air does not seem to be clearing as Master wishes it to. Does he imagine he can command it, like his dogs or the servants at home?

'I must take samples, Bessie. There will be injured creatures nearby, who pose no threat. You must accompany me.'

It is as if the smoke suddenly clears from Betty's eyes. Who is this man, who has aged so fast, standing before her? Certainly not her protector!

Betty looks back at the women, busy with their chores. She might not like how the 'mune live, their dress and the way they conduct themselves, but they would never knowingly put her in danger.

'We must help,' Betty says, thinking about the beast, the ruby in its hide and how, despite everything, Newt led her to its side.

She sweeps through the doorway, leaving Master open-mouthed behind.

STAR

*Confusion -
where answers
is found.*

Star moves away from the sleeping hut, uncomfortable under Betty's gaze. The air is getting hotter, and sometimes the grey dust that falls from the sky burns the skin on contact. Why does nature wish to harm the Mune when it ain't done so afore? Is it Star's fault for wanting to leave? Or the strangers for arriving? Is the island like the Elders, wanting always to stay the same—angry at change?

'Us must talk.'

Star's stomach shoots into their mouth at hearing Rainbow's voice, but quickly sinks again. Rainbow is back, safe. Why did Star ever doubt it?

'Where is Lightning?'

'At the shore with Clay,' Rainbow says.

Star nods. Clay was always going to try to help the beasts, even with the risk to emself.

'The Mune must leave the island,' Rainbow says. 'It ain't just the trees that sense danger, but us saw paintings that show it.'

Star nods. 'The doctors also showed me paintings of what might come to pass.'

'There is face coverings in *No Place* and the doctor brought berries. Enough I think?'

'Red berries?' Star asks, hopeful.

Rainbow nods.

'Those that is strong could manage without the coverings,' Star considers.

Rainbow sits down, blows out a breath. 'The doctor said the passageway is unstable.'

There is black rings under Rainbow's eyes and their skin is pale, which is worrying what with it already being as light as the shell path.

'We must act quickly but rest is needed,' Rainbow says. 'To be strong enough to journey.'

Star nods, wonders how any of em will manage sleep with the air still burning.

Star cannot rest. The Elders is carrying on as if nowt has occurred now that the island is silent neath their feet again. Fish and roots is being chopped and boiled for stew, even though it is hard to see where the smoke from the meeting place ends and the sky begins.

Betty is stirring the bucket of food, but sits some way away, as if they do not wish to inhale. Star is taken aback to see it. Betty helping?

Star draws in a breath. 'The Mune must leave the island.'

Betty sighs, nodding. 'And yet we will sit here and eat, and Master will continue with scientific discovery, instead of making plans for rescue.'

'Why do the Elders fear the outside?' Star asks.

Betty considers the question for some time before answering, giving the stew more attention than necessary, scraping the bottom of the bucket with the stick. 'It were not a good place for them.'

'But might it change, like the island?' Star asks.

Betty pauses. 'I do not think so. Those that could change it are happy to keep things as they are.'

'Why can *us* not change it?' Star asks.

Betty laughs so hard, it draws others forth, until they circle them.

Star wishes they could tell Betty bout the case, hidden in the cave. What the doctors said.

'We might as well eat.' Betty dismisses Star with a wave of the hand. 'Master is in the hut cataloguing goodness knows what but will not wish to miss a meal.'

BETTY

Master has joined the circle but is distracted by the child from before who is asking questions barely formed in Betty's mind. They do not seem to accept what is answered, even when it comes from Master's mouth. Has Betty been too eager to please? It is true, as evidenced since they arrived here, that Master relishes a challenge.

'If the fire has passed, why do the ash still fall?' the child asks, taking the offered bowl of stew.

'Well dear,' Master says, with authority. 'It is the nature of it.'

'That ain't no answer.'

'What an impudent young thing,' Master laughs, cupping a bowl to his mouth and slurping.

Betty winces, waiting for him to raise his hand, but he does nothing except wipe the juice from his beard.

'What is your name, child?' he asks.

'Star,' the child says.

Betty tries to hide her surprise by taking a mouthful of stew, knowing she must eat, despite nothing sitting well in her stomach. It has been the same since she touched the beast—a flickering deep within. She looks over her bowl at Star, now able to see the similarities to the infant she named, who was always looking up. Further thoughts about Star are interrupted by the arrival of Lightning and one other.

'Us must leave the meeting place,' Lightning says, seeming fearful. 'The beasts is coming ashore.'

'Where are the beasts now, and how long do we have?' Betty demands.

Tattio rises from the circle before any questions are answered. 'Ketch de spears. Us will fight dem. Us won't be forced from us home.'

Betty puts her bowl down and laughs, cannot help it. 'Our home has never been here!'

One of the babbys starts to cry at Betty's outburst, which was angrier than intended.

'We ain't got nowhere else to go,' Rosie says, comforting the child. 'We been safe here.'

'Safe! You are as stupid as I remember if you would choose to be eaten alive,' Betty barks.

There is murmuring around the circle and Betty sees some of the Elders frowning.

'Stop being so dramatic, Bessie. There is no risk here,' Master says, offering his bowl out for another helping. 'The beasts, like any creature, can be tamed with the right skills.'

'They are not dogs,' Betty is unable to stop now the words have started pouring out, which have been simmering for far too long, 'and you do not have your whip.'

'The island is dying,' Rainbow says, suddenly.

The 'mune's attention falls to Rainbow. Betty cannot bear to look at the creature as they speak and has a strong urge to make the sign of the cross.

'Explain,' Tattio says, too calmly for Betty's liking.

'There is another place, where us might be safe.' Rainbow seems to be measuring words as if they were ingredients for one of Cook's puddings.

'It is neath the sacred well. It is the truth,' Star adds. 'There is other peoples.'

Newt stands and places a hand on her heart, which causes Tattio to seem uncertain.

'De well?'

'That is also how Master and I travelled here,' Betty says. 'Through the sacred waters.'

'But we will drown,' Rosie gasps.

'The peoples there gave us these...' Rainbow has one of the masks. 'They help breath in the water.'

'Why would dey help?' Tattio says.

'It is cause of em, that you is here,' Star says. 'They said the island wants us to leave.'

As if the island is listening, the earth rumbles beneath them with such a force, the remains of the stew tips over, lost to the earth with Betty not quick enough to retrieve it.

Then the bowbirds rise from the trees in a mass, the sound deafening, before taking flight high above the grey rock.

The beasts' screams that follow are enough to make Betty's face hurt from screwing it up.

'They sense what is coming,' Rainbow says. 'It is a warning.'

Then it is silent again, but it is an uncomfortable silence, like that before Master erupts in anger.

'We can waste no more time,' Betty says, kicking the bucket away to draw attention to herself. 'We must act, not wait for things to happen.'

Tattio looks carefully around the circle, at the pinched faces, most of which are nodding.

'I made Lightning better with a berry given to me by peoples in the safe place,' Star says. 'It healed. They speak truth.'

Tattio stares at Star, then at Lightning, and Betty wonders what happened. Whatever it was, Tattio changes her mind.

'Gather de chillun,' Tattio says.

CLAY

Lightning and Thunder lead the Mune down the dust path, spears extended. The chillun is safe, strapped tight to the Elders' backs behind Clay. Betty is somewhere at the rear, looking for signs of Master, who took leave of the Mune when the decision was made to start this journey to the cave.

As they round the corner of the grey rock, Lightning pauses but the beasts have taken a new path out of the wood, and down rocks that have crumbled into the sea. They is swimming in the deeper water, which must be cooler than the pools near the shore.

Clay was right that their intention bin not to harm but only to survive, attracted to the shore by a scent they dun understand.

Clay is so busy looking at the beasts through the broken, smouldering tunic trees that they trips on a fallen rock. It is the last thing needed when the legs is weary.

Rainbow grabs Clay's arm and squeezes.

'The island will live on, as it always has,' Rainbow whispers. 'Even the trees. The bowbirds carry seeds to the next place.'

Clay nods, but it is hard to witness the beasts that have fallen, their skin blistered with heat, their flesh half-cooked, smelling of oily meat.

Inside the cave it is warmer than afore, but the air is clearer, so it ain't as difficult to draw breath as outside. Clay stands, back against the damp wall, between Rainbow and Star, so the Mune can crowd in.

Star leans in. 'This is how the Elders spent their first night, together in this cave, all em years ago. I saw pictures. Life is a circle.'

Clay thinks bout circles, how they never end. Perhaps the beasts will find a way to flourish when they is gone.

There is hush as Lightning climbs over the edge of the sacred well. Lightning will go first, to prove it is safe and return with the masks, which is needed for breath. Clay hopes the air here ain't made the task harder for em, but Lightning looks strong and determined. Their fire, lost after the childs' arrival, is burning again, reflecting the island.

'The water!' Elder Rosie gasps, as Lightning's skin touches the surface.

'It dun harm we before, when others bin through,' Tattio says, touching Elder Rosie's arm. 'It won't now.'

Betty pushes forward, nearly toppling Elder Rosie. 'What about Master? We will need a man when we arrive in Yorkshire. It is not the same as here!'

Lightning glances at Betty but dun pause to answer. Taking one last breath of island air, Lightning drops down into the water, seemingly shedding fear and the island from their body.

Clay stands by the sacred well waiting with Star, hoping for a sign that the beasts is safe. The mask brought back by Rainbow after the last member of the Mune travelled through, is clamped over the face. There is comfort in breathing in Rainbow's scent, imprinted inside the fabric. It is needed as the air is now dense enough to cut with a hand.

'Dun wait too long,' Clay says, climbing over the ledge. 'The Mune will need yer words to survive.'

Star nods but dun touch Clay, seeming at ease, even with the crashing noise outside.

'I do not know if I will travel on to the same place,' Star says, 'there is things I wish to know that ain't to be discovered there.'

'I think I understand,' Clay says, climbing over the lip of the well, the metal case that the doctors gave Star clutched tight, 'what you meant by stepping in footprints already sunk. I will do what is needed.'

Clay takes one last look at Star, just in case they dun witness their face again, but Star is looking at the cave entrance, their thoughts already moved on.

STAR

Stars—
ideas
waiting for collection.

Night falls, and outside the cave the island is hungry, rumbling discontent. The moon is shrouded in grey, and the sea is rising, lapping at the entrance, though it do not seem to wish to enter yet.

Where is Master? There ain't much time left to spare and with no mask clasped to the face, it must be hard to breathe.

Since the Mune all passed through the water, Star has had time to retrieve the other items neath the stone. When Clay agreed to take the doctor's case, with the scanner, the instructions, and the list of contacts inside, they decided it was best not to lay out all the truths in case Betty broke the promises made, being as changeable as the beasts. Clutching the glass pipe, Star's thoughts switch to the Elders. Hopefully, Lightning and Elder Tattio will have taken the first chillun safely through the second well by now, if obstacles bin tossed aside, and all is as hoped. What must it feel like to return to a place you once tried to leave?

There is splashing beyond the walls and a sound Star recognises as the call of the beasts. Not the pain as afore, but summat new, which do not tear at the ears.

Master is at the entrance of the cave, atop one of the creatures, which look familiar. Is it the beast Betty touched with the stone in its belly? Star would like to believe it is.

Dismounting, then patting it on the side, Master approaches Star. The beast seems happy to wait, riding the water, seemingly unafraid.

'I must stay awhile longer,' Master says, coughing. 'These creatures need categorising—their species must be protected. It is imperative.'

Star frowns, unsure what to do, cause Master's chest rattles like stones in a jar. Must they break their promise to Betty and the others?

'The Mune is waiting,' Star says.

Master coughs again. 'I will follow when my observations are complete. It is an opportunity that must not be wasted.'

Master ain't going to survive for long with the air so thick—not with breath already so stuttered and the face as grey as the beast's skin.

Star strips off the face covering, worn while waiting, and throws it, and the silver travelling suit, to Master. The doctors said the cloth was made for travel and it might keep Master's body safe for long enough to help the beasts. Clay would like that. Star has made the journey through the well afore with nowt but what nature afforded. There is more chance of Star's survival than Master's here—what with the island so heated and Master not as strong.

'You will be rewarded in heaven,' Master says, catching both cloths, and clamping the mask straight onto the face. Breathing seems immediately easier.

Star takes one last look around the cave: at the washed-out paintings of the beasts—the creatures they once feared, who finally seem to have found purpose; at the lightberries which is fading from lack of touch and the pile of discarded tunics next to the well.

There is much to discover beyond what is already known.

Nodding to Master, who has already turned back toward the beast, Star holds the nose, and lets the water drag em down once more, to meet the moon at the bottom.

EPILOGUE
Leicestershire, 1888

BETTY

It is not often that Betty has five minutes to herself in Master's study, such is the nature of the Manor now, which has taken on the air of a blacksmith's, rather than a place of quiet contemplation. The floor is littered with metal tools and the large mahogany shelves are crammed with leather-bound books in all manner of subjects of which Master would scarcely approve.

Betty sighs, supporting her stomach as she scrubs at a patch of starred, dried ink with one of Master's white handkerchiefs. Hertha never cleans up after herself properly after writing her mathematical notes, and as for Sophia, the woman who arrived just last week, the glass vials have begun to outnumber the quills, adding to the scent of industry. Betty wishes she were able to let the servants give it a good going over, but the 'mune's purpose here must remain guarded. It is hard enough to keep John, Master's manservant, at bay with his impertinent questions. He should consider himself lucky he still has a position, for they have no need of the extra hands now the Manor and farm cottages are full to capacity.

Betty sits down heavily on the leather upholstered chair. It was not hard to convince Master's friends of their private nuptials, and not one eye was batted by Master's absence, even with Betty now so obviously expecting, and so soon. It seems Master has desired for many years, not only an heir, but the opportunity for exploration and discovery. Anyhow, Society does not permit the asking of intimate questions, and the new powders do a fine job of masking the extra lines drawn on Betty's face by the island.

Glancing out of the bay window and into the grounds, Betty spies Rainbow, as usual, with their hands on the ancient Oak, mouth moving in conversation. The new muslin robes, created by Rosie, suit them well enough, and at least cover the limbs. Despite the many conversations about freedoms Betty has read in the new female suffrage pamphlets that Tattio likes to collect on trips to London with Jessie, it is something she may never warm to—this female man. But perhaps there is something in what the 'mune argue, that if woman is to be equal, to be truly free of the corsets that constrict, so must it also be for men.

Dipping her pen into the ink pot, Betty pauses before letting the nib touch the fresh sheet of paper. The words flow as fast as the newly installed tap in Cook's kitchen, which is truly a sight to behold:

'No Place: the island beneath the well,' by Lord Henry Harrington.

Soon, Betty will see her own name on the page under one of her scientific stories, but for now appearances must be maintained if they are to achieve their goal, written in the papers contained in Star's case. Betty sometimes wonders what happened to Molly's child, if they are safe, and why they did not return with the others. Clay does not offer up an explanation, even when pressed. Perhaps one day, they might see eye-to-eye and Clay might seek her confidence.

Pausing to flex her fingers, and admiring her newly purchased, diamond-encrusted wedding band, Betty continues to pen her tale, immortalising Master.

It will be enough, she hopes, to secure the 'mune's future at the Manor.

Acknowledgements

Firstly, thanks to the team at Gold SF for taking a risk on my PhD novel—especially Una McCormack for her excellent editing advice. Credit also goes to Matthew De Abaitua for the conversations, ideas, and reassurance that weird is good. Sarah Armstrong, author and friend, was the best beta reader a writer could hope for. I am also grateful to my other writerly friends for their ongoing support and edits: Helen, Clare, Eleanor, Pauline, Philippa, Jo, Emma, and Sue. Special mention to Petra who, even though she can't remember it, gave me excellent feedback whilst recovering from a serious injury—the morphine might have helped. Thanks to family and friends: Aly, Mary, Frances, Ilia, Fan Ying, and Sally for their unwavering belief in me, never questioning why I might want to torture myself with words. Lastly, but most importantly, my family: Blair, James, and Tom, who have travelled this journey with me and kept me grounded (potholes and breakdowns notwithstanding).

The Gold SF series

RECENT TITLES

Gold SF is a new imprint dedicated to discovering and publishing new intersectional feminist science fiction. Science fiction looks to the future and tries to imagine new ways of being in the world. Goldsmiths Press is a natural home for speculative fiction, and this new imprint promotes voices answering to our unprecedented times.

9781913380618
Empathy
Hoa Pham

9781913380786

The Ghostwriters
M.J. Maloney

9781913380823

The Other Shore
Hoa Pham

9781913380489
Mathematics for Ladies
Poems on Women in Science
Jessy Randall

9781915983053

Merchant
Alexandra Grunberg

9781915983077

Little Sisters and Other Stories
Vonda N. McIntyre

9781913380809
The Disinformation War
S. J. Groenewegen

9781915983183

Schrödinger's Wife (and other possibilities)
Pippa Goldschmidt

9781915983121

The Headland
Abi Curtis

GOLD SF°   Series editors *Una McCormack* and *Paul March-Russell*